A RECKONING OF SOULS

A RECKONING OF SOULS

The Battle for Humanity Has Begun

HARRISON EDWARDS

Printed in the United States of America
Published in Hellertown, PA
Cover design by Christina Gaugler
Library of Congress Control Number 2024912917
ISBN 979-8-894200-08-8
For more information or to place bulk orders, contact the author or the publisher at
Jennifer@BrightCommunications.net.

For Mary and Zach

In memory of Charlie.
I think he would have enjoyed this story
and the science behind it.

In memory of Rich.
Thank you for the classic line that
Epiphany delivers during a confrontation
that occurs later in this story. She may
have spoken the words, but they were all
yours. I will never stop missing you and
Charlie.

————————————

"There is good in this world; we just have
to learn how to see it."
—Tiorvi Eiken, sixteenth-century
sculptor and visionary

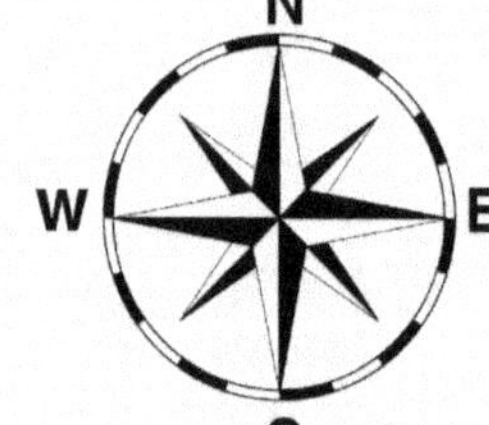

NORWAY
Lyfjord
Tromsø
Birtavarre
Overgård
Stamsund
Tjeldsund Church
NORWEGIAN SEA
Arctic Circle
Arctic Circle
Trondheim
Olso
N
W
E
S

PROLOGUE

Trondheim, Norway, Present day,
late afternoon

Aidan McCallum took off in an all-out sprint, glancing at the street signs for the intersection he was about to cross. He was two blocks away. The message he had received from the Otherworlds was abundantly clear. An attack at the Solsiden Mall in downtown Trondheim was imminent. If he moved quickly, there might be a chance to stop that from happening, or to at least warn people to clear the area. Lives were at stake, including his own and those of the two people he was due to meet. He hoped to God they hadn't gotten there yet.

The sudden blast of a horn from an onrushing car startled Aidan as he dashed in front of the large SUV bearing down on him. The driver hit the brakes, bringing the vehicle to a screeching stop, and then he laid on the horn a second time. Aidan cursed at himself as he finished crossing the street. *Getting run over isn't going to help the situation.* He leapt from the roadway onto the sidewalk and kept running. He nearly collided with two pedestrians and brushed the shoulder of a third, an elderly gentleman, who gave him an irritated look. *No time for apologies. Focus. Warn David and Epiphany and then call the police.*

His heart was pounding and his nerves were frayed as he came to an abrupt stop in front of a gift store. Aidan fished in his coat pockets for his cellphone and nearly dropped it in his rush to make the first call. "God damn it!" he swore out loud. His phone was dead. Yet again he had forgotten to charge the damn thing. The clock in his head was counting down the seconds. *Keep moving*, he told himself. One more block to go.

Aidan covered the distance quickly. His leg muscles were tightening. He was out of breath and regretting not having taken better care of himself. The Nidelva River was within eyesight. He was getting closer to the mall. *Push through the pain. Keep going.*

Another message from the Otherworlds reached out to Aidan's second soul as he approached the waterway. The soft voice in the back of his head informed him that a man in a black hoodie is carrying explosives and had just entered the mall area. The Moirae spirits who oversee the vast realms of the Otherworlds never contacted him like this—two messages in one day, both forewarnings of impending danger. Aidan had been born with a second soul, and in his fifty-seven years, there had been only one other time he had received a notification similar to these two. That was eleven days ago, when he had received a grave warning with global consequence.

Aidan sprinted across the Blomsterbrua, the pedestrian bridge that funneled people over the Nidelva into the downtown area of Trondheim. He came to a stop at the end of the bridge and surveyed the expansive area surrounding the Solsiden Mall. It was teeming with people. The outdoor seating areas of several popular restaurants were packed. He glanced at his watch: 3:57 pm. David and Epiphany were probably here already. They had agreed to meet at Ericson's Seafood Restaurant at 4:00 pm.

He scanned the walkway that ran the length of the mall. A man dressed in a dark hoodie placed his backpack on the knee-high brick wall at the corner of an outdoor seating area and then walked away from it. At this time of day, the sky had shifted into a twilight hue. Even with the outdoor lighting, it was difficult to discern the true color of the hoodie from this distance. Could be black. Could also be dark navy blue or possibly maroon.

Aidan ran toward the man. He had to get a closer look. No more than fifteen meters separated them when it became clear. The hoodie was black. The backpack probably had the explosives in it. "Hey! Stop!" Aidan yelled.

The man looked up, stopped for a second, and then turned and ran.

CHAPTER 1

Solsiden Mall, Trondheim, Norway

David Skye hurried out of the hotel lobby into the carpark. He hated being late. But today, a call from his chief technologist ran longer than anticipated. He had traveled to Trondheim for a meeting with Aidan McCallum and Epiphany. Aidan had suggested getting together for a meal at a popular seafood restaurant at the Solsiden Mall. It would be a nice way to catch up before diving into the details of the mission they had been asked to undertake.

Several cars were parked outside the main entrance to the hotel. The sound of flags rippling in the breeze drew his attention to five tall flagpoles at the edge of the parking area where it bordered the river. Another gust of wind kicked up. The ropes on which the flags were tethered clanked against the metal poles in rhythmic unison. Beyond the flagpoles stood the Blomsterbrua Bridge. David noticed a man sprint onto the bridge and begin threading his way between the pedestrians. He hadn't seen Aidan McCallum in nearly three years, but there was no mistaking that bright red hair when the man passed under a lamppost. It had to be Aidan. Worried that something was wrong, David picked up his pace.

As David reached the end of the Blomsterbrua, a bright flash erupted near a restaurant along the walkway, silhouetting a man wearing a dark hoodie and the man resembling Aidan. The sound of the explosion quickly followed. A loud thundering boom echoed off the surrounding buildings. The ensuing shock wave from the blast lifted the man in the hoodie and the man who had been running after him off the ground, hurling them like rag dolls. Charcoal-black smoke and debris swallowed the sky. For a brief moment, there was a strange silence, then chaos consumed the crowd. Screams of anguish and panic resounded down the long walkway.

The pedestrian bridge ended at a long esplanade along the water. David stood motionless as a swell of people began moving away from the site of the blast. Up ahead on his left he observed a string of restaurants along the outside of the mall, which was located on the site of an old shipyard that had once been one of the largest ship-building companies in Norway. The outdoor seating areas of each dining establishment were brimming with people. On his immediate right, David noticed boats of various sizes and types moored to one of the many piers in the harbor area. Farther ahead on his right, he saw the skating rink that had been built on a converted dry dock from the original shipyard. He spotted a female reporter and a cameraman standing next to a television news van near the main road. They had become unsuspecting witnesses to a major news story.

The sound of distant sirens brought David's focus back to the site of the bomb blast. A sudden pang of worry about the welfare of the two people he was supposed to meet overwhelmed his thoughts. David sprinted toward the restaurant where the explosion had occurred. His heart rate quickened as he ran. The anxiety overtaking his nervous system intensified. Each breath filled his lungs with stinging, frigid air. As he got closer, the true measure of the carnage became terribly evident.

The steel railing and metal panels around the raised seating area where the bomb had detonated were bent and twisted like misshaped, gnarled fingers. A huge gouge had been taken out of the brick wall. Beads of glass from shattered windows sprinkled the ground. Chairs and tables were overturned. Pieces of a shredded awning were scattered along the walkway. At least a dozen bodies were sprawled across the pavement. David stared at what was left of the sign with the name of the restaurant printed on it. The bomb had exploded between Ericson's Seafood Restaurant and an adjoining eatery. A sobering thought filled his head. Had he not been delayed with that work-related call, he'd be among the bodies lying on the ground.

People continued pouring out of the seating areas and from inside the mall building, moving in all directions to get to safety. Many were in tears as they observed the devastation—the magnitude of the atrocity a burden that even the strongest of wills failed to bear. David gazed at the ominous clouds overhead. Ash and burning debris drifted through the early December air. A light rain mixed with snow had started to fall. A cold breeze fanned the flames of several localized fires created by the blast. What had started as a peaceful afternoon of *friluftsliv*, the Norwegian practice of embracing year-round "free air life," had come to a violent end.

David reached the bodies of the two men he had seen get thrown through the air when the bomb had exploded. His worst fears had been realized. It was Aidan he had seen crossing the bridge. David quickly kneeled beside him and grasped his right hand.

Somehow, Aidan mustered a faint smile when he saw David crouching over him. A large piece of shrapnel had pierced his rib cage. Blood soaked through his clothes. He struggled to speak, choking on the acrid fumes that invaded his lungs, "The angel and the orb…" His voice tailed off before coughing out the last words he'd ever speak, "You have to find it." Aidan reached into his pocket and dropped his keys on the walkway. He took one final breath as his head lolled to the side and the last vestige of his life spilled away.

CHAPTER 2

Solsiden Mall, Trondheim, Norway

On the far side of the skating rink, the newswoman abruptly stopped in the middle of her prepared monologue. It had taken a few seconds for Celine Hove to register the enormity of what she had just witnessed. "Jesus Christ!" she gasped. Her human-interest piece about the Festival of Cultures in center city Trondheim would have to wait. She looked over at her cameraman. "William, please tell me you're recording this."

"Sure as hell am," the burly young man replied.

"Focus on the site of the blast. Capture as much of this as you can." Celine grabbed her cellphone and promptly made two calls. The first was to the police to report the incident. The second was to her boss. He'd want to know that she was front and center at one of the biggest news stories to hit the city in the past several years.

———

David Skye reached out and squeezed Aidan McCallum's right shoulder, grimly acknowledging the sadness of losing a man who had dedicated his life to bringing food and water to impoverished communities across the globe. He got up, pocketed

Aidan's keys, and quickly moved to the man wearing the black hoodie. His badly damaged body was crumpled on the walkway. David crouched next to him. A portion of the man's left arm was exposed, revealing a tattoo of Earth with a bloody dagger through it in front of a rising sun. David checked for a pulse. There was none.

The evolving chaos overwhelmed David's senses in a cacophony of sights and sounds. Dark smoke continued to drift along the esplanade. The sound of wailing sirens was growing louder. Most of the people were moving away from the mall complex in droves, looking to put as much distance between themselves and the site of the explosion as they could. Others were attempting to help the injured, while some stood in helpless shock, unable to comprehend such a senseless act of violence. David stood and did another scan of the seating areas. He hadn't seen anyone who resembled Epiphany among the victims of the explosion. Up ahead, on the ground between two park benches, David noticed a large duffel bag that had been left unattended. The blood ran from his face—a second bomb!

———

Celine stood facing the camera with her back to the mall area. She offered her best attempt at a serious, yet somber expression. William steadied the camera, trying to get as much as possible of the scene behind Celine in the frame with her. He motioned with his hand to indicate they were now broadcasting live.

"This is Celine Hove reporting live from the Solsiden Mall in downtown Trondheim. Moments ago, a huge explosion ripped through the outdoor seating area in one of the restaurants you see behind me. Police, firefighters, and emergency rescue teams are responding. Details on the cause of the explosion are not known at this time. We will …"

Before she could finish her sentence, a second deafening explosion tore through the mall area. Celine flinched and stumbled forward toward the camera. She turned to face the direction from which the second blast had originated.

William held the camera steady, keeping Celine in the frame while capturing as much of the second explosion as possible. Swollen clouds of thick, black smoke engulfed the entire area. A new wave of panicked cries rang out, competing with the blaring sirens from approaching police and rescue teams. The mix of precipitation had switched over to a steady snowfall. The gray clouds had grown more intense. Darkness had overtaken Trondheim.

A clearly distraught Celine regained her composure and continued her coverage of the incident. "Once again, this is Celine Hove reporting live from the Solsiden Mall in Trondheim. We have just witnessed a second explosion along the walkway that borders the mall. As I mentioned earlier, we don't have any details on the cause of these explosions at this time. Police and rescue teams are on their way. We will continue to follow this story as it unfolds."

William kept the camera focused on the area where the second bomb had been detonated for a few more seconds and then ended the live feed. "Okay, we're off the air," he said.

Celine bent forward at the waist and placed both hands on her knees, the microphone still tightly gripped in her right hand. Her entire body trembled. She looked over at her cameraman and asked, "What kind of world do we live in, William?" She took a deep breath and quietly wept.

The percussive shock wave from the blast nearly knocked David over. He stumbled sideways and struggled to maintain his footing. Fortunately, he was far enough away to avoid serious injury, but anyone within close proximity to the bench where the second bomb exploded had most likely perished. That thought hit him hard. He had seen a family, both parents and their two young children, somewhere in the vicinity of where the second bomb went off.

Strong winds quickly ushered the dense smoke down the long walkway. David could barely see through it. He convulsed as he inhaled the foul-smelling fumes. His ears were ringing. Sounds all around him were muffled, and he felt slightly dizzy. He raced down the walkway to find the parents and children. When he reached the site of the second explosion, he saw five more bodies on the ground. The two side-by-side benches where the bomb exploded had been obliterated. Shards of splintered wood were scattered everywhere. A shallow, charred crater occupied the space where the benches once stood. David continued onward, fighting through the smoke, to locate the family.

He found them farther down the walkway. All four were alive. The petite six-year-old girl with blonde hair in a ponytail peeking out below her bright red hat sat on the ground next to her mother. She was crying while she held her mother's hand. The little girl's nose was bleeding, and her cheek was scraped. Her mother was lying on her back with the soles of her shoes planted on the sidewalk and her knees raised. She looked stunned, staring blankly at the sky. The father was tending to their eight-year-old son. The boy's knuckles were badly scraped and bleeding as he wiped his tear-filled eyes.

The first of the police and emergency responders had arrived. Roaring sirens, the sounds of people running by, and the cries for help momentarily faded into the background, becoming a faraway, swirling cloud of muffled noise. The activity of David's second soul had intensified. A complex, harmonious tone reached his ears. He recognized it as a signal of another second soul. *Epiphany?* He turned his head in the direction from which the sound was emanating. His eyes drifted to the long esplanade along the water.

Epiphany was sprinting toward him. Her long, fluid strides covered the distance between them quickly. She stopped beside David. He was trying to calm the little girl. Epiphany bent down and buried her nose in her coat sleeve to avoid breathing the noxious fumes from the smoke. "I'm so glad you're alive. Are you okay?"

David looked up. Her voice sounded muffled. "Yeah, I'll be fine, just a little shaken up. Help me with these guys." David and Epiphany assisted the parents and children until the EMTs arrived. A pair of first responders took over, quickly assessing the condition of each family member. *Thank God they are okay,* he thought. The others who had been too close to the benches weren't that lucky.

Epiphany grabbed David's arm and pulled him aside. "Let's get out of their way."

David coughed several times, still feeling the effects of the smoke he had inhaled.

"Are you sure you're going to be okay?" Epiphany asked.

"I'll be fine," he said. "I'm glad you weren't hurt."

"I'm lucky I was late," Epiphany said. "I was taking a walk along the river and lost track of time. When I heard the explosions and saw the smoke, I came running as fast as I could. How about Aidan? Is he okay?"

"He didn't make it. He was killed by the first explosion."

Epiphany bowed her head. "That's terrible. He was such a good guy. I'm going to miss him."

"Yeah, me too. It'll be hard to imagine a world without him in it."

Noticing that David was a little wobbly from the second blast, Epiphany grasped his arm to steady him. "Was Aidan still alive when you got to him? Did he say anything before he passed away?"

"He was alive when I saw him, but only for about a minute or two. He did say something, but it was a bit cryptic. He said we have to find the angel and the orb. Any idea what that means?"

"None."

David reached into his pocket and held out the keys that Aidan had dropped on the pavement. "He gave me these before he died. I think we go to his place and find out."

CHAPTER 3

Oslo Headquarters of the Citizens for a Peaceful Planet Foundation

"How bad is it?"

Demetrius Wolffe glanced out the window at the Oslo skyline before answering his longtime friend and associate, Christian Slagg. The city's lights sparkled in the crisp winter air. Demetrius had fallen in love with Oslo from the moment he first arrived over two decades ago. It had everything he loved: a sense of history, friendly people, and a vibrant culture. He returned his gaze to the man sitting across from him. "We're hemorrhaging money, Christian." Demetrius glanced down at the floor from the seat behind his desk, almost ashamed to relay the next bit of information. Christian had been with him since the very start when Citizens for a Peaceful Planet officially opened its doors twenty-five years ago. Their mission had been to foster a peaceful global community that embraces cultural differences. The *One World, One Family* slogan had been Christian's idea. And now, everything was falling apart. Demetrius sighed, "I just closed our offices in San Diego and Dublin. Oslo's the last one left."

The grimace on Christian's face told Demetrius everything he needed to know. The man looked back at Demetrius and replied in a quivering voice, "That's five offices in the past two-and-a-half years."

"I don't know whether to scream or cry," Demetrius said.

"Under the circumstances, I think both would be okay."

"My dreams of making this planet a more peaceful place …" Demetrius paused and added wistfully, "a better place … are crashing down around me." Then he settled into a moment of sullen, inner reflection. "I feel like a man with no alternatives and nothing left to lose."

"That's a dangerous combination," Christian warned. Trying to be as reassuring and positive as possible, he added, "You always seem to find a way, Demetrius."

Demetrius pursed his lips, nodded, and remained silent.

"Where do we go from here?" Christian asked.

"We can't go down without a fight. We've invested most of our adult lives in this venture." Demetrius had been looking over the latest set of statistics. "Citizens has had a positive impact in the cities where we've set up offices. Hate-related crimes have been on the decline in those cities, and we've seen an increase in annual cultural festivals that bring people of different nationalities together. Well," he paused, "up until the last few years anyway."

"What changed?"

"The COVID pandemic hit us hard for one thing. People stayed at home. Large gatherings for things like cultural festivals became pretty much nonexistent. Employees worked remotely and got comfortable with the freedoms that brought. A lot of people found they could live on less. They achieved better work-life balances and had more free time to enjoy the things they like to do when not working." Demetrius managed a contemplative smile as he finished speaking. "Many of them used that free time to look for more gainful employment. We couldn't find people to staff our offices, or keep them very long if we did."

"Yes, and the downturn in the global economy didn't help either," Christian added.

"Right. Donations dried up pretty quickly because of that."

"What about that philanthropist you're meeting with? Any possibilities there?"

"Gerd Schumann. Possibly. He's a wealthy businessman. Owns an international shipping and transportation company. I'm due to meet him in Tromsø in a couple of days. He's chartered a small bus to go on a northern lights expedition in the mountains outside of the city. He invited me to join them. Apparently, he wants to use the occasion to get to know me a little better and to discuss the details of a possible donation."

"What kind of donation are we talking about?" Christian asked. "Would it make a difference?"

"Two million, U.S., and yeah it would keep us afloat a little while longer. Long enough to work out a long-term plan to keep Citizens for a Peaceful Planet alive."

"Wow! That much? That certainly would help."

"Yeah, it would. The spike in inflation has really hurt our bottom line. Our cost of doing business has taken a hit. That kind of money would help us bail out. You know, the other thing that's hurt our ability to make an impact is the direction the world seems to be heading. People and countries as a whole are taking more of an inward focus."

"More of a me first approach to life," Christian added.

"A world where individual personal rights and freedoms are more important than what's right for society as a whole. There seems to be less of an appetite for things like diversity and inclusion."

"Then you throw in huge problems with immigration, record numbers of government coups in Africa, wars in Eastern Europe and the Middle East, and terrorist attacks," Christian added. "It makes it difficult for people to see what we're trying to do as a priority."

"You're right about that. There just doesn't seem to be much bandwidth for our message."

A loud bang interrupted their conversation. Both men turned to face the door to Demetrius's office when it swung open and hit the wall. Hanna Ortiz rushed over to the end table next to the sofa and picked up the remote. "Have you seen this?" she blurted out as she turned on the wall-mounted television and frantically scanned through the channels until she found the one she was looking for.

Demetrius and Christian got up from their chairs and walked over to stand next to her. "Hanna, what's going on?" Demetrius asked.

Choking back tears, Hanna replied, "There's been a bombing at the Solsiden Mall at our cultural festival. I just got a call from Brita Pederson. She was there when it happened."

"Is she okay?" Christian asked.

Hanna nodded, keeping her eyes on the television. "Yes. She was inside the mall building when the bombs went off outside."

Images from a news crew filled the screen. They watched in silence as the video replay of the devastation unfolded on the television. "What is wrong with our society?" Demetrius exclaimed. "Why do things like this keep happening? This was supposed to be a celebration, an opportunity to rejoice in the things our different cultures have to offer."

Demetrius glanced at Hanna. She had turned forty-seven at the start of the new year, but he'd always see her as the young thirty-two-year-old Bolivian native whom he interviewed for the Director of Events position fifteen years ago. Her effervescent, high-energy personality had won him over. She had come to Norway looking for new challenges and had brought with her a rich culture that influenced the early direction the Oslo headquarters of Citizens for a Peaceful Planet had taken. He moved closer and put his arm around her shoulders while she wiped tears away from her eyes. She looked up at him and smiled.

"Were any of our other people there, Hanna?" Christian asked.

"Brita was the only one there at the time."

Demetrius took the remote, turned off the television, and motioned for everyone to take a seat. Christian and Hanna sat on the sofa, and Demetrius sat in a wingback chair facing them. "We need to help in any way we can."

Hanna's facial expression changed from solemn reflection to positive determination as she spoke. "Absolutely."

"I can take the train to Trondheim tomorrow," Christian said.

"I can go with you if you'd like," Hanna added.

Christian looked over at her and nodded approvingly. "That would be great."

"Offer them whatever assistance they're willing to take," Demetrius said. "I need to travel to Tromsø to meet with Mr. Schumann, so please pass along my humblest condolences and regrets for not being able to go with you."

"Will do," Christian said.

Hanna got up from the sofa. "I'm going to check into travel arrangements for tomorrow."

"Thanks, Hanna." Christian waited until she left the office, then he asked in a low voice, "What happens if Schumann doesn't come through with the donation?"

Demetrius returned his gaze to the window, to the view of the city that had become his home. "Well, I'm afraid we just might be finished."

CHAPTER 4

Gimsøya Island in the Lofoten Archipelago, Norway

Punching a hole in the fabric of space-time and tapping into an infinite source of primordial energy was well beyond the farthest reaches of current science, yet Johannes Stinar was about to make the attempt. If he was successful, he'd change the world for generations to come. If unsuccessful, well, he didn't want to think about that. These notions consumed Johannes's thoughts as he drove along a remote stretch of roadway on the tiny island of Gimsøya in the Lofoten Archipelago. Johannes had chosen Gimsøya for the first trial run of his quantum-well device for one primary reason: its seclusion. On an island of fewer than two hundred people, no one would be around to see what he was up to, which was good because if his device failed, or worse yet, failed catastrophically, no one would get hurt—hopefully.

Johannes slowed his Range Rover and pulled off the road onto a patch of gravel next to a long stretch of woods. This part of Norway was a day or two away from entering the period from early December through early January when the sun would remain below the horizon. During that span of time, a typical day would cycle through nothing but varying degrees of darkness. Johannes noticed that the sky had dimmed to a duskier shade. In the distance, in the fading light, he could still make out the neighboring mountain peaks. Hidden beyond them was the Norwegian Sea.

He got out of the vehicle and took a deep, cleansing breath to collect his thoughts and calm his nerves. The brisk winter air felt refreshing. His emotions teetered between energizing excitement on one end of the spectrum and fearful anxiety on the other end. He walked to the back of the vehicle, opened the rear door to the storage compartment of the car, and removed everything he'd need for his trial run. With a flashlight in one hand and a backpack slung over his insulated coat, he started his trek into the woods.

His kilometer-long hike into the caldera-like cutout in the mountains ended at a deep swale where he could operate hidden from the rest of the world. He carefully removed the quantum-well device from his backpack and set it on the snow. If it worked, it would mean his theories were correct. The technological advancements to follow would be historic. At the top of the list would be an unlimited supply of energy to power the planet with no waste products or pollution. And if humanity makes it far enough into the future, it would provide a new source of near-light-speed propulsion to colonize other worlds beyond this one.

This version of his quantum-well device was a working prototype small enough to test, but nowhere near large enough to power a city or a spacecraft. He had labored over the calculations for the trial run for days. On paper, everything looked good, and if there was one thing in this world that Johannes had faith in, it was mathematics. Like Leibniz and Newton, who had independently developed calculus during the seventeenth century, Johannes had developed a new math. His was an extension of calculus, one capable of dealing with the difficulties of an eleven-dimensional version of reality. According to his calculations, his trial run should work. There were risks, however. If he slipped a digit, his device could swallow half the island in an eleven-dimensional void of pure energy.

Johannes mounted his high-speed video camera, capable of recording in low-light environments, on a tripod. He recorded the time, day, month, weather conditions, and the settings of his device in his lab notebook. Everything was ready. He flipped the power switch on. The microelectronic circuitry at the core of the quantum-well device came to life, feeding energy to a series of miniature toroids, tiny doughnut-shaped rings that formed the heart of the apparatus. The international patents on their unique design had made Johannes a rich man. The money, which enabled him to concentrate on his work full time, was about to pay off.

He positioned himself behind a rock outcropping in case something went wrong. The green Ready light turned on, indicating the device had warmed up. A revolutionary advancement in science was the push of a button away. This would be his moment of truth, the instant where success or failure would be decided. Johannes pressed his thumb into the Start button. The toroids kicked in, generating an intensely strong energy field tearing at the fabric of reality. A small sphere of light the size of a golf ball appeared above the quantum-well device. Within seconds, it expanded to a diameter of three meters. Its surface undulated and transitioned through the colors of the spectrum. The three-meter sphere rotated in the air like a small planet. Inside the rotating shell, the primeval energy present at the birth of the universe rippled through eleven dimensions. An onboard computer inside the quantum-well device transmitted readings to Johannes's laptop. He'd have several minutes of run time before the power required to keep the device operational would drain.

Johannes worked up the courage to move closer to the multicolored sphere. He cautiously reached his hands into the hazy, plasma-like atmosphere surrounding its outer shell. Waves of energy streamed through his fingertips. The surface of the sphere had similar properties to an event horizon around a black hole. Everything outside the horizon remained safe. Crossing that boundary, however, meant being pulled inexorably inward, never to leave. As the power in the quantum-well drained, the surface of the sphere went pitch black. Johannes stared in awe. At the moment his device relinquished its last bit of energy, the sphere collapsed into a small violet orb the size of his fist. Two seconds later, it vanished.

Johannes waved his hand through the open space where the sphere from the quantum well had been. He felt residual energy in the space it had once occupied. A long, thin bolt of light arced through the air and then dissipated—an aftershock of some kind perhaps. The unexpected event bothered him. *Why didn't I anticipate this?*

The sky overhead had grown much darker. Johannes suddenly became aware of how quiet it was. He placed his hand over his chest and felt his heart hammering away. He'd have reams of data to sift through to confirm the results, but it appeared that he had delivered what was arguably one of the most monumental scientific breakthroughs in the history of humankind.

CHAPTER 5

On the outskirts of Trondheim, Later that evening

The navigation app on David Skye's phone interrupted the last few minutes of silence. A female voice with a British accent announced a left turn in two hundred feet. Epiphany slowed the vehicle and turned onto a driveway that hadn't been plowed in some time. The SUV fishtailed on an icy patch as she transitioned from the paved road surface to the deeper snow on the gravel driveway. Epiphany steered through the slide and navigated the winding path until she came to a stop in front of Aidan McCallum's cabin.

Most of the thirty-minute drive from downtown Trondheim had been spent discussing the attack at the mall. David was thankful to have had someone to talk to about it, to help unburden the weight of what they had experienced. Although the actual event was behind them, he knew the memories and shock of what happened would linger on. He got out of the vehicle and stood in silence for a moment. The cabin was set back in a remote section of woods near the Bymarka Nature Reserve. The natural wood siding of the unimposing structure blended into its surroundings. It seemed like a natural part of the forest—a haven for the man who once inhabited it. Evergreens dominated the property, their branches sagging from the weight of the heavy, wet snow. The noise of the city and highway traffic was lost in the distance. David reveled in a moment of serenity following what had been a few chaotic hours.

Epiphany walked over and joined him. "You okay?"

David turned to watch the snow drifting through the fir trees. "It's peaceful here."

"It's a far cry from the chaos we just left behind."

"I know we discussed this in the car, but what did killing those people accomplish?"

Epiphany looked over at David. "It was a senseless act by an insensitive person. Who knows what goes through the mind of someone capable of doing something like that."

"You're right about that," David said. "I can't help but wonder about those two young children we helped. Physically, they'll recover, but what long-term emotional scars will be left behind?"

Epiphany put her hand on David's shoulder. "Let's hope a youthful resilience will carry them through this. With the help of their parents and whatever counseling they might need, they'll be able to move on with their lives."

David nodded. "I hope you're right."

"Come on; let's go inside," Epiphany said.

David unlocked the front door with one of the keys that Aidan had given him, knocked the snow off of his shoes, and stepped inside. Epiphany walked in behind him. They entered a living room to the right of the front entrance. A lamp on the end table next to the sofa had been left on. It cast enough light to illuminate the other rooms. David glanced at the dining area to his left and the kitchen beyond that. A hallway to the right of the kitchen led to several more rooms at the back of the house.

"It feels odd to be standing in someone else's house when they're not here," David said as he dropped Aidan's key ring on the coffee table in front of the sofa. "Even though Aidan gave me the keys, it still feels like trespassing."

Epiphany nodded as she removed her wet shoes and walked into the center of the living room. "Aidan took a minimalist approach in decorating the place," she said while scanning the room. "Not many personal items, no pictures on the walls. When we came in, I was expecting to get more of an insight into the man who lived here by the way his house was furnished and decorated, but there's not much to go on."

"To me, his home and the property it sits on tell a story, nonetheless. Sparse furnishings in a house that's nestled in the woods tell me that Aidan was a man of simple pleasures who didn't need material things to get enjoyment from life. He found contentment in the solitude of living among the trees surrounded by nature." David removed his coat and eased himself into an oversized club chair.

Epiphany smiled at the notion. She took off her coat, dropped it on the sofa, and sat down. "So, what do we expect to find here?"

"Hopefully more detail on what Aidan meant when he told me to find the angel and the orb."

"The orb probably has something to do with the warning Aidan received from the Otherworlds," Epiphany said. "I think it was ten or eleven days ago. He called me immediately after receiving that message."

"I think he called me shortly after talking to you. He told me that a Moirae spirit had contacted him—something about how the only Ebony Sphere of Vayla Isarrus that had not been destroyed had recently been detected here on Earth. That was the first time I had ever heard anything about Ebony Spheres—or Vayla Isarrus."

"It was the same for me. Never heard of either of them. He told me the sphere has the power to change every soul on the planet, or worse to destroy every last one if used improperly."

"The notion that some ancient artifact can alter or destroy all of humanity is scary," David said as he recalled the distress in Aidan's voice when they had talked about it during their phone call. "Aidan was practically begging me to come to Norway to help him find it. He was frantic. The Moirae told him that finding and destroying that sphere would be the most important thing he would do in his lifetime."

"Yeah, no pressure, right?" Epiphany said with a hint of sarcasm. "So, realizing the magnitude of the task, he reaches out to us for help."

"It makes sense the Moirae would want him to find this sphere and destroy it somehow. It's unfortunate they couldn't tell him exactly where it is. The closest they could get was to tell him it's in Norway somewhere. Something about the sphere's signal being too weak and diffused to locate it precisely," David said.

"There was another thing I found interesting. Aidan mentioned the spirit who contacted him was concerned about breaking the eternal vow of the Moirae to never interfere in the lives of sentient beings. It feared it would be censured and banished to the Valley of Shadows."

David shook his head, acknowledging what Epiphany had just said. "Aidan said that's why he was the only one contacted about this. You would think if the sphere was that dangerous, they'd make an exception to their vow, but I guess not."

"So, going back to the angel and the orb, it must have been something Aidan uncovered that would help us find this Ebony Sphere. I'm glad he had offered to dig into the details so we didn't have to. It lessened the burden of preparing to travel to Norway for what could be an extended period of time. Between making travel arrangements to get here, passing off assignments to my direct reports, and making preparations to have someone periodically check on my house while I'm gone, I didn't have time for much else."

"He told me he was in between projects and had the time to investigate more of what we'd be up against," David added. "That freed me up to focus on working with my staff so they could continue progressing several big projects my company is working on—without me around."

Epiphany stood. "Let's check the other rooms in the house. Maybe Aidan left behind some notes." She walked down the hallway at the back half of the house. "Two bedrooms, a bathroom, and a study. I vote we start in here."

David followed her into the study and flipped the switch next to the door. A dim light in the center of the ceiling flickered to life. He walked over to the only furniture in the room, a long work table with two chairs and a desk lamp. What appeared to be a diary of some type caught his eye. Its leather cover was worn from heavy use. David took a seat, turned on the desk lamp, and began paging through Aidan's journal. It felt a little odd getting a glimpse, that he might not otherwise have seen, into another person's life. "It looks like this goes back about six months." He scanned the pages for the last ten days. "Look at this. His journal entry for yesterday mentions the angel and the orb." Reading the words brought back a vivid image of Aidan in blood-soaked clothes uttering his last words. David shivered at the thought.

"What did he say about it?" Epiphany had taken a seat to David's right and was going through the stack of papers on the work table.

"That's the odd thing. He simply wrote 'The angel and the orb.' He didn't elaborate beyond that. Did you find anything?"

"There's a lot of work stuff here. Invoices for equipment used on recent trips. Looks like he spent a lot of time in Africa working on projects to dig new wells and collect and purify drinking water." Epiphany removed a file folder from the bottom of one of the piles of papers and opened it. She removed three letter-sized pieces of paper from the folder and laid them out on the table. "Look at these sketches and the date they were drawn."

"Yesterday," David observed. "On all three of them."

Epiphany touched the most detailed sketch with her index finger. "Looks like an angel and an orb to me. Aidan had some artistic talent." She slid the sketch of a man in long robes, holding an orb up in front of his face, across the table to David.

David glanced at it and then turned to the next page in the journal. "Aidan noted here that on his most recent forays into the Otherworlds to search for the angel and the orb, he kept coming across the name 'Eiken,' but that's where the trail went cold."

"It's not what I was hoping for, but at least we have one more clue. I think our only option at this point is to search the Otherworlds for more information," Epiphany suggested.

"I agree," David said. "I'd really like to learn more about the sphere we've been asked to find.

How about you search for the angel and the orb and anything you can find on the name Eiken, and I'll look into Vayla Isarrus and the Ebony Spheres that she had created?"

"That works for me. I'm curious, how often do you send your second soul into the Otherworlds?"

David paused a moment to think about his answer. "A lot when I was really young. It was like being a child with a new toy. But now, I've been busy running my company. I don't think I've had a need to explore the Otherworlds more than once a year. A lot of times it's for some arcane piece of knowledge about a technology we're investigating that I couldn't find any other way."

Epiphany nodded in agreement. "I'm about the same, maybe even a little less frequently than you. When I started the Samantha Foundation fourteen years ago, we had just begun developing programs to help immigrants commence new lives, to find their way in the countries where they had resettled. Immigration problems have only gotten worse since then. Anymore, there aren't enough hours in the day."

"Journeying into the Otherworlds comes back pretty quickly though," David said. "Do you remember when you first realized you had a second soul?"

"I can't remember a time when I didn't have one. I couldn't have been any older than four or five when I started having the dreams."

"You too? That's how it was for me." David smiled as he recalled those early years of his life. "When I was about five years old, I'd have what I thought were dreams about flying under my own power through magical lands. That turned out to be how my Moirae guide introduced me to the various realms within the Otherworlds."

"The Moirae who eased me into a life with a second soul did an amazing job of making it seem normal," Epiphany said. "Let's see if we can use the gift we've been given to get some answers. I prefer solitude when I do this. Do you mind if I take one of the bedrooms?"

"That's okay with me," David said. "I'll use the living room. Let's meet back here when we're finished."

David walked out to the living room and sat back down in the club chair. He sank into the plush, cloth-covered beige cushions and covered himself with a heavy, red-and-black plaid blanket that was balled up on the sofa. The warmth of the blanket felt comforting. He reached over and turned off the light. It had been a while since he made this journey, and he needed to prepare himself for what he was about to do. To reach the Otherworlds, he'd have to first cross the Black Void, the barrier between physical existence on Earth and the spirit realms that lie beyond. He leaned back, steadied his breathing, and cleared his mind. His thoughts drifted into the ether. His second soul stepped beyond this world.

———

David drifted through the Black Void—no light, no sound, an emptiness so utterly deep and complete. The scariness of a great, infinite darkness wrapping itself around him quickly set in. Although the journey was being made by his second soul in its spiritual incarnation, he had a strong sense of the impact on his corporeal self. His heart rate and anxiety level noticeably increased. His blood pressure had risen slightly.

Falling deeper into the abyss, he felt a presence approaching him. The Moirae who would guide him across the great void was now by his side. She reached out and touched his arm. Her embrace was warm, reassuring. As soon as David's second soul crossed through the void into the Otherworlds, an eternal symphony erupted. His mind was everywhere all at once, overwhelmed by the cosmic flow of primordial energy. The overpowering flood of information that thundered through his brain eventually receded. His breathing and heart rate steadied. Having completed her task of leading David across the Black Void, his Moirae guide returned to one of the many realms within the Otherworlds.

David stood at the bank of a great river. The gentle flow of its water meandered through a broad meadow of tall, green grass. Trees lined both sides of its banks. Long, twisted limbs arched over his head. Rays of light from a brilliant sun sliced through the canopy of leaves that blocked out most of the sky. The air was laden with the fragrant aromas of local plant life. David relaxed his mind. His second soul connected to the Mesh—the holographic structure that threads its way through the fabric of reality, through which he'd see the unseen. At his avail was the universal record, a complex mosaic of all things that ever were, currently are, and could possibly be.

The problem with accessing the nearly infinite amount of information in the vast reaches of the Mesh was finding something. David knew he'd have to focus his search. He concentrated on Vayla Isarrus and the Ebony Spheres. Visions pertaining to the spheres streamed through his head, rapidly, like a surreal video on fast-forward. The landscape around him had changed. He was in a different place than where he started. David's second soul was standing on a plateau, overlooking a valley of rolling hills. The cloudless sky was an unusually deep shade of blue. Vayla Isarrus, the ancient spirit who existed on the other side of time, came into view. She held one of the Ebony Spheres in her hand. The energy of the sphere radiated through David's second soul. A deluge of information about the spheres filled his head: the reason they were created, how they were intended to be used, and the ungodly power they possessed.

David's eyes fluttered open. His shirt was soaked in sweat. He reached over to the side table and switched on the light. "Jesus, how long have you been sitting there?"

"Fifteen, twenty minutes," Epiphany said.

"How long have I been out?"

"It's 11:15. What's that make it? About two hours?"

David leaned forward. "That was intense." He removed the blanket and tossed it onto the sofa.

"Did you find anything we can use?" Epiphany asked, yawning as she spoke.

David ran his hand through his shoulder-length, dark brown hair and took a deep breath before beginning. "Yeah. I felt like I was fed through a fire hose. How much do you know about the Moirae?"

"I remember most of what I learned about them when I was younger. When the spark of life is ignited, the Moirae bestow a soul to each sentient being at the time of birth. They believe in free will and the notion that we all have an existential right to live out our lives without interference from any external source, which includes the spirit realms."

"Yeah, that's essentially what I was taught. Their existence is predicated on maintaining the natural harmony and balance of the universe, where all souls are free to fulfill their destiny. Well, I just discovered that a small, breakaway faction of Moirae, six of them, had foreseen the true nature of living, thinking beings and the possibility that entire societies could drift far from that natural balance that the Moirae strive to achieve."

"You mean, like the current path the people of our planet seem to be heading down," Epiphany said with a sardonic tone.

David smirked. "Yes, like that. Anyway, for Vayla Isarrus, the leader of this renegade alliance, a laissez-faire, whatever-happens-happens approach wasn't good enough. She created the Ebony Spheres, which are literally drops of the primeval energy from which everything, including our souls, was created."

"What were they designed to do?" Epiphany asked.

"They were meant to be used by the apostles, people like you and me, to alter society if it lost its natural order and harmony and started drifting in a direction that was perceived to be too unstable, spiraling out of control, self-destructive. That kind of thing."

"Like I just said ..."

"Yeah I know, like the path the people of our planet seem to be heading down." David completed her sentence with a wry smile. "I can't argue with you there. The intended purpose of the Ebony Spheres was to alter all living souls to the desire and specifications of the apostle who controls them—things like eliminate the ability to commit murder, end hate, stop racism. The first apostle to touch a sphere is the one who controls it. If its use and purpose are not fully understood and mastered, instead of altering all souls on a planet, it could wipe them out. Essentially end all human life. And here's the other thing the Moirae were concerned about. To activate the spheres requires energy. Spiritual energy. So, even if the spheres were used properly, to alter every soul on an entire planet would require the sacrifice of tens of thousands of lives."

Epiphany's facial expression morphed into one of profound thought. "So, if I follow this, to change the souls of billions of people, to create a better world in the eyes of the person who controls the Ebony Sphere, would require that tens of thousands of lives be sacrificed. Do I have that right?"

"Exactly. Think about it. If you had the power to make the world a better place, where no one kills anyone anymore, where there's no more hate, where everyone gets along with each other, would you do it, even if you knew that tens of thousands of people would have to die to make it happen? It's a hell of a moral quandary."

"You look around at the direction our world is taking, the wars, terrorism, hate, and it seems to be getting worse with every year that goes by. I could see where some people might say the sacrifice would be worth it," Epiphany said.

David nodded. "The reason the Moirae also bestow a second soul to a small handful of people every generation or two is to give them a connection to the Otherworlds. Those born with a second soul have the tools and knowledge to help guide the world in a positive way to maintain the harmony and balance that the Moirae want to achieve. It was their way of addressing the problem that Vayla Isarrus wanted to solve with the Ebony Spheres. When the Moirae discovered the plans of Vayla Isarrus and her followers, they imprisoned them in a distant realm and destroyed all of the spheres, or so they thought. Apparently, they missed one. And if we don't find it and determine how to destroy it, well you now know what the repercussions could be."

"How many apostles are there that you know of?" Epiphany asked.

"There's you and me, there was Aidan, and there's Demetrius Wolffe. That's four that I know of. Why do you ask?"

"That's what I thought. So, why isn't Demetrius here?"

"If I recall correctly, Aidan had talked to Demetrius after he called you and before he talked to me. Aidan told me Citizens for a Peaceful Planet is on its last legs. He said Demetrius really needed to focus on keeping it alive and thought that the three of us should be able to handle this."

"Well, I hope he's right. Although now it's just you and me. The other reason I asked was that in my trek into the Otherworlds, I learned there might be one more of us."

"Really? I never knew that. Who? Do you know?"

"No, but I'm going to keep looking." Epiphany stood and stretched. "After the day we've had and after hearing everything you just shared, I think I need a drink. Do you think Aidan has any beer in that fridge of his?" She wandered into the kitchen and rustled through the refrigerator. "Ah, here we go. Do you want one?"

"A beer sounds good."

Epiphany brought two cans of beer back to the living room and handed one to David.

David took a long swig then asked, "Did you have any luck with the angel and the orb?"

"Eiken was the key; the surname of Tiorvi Eiken, a sculptor who lived in the 1500s. He created a life-sized marble sculpture of an angel holding an orb. Only Tiorvi wasn't just a sculptor. He was also a Moirae spirit who stepped through the Black Void to come to Earth to find the last remaining sphere. In making that journey, he lost many of the powers he had in the Otherworlds."

"Given that it still exists, I'm guessing that left him without the ability to destroy the last Ebony Sphere?" David surmised.

"Exactly. He couldn't destroy it, but he did the next best thing. He decided to hide it in plain sight, in the only way he knew how with the limited powers and tools he had. He sculpted a life-sized statue of an angel and placed the orb in its outstretched hand. He sealed the sphere in a cement-like substance then donated the sculpture to a church. He told them it must always be kept in a house of God. Tiorvi believed doing that would protect it from the spirits who created it."

"Is that church still around? Do we know where it is?" David asked with an air of excitement in his voice.

"No and yes," Epiphany replied. "The original church was on an island in Norway called Tjeldøya, in the municipality of Tjeldsund. The old church no longer exists, but when they built a new one to replace it, they moved the statue into it. It's still there today."

"But how did placing the orb in a statue's hand and sealing it in cement hide it?" David asked, looking a bit puzzled.

"After the statue was placed in the original church, they found Tiorvi's dead body on scaffolding next to it. Tiorvi's outstretched hand was gripping the orb.

He took his own life and imbedded the essence of his spirit into the cement coating that covered the orb, which created a veil that smothered the signal radiated by the sphere. The Moirae lost touch with Tiorvi and the orb. Until eleven days ago."

Despite David's attempts to hide it, his expression and physical demeanor revealed the uneasiness he had been feeling for the past several days. "Now that we know where to find the last remaining sphere, there's something else that I've been thinking. It's really been bothering me. I'm worried that we're a bit out of our element, don't you think? We're not trained for this kind of thing. I'm an engineer. I run my own company. I came here out of a sense of duty to the Otherworlds. But are we really geared to do something like this?"

"I've had similar doubts," Epiphany said. "You and I are trying to fulfill our roles as apostles. It's a big ask to step away from that for however long it takes to find the sphere. We don't know what risks we might face. If we do find it, how the hell do we destroy it? But I do know this. I've seen people who start out as decent human beings, and then something happens in their lives that causes them to do a one-eighty. Like a switch had been flipped. They become demagogues indulging the deepest of people's fears. That could just as well happen to a person with a second soul. If a person like that gets a hold of the last sphere, they could wreak havoc on humanity. I don't think we have a choice, David. There's too much at stake not to try. We have to see this through to the end. Knowing what we know now, I'm in. One hundred percent."

David thought about what Epiphany had said. "You made some good points, and I trust Aidan's instincts on this. There are enough unknowns and downsides in using the Ebony Sphere that we should make every effort to find it." David raised his beer toward Epiphany in a toast. "I'm willing to keep trying if you are. First thing tomorrow morning we're making travel arrangements for Tjeldsund."

CHAPTER 6

Kripos Headquarters, Oslo, Norway, Next day, 7:30 am

"Four attacks in the last three months. Bergen, Oslo, Drammen, and now the one in Trondheim. Twenty-seven killed in the first three incidents. The death toll in Trondheim was confirmed about an hour ago. Twenty-three people died. Over twenty more were injured, several of whom are in critical condition." Detective Kari Salversen paused for a moment. That number of deaths in such a short period of time was disturbing. "These cases need to be solved quickly and methodically. I don't want the people of Norway living in fear every time they leave their homes."

Kari nodded at Liv Royse, one of the department's tech experts, and then said, "Let's review the video footage from the news crew that was at the mall. Start at the point where our suspect first comes into view."

Liv sat across the table from Kari. Sitting to Liv's right was the only other person in the conference room, Jens Tofte, a detective in his early fifties. Jens would be working with Kari until the string of attacks was solved and arrests were made.

While Liv cued the video, Kari scanned the conference room, which had become the de facto war room for the recent set of attacks. Multiple sticky-backed flip chart pages for each of the incidents were posted on the walls. Despite the plethora of information that had been collected, little progress had been made in determining if these were random, one-off events or a series of coordinated attacks.

At the age of forty-three, Kari had quickly become a well-respected senior police attorney and investigator with the National Criminal Investigation Service stationed in Oslo. Also known as Kripos, an acronym for KRIminal POliti Sentralen, criminal police central, it was the specialized branch of the Norwegian Police Service that focused on complex criminal activity. Kari's sharp mind and insights had led to successes on several difficult, high-profile cases, resulting in a quick rise through the ranks. Not surprisingly, she had been assigned to be the lead on these recent attacks.

Liv paused the video playback at the spot requested by Kari. The Solsiden Mall was displayed on a large flat screen that filled the front wall next to the door. "We received a copy of the video footage from the television crew that was covering the last day of the cultural festival in Trondheim. The cameraman was recording scenes of the mall area prior to going live with the reporter. He managed to capture useful bits of information about the bomber." Liv hit Play. "Watch the man in the black hoodie enter from the right. He's carrying a large duffel bag and an oversized backpack." She stopped the video at the point where the hooded man sat on a park bench along the skating rink. "He sets the duffel bag on the ground between the bench he is sitting on and the one next to it." She hit Play again. "Then he walks over to Ericson's Seafood Restaurant, where he sets the backpack on top of the brick wall. The news team was on the opposite side of the skating rink when this was recorded, far enough away not to be injured by either of the bombs. The cameraman had the camera zoomed out to get a broader picture of the overall area and festivities. We were lucky that he captured this guy setting the bombs in place."

Kari watched the hooded man walk quickly in the direction of the pedestrian bridge, and then all of a sudden he turned and started running the other way. "Why did he turn around and start running like that?" she asked.

Liv hit the Pause button on the video playback. "I've reviewed this footage several times in preparation for our meeting today. Watch the left side of the screen. A red-haired man comes running from the direction of the pedestrian bridge." Liv hit Play.

"Yeah, it does appear that the red-headed guy is chasing the bomber," Jens said. "I'll check with the Trondheim station to get his ID. He may have been a concerned citizen who put two and two together. Maybe he saw the guy leave the backpack and walk away, and he tried to put a stop to it."

The video kept rolling. Kari flinched when a bright flash filled the screen, followed by the noise of the explosion.

"Both men were close enough to the backpack when it exploded that the force of the blast lifted them into the air," Liv noted. She stopped the video.

"Okay, so it's clear that the man in the hoodie brought the bombs," Kari stated. "Jens, what did you find out about our attacker?"

"We don't have much on him yet. His name is Lars Bohle. Local police are looking into his background. He is a Trondheim resident. Doesn't have an arrest record, so pretty clean up until yesterday. A search warrant has been issued for his residence. We should have information sometime later this morning.”

“Good. Let me know as soon as we have the results,” Kari said.

“There is one more thing,” Jens said as he slid a picture of a tattoo across the table to Kari. “I got this from the Trondheim office. Bohle had a tattoo on his wrist—an image of Earth with a bloody dagger through it and a rising sun in the background.”

Kari got up from her seat and walked over to the flip charts posted to the wall behind Jens and Liv. “We’ve seen that tattoo before.”

Jens swiveled around in his chair and pointed to a specific flip chart page. “There it is, the first attack, in Bergen. Rutger Solberg. He had the same tattoo.”

“Of the previous three attacks, he was the only perpetrator who did not manage to escape,” Kari noted.

“Right, he was shot and killed by police when he attempted to take a hostage,” Jens added. “So, it’s possible the other attackers have the same tattoo.”

Finally, a solid connection between two of these attacks, Kari thought. “Let’s explore the tattoo connection between these two men. They had to get that ink somewhere. Jens, have your team work with the local police in Trondheim, Bergen, Drammen, and Oslo. Check the tattoo shops. See if someone remembers making that design.”

“The first three attacks occurred at gatherings that would have had a large mix of non-Norwegian-born people, including one at a refugee and immigration service center. The Trondheim attack was at a cultural festival,” Jens said. “Has counterintelligence provided anything we can use?”

“I’ve been working with them, following up on the far right, radical group angle, but so far nothing concrete," Kari stated. "None of the known groups that espouse keeping immigrants and refugees out of the country have taken credit for the attacks. We haven't seen anything posted online about the previous attacks from any of these groups that would suggest they had something to do with it. Jens, while your team follows up on the tattoo shops, I'll double back with my contact in counterintelligence to see if they have anything on the tattoo. It's looking like we may have a new radical, fringe group that is intent on operating under the radar."

Kari walked around the table and sat down again. "Do we have anything on the explosives that were used yesterday?"

Jens scrolled through the file structure on his laptop until he found the report he was looking for, and said, "Both explosives generated a huge amount of black smoke. Our ballistics guys suggested that a heavy fuel, or possibly a synthetic one, might have been used."

Kari nodded, "When I talk to counterintelligence, I'll see what they have on file about bomb makers." She glanced at Jens. "Do a deep dive into the backgrounds of Lars Bohle and Rutger Solberg. See if they have a connection to anyone with expertise in explosives. Liv, run through the video footage from Trondheim and look for any matches with people who were at the three previous attacks."

Kari spoke as she stood and walked toward the door. "This continues to be our top priority. No vacation time or personal leave until we solve this."

CHAPTER 7

Tjeldsund Church, A day later, mid-afternoon

Demetrius Wolffe entered the church, leaving the howling wind and snow squalls behind. Would it be here that he might find his salvation, a pathway to a future he could only dream about? Two days had passed since the Trondheim bombing, which had given him plenty of time to rethink the request he had gotten from Aidan McCallum nearly two weeks ago. At that time, the idea of diverting his energy to recover an ancient artifact was of little to no interest. Now, with Citizens for a Peaceful Planet on life support, it was presenting itself as the only way forward.

He dusted the snow off his clothing and removed his winter cap and gloves. The chatter from a group of people, a dozen or so, made its way down the central aisle to the vestibule where he was standing. One of the men turned his head and smiled at him then walked toward Demetrius to greet him.

"Hello, I'm Pastor Lund. But please, call me Patrik. Are you Demetrius?" The man extended his hand.

Demetrius shook the pastor's hand and smiled. "Yes, I am. Thanks for agreeing to let me stop in and see the statue."

"I'm honored to have you here. I've read a lot about the wonderful things you and your organization are trying to achieve. The world needs more people like you."

"We're doing what we can, but I have to admit, the journey we're on is long and arduous," Demetrius said, feeling a bit worn down by the events of the past few days.

The pastor smiled again and said, "In the words of Tiorvi Eiken, the man who sculpted *The Angel and the Orb*, 'There is good in this world; we just have to learn how to see it.' That quote has always stayed with me. Your mission is a good one, Mr. Wolffe. I hope you continue that journey."

Demetrius pointed to the gathering of people and said, "Patrik, am I interrupting something? I can come back some other time if you have something else planned."

"Nonsense," Patrik replied. "You're here now. I'll show you what you came to see. Besides, we're waiting for two more people. This is a weekly meeting of our volunteers who run the annual Christmas Festival."

Demetrius followed Patrik down the center aisle, smiling and exchanging hellos with the volunteers as he passed by them.

Patrik led him to the altar. "Here it is," he said as he pointed with a sweep of his right arm through the air, "*The Angel and the Orb*."

"It's exquisite," Demetrius said. His eyes were transfixed on the life-sized marble sculpture of an angel in long flowing robes with shoulder-length, wavy hair and a full beard. The figure was holding a grapefruit-sized orb in his right hand with his arm extended upward toward the sky. "The workmanship is incredible. His expression, that look of anguish and despair, is so vividly real. I haven't seen anything like that before."

"Tiorvi Eiken had exceptional skills. This is his only work that we know of. The sculpture was made in the early to mid-1500s to the best we can tell. Not many records of the man exist, I'm afraid. The statue was donated to the original church in the last decade of the 1500s. Mr. Eiken was adamant that it remains in a house of God. He insisted upon it as a condition of donating it to our community. When we built this church, we moved the statue in here to stay true to Tiorvi Eiken's wishes."

Demetrius moved around the statue to view it from different angles. "In all of the pictures I've seen online, the orb he is holding was a similar color as the rest of the white marble sculpture."

"You're correct. About two weeks ago, our caretaker was making repairs on the wall behind the statue. He was up on an extension ladder and dropped a hammer. It glanced off the orb and shattered the outer shell, revealing this inner sphere. The poor man was mortified. Couldn't stop apologizing."

Demetrius was spellbound by the lustrous ebony-colored sphere in the statue's hand. A rich sonority emanated from somewhere deep inside it, resonating in a complex waveform that only a person with a second soul could detect. The lush harmonies were absolutely enchanting.

Pastor Lund reached out, lightly grasped Demetrius's right forearm, and nodded in the direction of the main entrance. "The last two members of my group have arrived. I need to step away and get them started. Take as long as you need." He walked to the center of the nave to talk with the volunteers.

The night of the attack in Trondheim, after Demetrius had left the office and gone home, his emotional state was at an all-time low. He was a desperate man seeking desperate solutions. He had spent the remainder of the night searching the Otherworlds for the whereabouts of the mysterious sphere. Perseverance had paid off and led him here to this small village in Tjeldsund. And now he was staring into the beauty of the sphere, bathing in the warm radiance of its song.

The Angel and the Orb had more than captured his imagination. Demetrius felt connected to it. He desperately wanted to touch the surface of the ebony sphere with his fingertips, to feel its energy in his hand. *Had Vayla Isarrus designed the sphere that way,* he wondered, *to capture the mind of an apostle, to entice him to use the sphere?* Demetrius glanced back at the church group. They were busy with their discussion. He extended his hand, slowly reaching for the sphere. Someone coughed. Demetrius retracted his hand quickly and looked back at the volunteers. No one was paying attention to him.

With an emboldened sense of purpose, Demetrius reached out and grasped the sphere with his right hand. The impact was instantaneous. The sphere came alive in his grasp. Energy from deep inside its core radiated throughout his body. His soul resonated with the ancient song that filled his head. The surface of the ebony sphere erupted in shades of light covering the full spectrum of colors. A roiling orange haze engulfed its surface. A protective shell of energy encapsulated Demetrius's body in a thin violet sheen. Shafts of light shot outward from the orb. They filled the church and spilled out through the windows. Within seconds, the light from the sphere subsided, and everything fell silent. The lights in the church flickered, and then they all went off at the same time.

Demetrius released his grip and dropped to his knees. His entire body was numb. Somehow, he found the strength to stand and turn around to see what the volunteers and pastor were doing. The room was filled with darkness. He turned on the flashlight on his cellphone and scanned the room. Every one of them had collapsed. Demetrius rushed over to the pastor. He gasped when he saw the man's face, twisted in agony, with an uncanny resemblance to the facial expression of the statue. He turned to face each of the other people. Every one of them had the same shocking expression on their faces. Demetrius reached down and felt for pulses on several people. Nothing. They were all dead, and somehow, he had triggered the event that did this.

Panic set in quickly. *What have I done?* he thought. Even if it was an accident, he was the one who brought it about. Myriad thoughts streamed through his head. If he called the police, how would he explain what happened? Would he become a suspect? His foundation was struggling. He couldn't jeopardize his meeting with the wealthy potential donor. The last thing he and Citizens for a Peaceful Planet needed was a scandal. Even if he wasn't arrested, the optics wouldn't look good if it got out that the man who founded the organization was brought in for questioning by the police for an incident in which at least a dozen people were killed. His first instinct was to leave, put as much distance between himself and the church as possible. He started toward the main entrance, but the connection to the sphere latched onto his second soul, drawing him to it.

Demetrius ran to the statue and removed the orb from the outstretched hand of the angel. He sped down the center aisle and burst through the doors into the swirling winds and snow. Getting off the island was his only concern. He'd figure out the rest later.

CHAPTER 8

Tjeldsund Church, Minutes later

Beyond thick veils of falling snow, a darkness awaited. There was no avoiding it, no turning back. David Skye had an uneasy feeling about what he'd find, yet he pushed forward anyway. Visibility worsened with each pass of the wiper blades as they swished from side to side, leaving smears of frozen snow across the windshield. He wrapped his fingers tightly around the steering wheel, doing his best to keep the vehicle from veering off the slick, snow-covered road. David desperately wanted to press down harder on the accelerator, but he thought better of it as he fought to guide the Toyota 4Runner along the deserted stretch of highway that hugged the northern coastline of Tjeldøya Island.

"There it is, up ahead, on the right," Epiphany said.

The sound of her voice momentarily broke David's concentration. The silhouette of the old church, its spire reaching into the cold, cloudy sky, stood out against the backdrop of the waterway and the mountains. A heavy, gray fog rolled in off the water. David slowed the vehicle and slid to a stop in the church parking area just off the main road, where he saw six or seven parked cars. The vehicle had barely stopped when Epiphany flung open the passenger door. She leapt out of the 4Runner, swung the door shut, and sprinted down the path leading to the church. David watched her disappear into the snow and mist, vanishing like a specter leaving this world for the next. A transient thought darted through his mind. He had barely been with Epiphany for more than a few days, and given their circumstances, he hoped they'd somehow manage to stay alive for a few more.

David shut off the 4Runner's lights, turned off the ignition, and slipped the keys into his pocket. He took a deep breath to calm his jagged nerves. An unexpected series of snow squalls battering the region had dogged them the entire length of their drive from the airport in Evenes. It felt good to no longer be driving in this messy weather. A gust of wind startled him when it pelted the driver's side of the SUV with small pellets of icy snow. It drew his attention back to the pathway leading to the church—a hundred yards between himself and the darkness that had been consuming his thoughts. That same sickening feeling that filled the pit of his stomach in Trondheim had made a return appearance. Reluctantly, he swung the car door open and exited the vehicle. A blast of wintry air blanketed his body with a spray of snow and mist. His senses came alive as if they had been charged by an unexpected surge of electricity. David zipped up his coat, pulling it in tightly around his neck, hoping to fend off the frigid weather. He turned and sped down the pathway after Epiphany.

His footfalls crunched through the icy snow. The wind whipped at his body. The fog grew thicker with every step. By the time he reached the church, it was difficult to see his hand in front of his face. He entered the vestibule at the front of the building. The door closed behind him, leaving the harshness of the storm outside. All of the lights were out. David saw the beam from the flashlight on Epiphany's cellphone as she scanned the pews in the main seating area. He noticed the mist from her breath billowing through the beam of light.

Epiphany yelled back to David. "They're all dead." Her voice echoed off the hard surfaces of the church interior.

David removed his cellphone from his coat pocket and turned on the flashlight. The beam revealed several light switches at the back of the vestibule. None of them worked. *Maybe there was a power failure from the snow storm,* he thought. He proceeded down the center aisle. There must have been a dozen people in the church, their bodies sprawled across the floor and church pews. He shined the flashlight on the body of one of the victims, a male probably in his late sixties. His face was contorted in what appeared to be agony. It was an unnerving, eerie sight. In his best assessment, the attack at the Solsiden Mall had killed over twenty people. Seeing the faces of the dead in Trondheim and now here in the church was unsettling. He hoped that he'd never become so desensitized to it that someday it wouldn't bother him. "What the hell happened here?" he asked in astonishment.

"I counted fourteen people." Epiphany walked over to join David. "No signs of physical trauma, other than the distressed looks on their faces."

David sat in one of the pews and shook his head in disgust. The darkness that had been tearing at his soul over the last mile of their drive to the church had firmly taken hold. An emptiness had overtaken him.

Epiphany walked toward the altar at the front of the church. "David, come here. Take a look at this."

David pushed his sullen thoughts to the back of his mind and joined Epiphany. The statue was illuminated in the glow of her flashlight. "Look familiar?" she asked.

"Yeah, it looks just like the sketches that Aidan had drawn."

"The angel and the orb. Only there's no orb," she said.

"Do you think what we're seeing here in the church was the work of the Ebony Sphere of Vayla Isarrus?" David asked.

"I can't imagine what else could have caused this," Epiphany said. "Someone beat us to the sphere. We learned about it less than two weeks ago, and now it's gone. Who else knew about it?"

"You, me, Aidan, Demetrius, and possibly the other apostle you came across," David said. "It probably wasn't Demetrius. He's not the type, and he's focused on keeping his foundation afloat. So, that leaves the other person."

"Yeah, only I still don't know who that is. At least not yet, anyway," Epiphany said. "And we don't know if Aidan knew about him or contacted him."

"I think we should get out of here," David suggested.

"Shouldn't we call the police and stick around until they show up?" Epiphany asked.

"What could we possibly tell them, that some otherworldly orb may have killed these people?"

"No, but it doesn't feel right to leave."

"I agree. It doesn't feel right, but the police are going to focus on finding the killer—not on a missing orb from a sculpture." David turned and pointed to the dead bodies on the floor and in the pews. "We have to find that orb and prevent it from being used to do something like this again. And we can't do that if we're taken in to be questioned or, worse yet, jailed."

"You're probably right. Let's get out of here, regroup, and figure out what to do next," Epiphany agreed.

They exited the church, running headlong into the snow, following the path leading back to the 4Runner. When they reached the vehicle, David got into the driver's seat. He fired up the engine, turned the vehicle around, and drove away in the direction from which they had come.

As David drove, his thoughts drifted to the faces of the people sprawled across the pews and on the floor. The expressions on their faces were ghastly. He looked over at Epiphany and asked, "What have we gotten ourselves into?" as he drove through the squall. He headed northward to the only bridge leading off the island. An unnerving realization crept into David's thoughts: This was the start of something much bigger than he ever could have imagined.

CHAPTER 9

Gimsøya Island in the Lofoten Archipelago, Norway

Another round of gusting winds and intense snow squalls battered Gimsøya. Hidden from view, a kilometer from a deserted stretch of highway, a misshapen sphere nearly three meters in diameter violently twisted and turned. It hovered just above the ground in a swale at the base of the mountains. Remnant aftershocks from the trial run of the quantum-well device tore at the fabric of space and time. A brief burst of violet light erupted at the core of the churning sphere. The Black Void that separated this world from the Otherworlds had been breached.

An entity stepped through the rift and set foot on the snow-covered earth. It turned to watch the sphere dissipate and snap shut. The sharp crack of an electrical arc pierced the air. The entity transitioned into something more fitting for this world—a man, six feet tall with shoulder-length brown hair and a thick beard. He was dressed in jeans and a heavy red-and-black plaid coat. Crossing through the Black Void had been a treacherous journey that drained him of his energy. Tiny pinpricks of pain radiated in waves across his now-human body. He lumbered over the rough terrain to the roadway in search of a human soul to replenish the energy he had lost.

"Jesus Christ!" The driver of a white delivery van shouted as he rounded the curve in the road. He instinctively hit the brakes. The van swerved, slid on the snow-covered road, and came to a stop perpendicular to the direction in which he had been driving. A man, barely visible through the near-white-out conditions, had been standing in the middle of the road when the van rounded the curve. There was no time to react. *Did I hit him?* the driver wondered. His heart thumped through his chest, and his hands shook as he released them from the steering wheel.

The driver unbuckled his seat belt, kicked open the door, and stepped out of the van. He placed his hand above his eyes as a makeshift visor to block the swirling snow. If there was a body somewhere along the roadway, he wasn't seeing it. Come to think of it, he didn't hear the loud thump of a vehicle hitting a person. Maybe he didn't hit the man after all. The wind shifted again. Another gust whipped at his body. "Should have put my damn coat on before getting out," he mumbled to himself. He turned to look toward the back of the van. A large hand reached out, grabbed him by the throat, and shoved him into the side of the vehicle. The driver attempted to speak, but the man's grip was too strong.

A jolt penetrated the driver's upper body when he grabbed his attacker's hand in an attempt to break his grip. It felt as if he had latched onto a high-voltage line. The attacker said nothing. The driver stared into his eyes; it felt as if he were gazing into the empty depths of hell. His entire body spasmed in fits of pain that no human should ever feel. In the passage of a few seconds, the driver's soul had been ripped from his body.

The attacker released his grip. The driver's limp body dropped to the ground. His attacker dragged his soulless body to the side of the road, leaving it twisted like an old rag discarded in the snow. An expression of horribly unbearable pain was etched into his face.

The entity from the Otherworlds stepped into the van. The knowledge of its driver was now his. Everything the driver knew, every memory, every bit of learning was at his command. The entity put the van in reverse, turned around, and navigated the roadway to his destination, driving as if he had been doing it for all of his existence. The harmonious sound of a distant beacon had brought him to this tiny rock orbiting a small star at the edge of its galaxy. That same beacon, the soft waves from the only known Ebony Sphere of Vayla Isarrus to have survived, would lead him to his destination.

CHAPTER 10

Evenes, Norway

David Skye pulled over at a small convenience store and diner across from the Harstad/Narvik Airport in the municipality of Evenes. The drive from the church to the airport had been forty minutes. It had taken every bit of that time for David's nerves to settle down. Fortunately, the snow squalls had eased into light flurries, which made the trip much less treacherous. He parked the 4Runner at the front of the lot bordering the highway and let out a sigh of relief.

On the opposite side of the road, airport maintenance crews were busy trying to stay ahead of the snow. Several large plows were clearing one of the long runways, driving in an orchestrated formation that appealed to David's engineering sense of order and precision. He watched a small commuter plane lift into the air and bank right to head in a southerly direction. It disappeared into the twilight sky over a range of snow-capped mountains. *What a beautiful country*, he thought. The more of Norway he saw, the more he imagined what it would be like to live here someday, but he doubted there'd ever be a time in his life when he could settle down and enjoy retired bliss. For the time being, he'd have to leave the dreams of a post-work life behind.

The slight lurch of the SUV coming to a stop had brought Epiphany out of her brief trance. Shortly after leaving the church, she had told David about a few ideas she had for finding the fifth apostle. Epiphany had used the time on the drive back to the airport to search the Otherworlds. David reached over and lightly nudged her shoulder. "Any luck?"

"Yeah, I think so." Epiphany shifted in her seat. She spoke in a sleepy voice. "The information is kind of minimal, but it should be enough to go on. I saw vivid images of a place called Stamsund, somewhere in the Lofoten Islands. There's a house in the woods at the base of a mountain. More importantly, I got a name. Johannes Stinar."

"That's great! Let's go inside. We can get something to eat and lay out a plan for finding him." David zipped up his coat and got out of the car. Epiphany joined him as they walked toward the diner.

The damp air was laced with a touch of diesel fumes from two tractor-trailers that had just pulled into the lot. The drivers of the trucks conversed in their native Norwegian language as they walked toward the entrance of the diner. Among the benefits of having a second soul was the ability to understand and speak most modern languages presently in use on the planet, enabling apostles like David and Epiphany to do their work no matter where they found themselves. David listened to the drivers talk about looking forward to a good meal and some hot coffee before continuing on the remainder of their trip. Another gust of cold air drifted across the parking lot, whipping around the freshly-fallen snow. David shivered as the spray dusted his face. A hot cup of coffee sounded good right about now.

Epiphany picked a table in the far corner of the diner. David dropped his weary body into the chair across from her. A waitress wandered over and took their orders.

"I still feel uneasy about leaving the church," Epiphany said, keeping her voice down.

David looked around the diner. The two truck drivers were the only other patrons, and they were sitting on barstools at a raised counter facing the window—not close enough to overhear what he and Epiphany were talking about. "I agree. It didn't feel right to leave. That's part of what I meant when I questioned whether or not we're cut out to undertake a task like this. We're going to be in situations where we'll need to do things like that. Bottom line, we didn't do anything wrong, didn't see what happened, so there wasn't much we could tell the police anyway."

The diner wasn't very busy. It didn't take long for the waitress to bring their coffee and food to the table. David took a sip, inhaling the pleasant aroma of the dark roasted beans. "There's only the two of us. Finding the sphere is going to be a lot harder now that it's been taken, and we don't know for sure who has it."

"We'll find it. It has to be Johannes Stinar or Demetrius Wolffe."

"Right. We'll start with Stinar and go from there."

Epiphany leaned forward and finished the last of her sandwich. "I've been thinking about this a lot over the last two days. About that question you posed: Would you sacrifice the lives of thousands if it would make the world a better place for billions? My sister was killed right before my eyes by a young teenage boy with a gun. She was only fifteen. I was barely thirteen. She never hurt anyone. Samantha was the most decent, the most important person in my life, and she was taken from this world. I truly believe she would have gone on to do great, meaningful things with her life. But that's never going to happen. We'll never know, and I believe this world is less better off in her absence."

David reached across the table and gently grasped Epiphany's hand. "Jesus. Epiphany, I'm so sorry about what happened to your sister."

Epiphany let her gaze wander to the view outside. "We'd walk to school together. She'd always say, 'Yo Piph, knock 'em dead.' Samantha was the one who gave me the nickname Epiphany. When I was entering my teens, my second soul was becoming more active. I'd have these premonitions of something big that was going to happen, and in many cases what I predicted came to be."

David smiled. "I've gotten so comfortable calling you Epiphany, I sometimes have to stop to remember that your given name is Jade Hendrix."

"Going by the name Epiphany keeps a part of Samantha alive in me."

Another patron entered the diner. A wave of frigid air drifted through the seating area when the door opened. Epiphany shivered. "I still remember the day it happened. It was on a winter day like this one. We had just entered the school grounds when the shooting started. Samantha ran toward me and wrapped her arms around my waist. She was shot in the back. Took a bullet that would have killed me. I fell backward onto the sidewalk. She landed on top of me. Samantha's eyes seemed so distant." Epiphany paused as she recalled that exact moment in time. "She managed one last gasp of air before she died and whispered, 'I love you, Piph.'"

David watched Epiphany wipe the tears that had formed in the corners of her eyes. Maybe it was the particular lighting in the diner or the fact that she had been crying that drew his attention to how rich the blue color of her cerulean eyes really was. David squeezed her hand one more time and released his grip. "That's such a sad thing to have to carry with you."

Epiphany brushed her shoulder-length black hair away from her face and continued on her original train of thought. "What I'm trying to say is that the world would have been a better place with Samantha in it. I know it would have. If whoever uses this sphere does, in fact, attempt to change the eight billion souls on this planet, he's going to do it by killing tens of thousands of people—people like Samantha, who could enrich this world with their lives. We can't let those people die in the hope that society will somehow be better. And who's to say that the person who uses the sphere has a view of a better future that everyone else would agree with?"

David sat back and crossed his arms. "That's a lot to think about. When we talked about this earlier, when we first learned what this sphere was capable of, I wasn't sure which side I was on—do we let whoever controls the sphere succeed, or do we try to stop him? But what you said really strikes a chord with me. Whoever uses the sphere doesn't have the right to decide who is going to be sacrificed for the greater good, and you're right, we don't know that his view of a greater good is what the rest of us would want. I think we have a moral obligation to prevent the sphere from being used, for all of the Samanthas of the world."

Epiphany leaned back in her chair and spoke with a sense of weariness in her voice. "If the last couple days are any indication—the carnage in Trondheim and what we just witnessed in the church—this task is going to be a rough ride."

"I agree. A business associate of mine would always say, 'We have ten miles of bad road ahead of us.'"

The waitress came back to the table with the check and started to clear their dishes. Epiphany left enough cash for the bill and the tip.

After the waitress left, David asked, "Where do we start? We know the sphere has been taken. We've seen what it can do. It could be one of two people who has the ability to use it, and we doubt that it's Demetrius."

"You have Demetrius's cellphone number, right?" Epiphany asked.

"Yeah, why?"

"Let's call him again. See if we can rule him out for sure."

David called Demetrius and waited for him to answer. "Hi, Demetrius. This is David Skye. I'm just checking in to see how things are going on your end. Thought I might give you an update. Give me a call when you get a chance. Thanks. Bye." David ended the call. "It rolled over to voice mail."

Epiphany shrugged in disappointment. "I was hoping you'd get him."

"No such luck."

"That leaves Johannes Stinar."

David opened Google Earth on his cellphone and entered his search criteria. The app zoomed in on the location and provided a pop-up window with additional information. "Says here that Stamsund is a small village on the island of Vestågøy in the Lofoten archipelago."

"Right now, Johannes Stinar is the only lead we have. Let's see where it takes us." Epiphany opened the web browser on her phone and typed in his name. A list of search results came back. She opened the third one in the list. "I'm looking at an interview with Johannes Stinar in a popular physics magazine. Says here the guy's a physicist. Apparently scary smart. The interviewer wrote that Johannes Stinar is a genius recluse who prefers the mysteries of quantum physics over human interaction."

"While you were looking for info on Johannes, I did a route search on my phone. Stamsund is just under four hours from here." David stood. "Ready to go?"

Epiphany nodded.

"During your journey through the Otherworlds you said you saw vivid images of Stamsund. Think you'd recognize the landscape where Johannes Stinar lives?"

"Absolutely," she replied. "Let's find this guy."

CHAPTER 11

Tjeldøya, Norway

Kari Salversen sat comfortably in the cushioned seat located in the central cabin of the Leonardo AW169 helicopter as it glided through the night sky. She looked over at Jens Tofte, who was in the seat next to her, and commented, "The search of Lars Bohle's residence yielded some tangible results."

Jens smiled. "It's nice to occasionally catch a break. Hopefully, the email string our tech analysts discovered between Lars Bohle and Anders Gustason, his associate in Tromsø, will get us a step closer to the people coordinating these attacks."

Located directly in front of each of the two side-by-side seats in the central passenger compartment of the helicopter was an impressive state-of-the-art computer system. Each system had its own CPU, keyboard, and two large monitors mounted one above the other. The components were contained in a heavy-duty console. Kari fired up the computer in front of her seat. She navigated through the network folder structure and opened the sub-folder labeled "Bohle emails." "This is what our tech guys recovered. Bohle and Gustason communicated every day for the seven days leading up to the attack in Trondheim. An attack of any kind had never been explicitly mentioned. They danced around the topic using code words. Gustason mentioned that he was not aware of any 'upcoming festivities' in Tromsø similar to those planned for Trondheim. But he did suggest that he'd like to see that happen."

"It was enough to justify an arrest warrant for Gustason," Jens said.

"Except we have to find him first. Martin Kolbeck, the chief of police at the Tromsø Station, is coordinating the arrest. He called me earlier. Gustason did not show up at work today, and they haven't been able to reach him at his residence. Kolbeck has a patrol officer watching his house."

"Gustason may have heard about Bohle's death. Maybe he anticipated we'd find out about his connection to Bohle and decided to go into hiding."

"That makes sense," Kari said. "It's possible another accomplice of Bohle's heard about him being killed in the attack and tipped off Gustason. Either way, his whereabouts are unknown."

"Nevertheless, it seems like we are finally making some progress. I wasn't sure Chief Nord would approve the use of the helicopter to go to Tromsø," Jens said.

"It surprised me as well. I laid out all of the facts and pushed pretty hard," Kari said, then thought, *Coerced was more like it.* "He wants these attacks to be stopped as soon as humanly possible and sees our efforts to solve these cases as paramount. Success is riding on how quickly we move to achieve that goal. Budget constraints notwithstanding, albeit with all the usual concerns about frugality and getting things done efficiently, Nord told me to do whatever it takes to put an end to these killing sprees."

"So we arrest Gustason when we find him, bring him in for questioning, and see if that leads us to the people behind these attacks."

Kari nodded. "That's the plan. We're going to push pretty hard on Mr. Gustason to see what he knows." She was about to continue her thoughts when a message came through over their headsets.

The pilot spoke in short, concise sentences, "Detective Salversen. Change of plans just came through. New orders from Kripos headquarters. Received an urgent call from Chief Nord regarding an incident at a church in the municipality of Tjeldsund. Should be there in thirty minutes."

"What kind of incident?" Kari asked.

"Multiple people found dead inside the church. Local police and forensics are on the scene. Chief Nord wants your opinion," the pilot replied before ending the communication.

Kari looked at Jens again and said, "Looks like we need to make an interim stop before we get to Tromsø."

Jens swung the keyboard mount downward to lap-level on the computer console in front of his seat. He brought up a map on the lower of the two monitors. "Tjeldsund is on the island of Tjeldøya. I've never been there. Have you?"

"Me neither," Kari answered. "Unfortunately, the first time to a new place for me typically seems to be the result of a crime that's been committed. One of the hazards of our profession, I guess."

Using her keyboard, Kari keyed in criteria to search online for more information about the church. It was located along the coastline in the village of Hol. She scrolled through several pictures showing the inside and outside, along with the surrounding grounds. The wooden church was constructed at the beginning of the 1900s. The site of the original church, dating back to the 1500s, was sixty meters to the east on the shores of the fjord. As she scrolled through a gallery of photographs, a particular set of images caught her eye—several pictures of what appeared to be a life-sized statue of a man in long robes, holding a sphere skyward. What grabbed her attention was the lifelike expression of anguish on the statue's face.

Jens pulled up several satellite images. "There are open fields on either side of the church where we can land." He opened a GPS map showing their position. "We're probably ten, maybe fifteen minutes out."

The helicopter flew in low from the south, following the coastline—its spotlights cut through the dissipating fog. The pilot set the copter down in one of the fields that Jens had observed and then indicated over their headsets that it was safe to depart. Kari and Jens donned their winter outerwear before exiting the warmth of the passenger compartment. They stepped down into several inches of fresh snow, which was whisked about by the downburst of air from the whirring props.

Kari led the way, shining her flashlight across the ground in front of her as they marched toward the church. After entering through the vestibule, they brushed the snow off their clothing and removed their coats, hats, and gloves. A forensics specialist handed them protective foot coverings to put over their shoes, pairs of exam gloves, and hair nets.

Kari and Jens passed through the doors from the vestibule into the main seating area, where they were greeted by Police Superintendent Fredrik Rindahl. Kari and Jens exchanged greetings with him. Superintendent Rindahl led them down the aisle to the middle of the nave. Several forensics technicians were milling about the victims.

"It was cold as hell in here when we arrived," Rindahl said. "The power was out. When we checked, all of the breakers had been flipped to the off position. We can't figure out what caused it; maybe it was a huge power surge from the storm. This is one of the most unusual scenes I've come across in a long time. After we got a better sense of what we were dealing with here, I notified Kripos. We know you've been leading the investigation on that recent string of mass killings, and this sure as hell qualifies as one. I thought it would be a good idea for you to take a look at it."

"We were on our way to Tromsø when we got the notification from Chief Nord to stop here," Kari said.

Rindahl pointed to several of the victims. "Look at the expressions on their faces. It's like they were scared to death."

Kari leaned in closer to a woman in her fifties sprawled on a church pew. "They all look like this?"

"All of them," Rindahl said.

"How many victims?" Jens asked.

"Fourteen," Rindahl replied. "No signs of what killed them."

Jens crouched to take a closer look at one of the victims. "What were they here for?"

"According to Stein Bensen, the caretaker for the church, this was a weekly planning session for their annual Christmas Festival. He's the one who found the bodies and called our station."

"Any witnesses?" Kari asked.

"Not directly. In addition to his duties as caretaker, Bensen is also the local handyman on the island. He was working on a ruptured water line at a bed and breakfast about five minutes down the road when he received a call from Eva Kaasa. She's an elderly woman who lives near the church. Bensen said Eva mentioned seeing a flash of light outside her home, in the vicinity of the church. When she went to her window to look outside, she noticed the lights were out in the church and called Bensen, figuring that he'd want to look into it."

"Did anyone talk to Eva about the flash of light?" Jens asked.

"Yes, we did. Not much to tell really. She said it was a bright flash that lasted a second or two. She couldn't say for sure that it came from inside the church. After Bensen received her call, he finished his work at the B&B before heading to the church. He figured it took him fifteen, maybe twenty minutes to finish what he was working on, and another five minutes to drive here."

"So as far as we know, was Bensen the only one to enter or leave the premises at the time of the incident?" Kari asked.

"When Bensen arrived, he pulled into the parking area and got out of his work truck. That's when he saw two people sprinting out of the church. A man and a woman. Late thirties, early forties was his best guess. He said it really took him by surprise. He didn't know what to make of it, so he decided to play it safe by staying out of sight behind his vehicle. He did get the make and model of the car they left in, along with the license plate number. Said they headed north. Probably to the only bridge off the island would be my guess."

"Based on the timeline you just laid out, if the two people Bensen saw leaving the church were the perpetrators, then they were in the church for twenty to twenty-five minutes from the time the flash of light was noticed by Eva Kaasa," Kari surmised.

"That sounds about right," Rindahl acknowledged.

"Superintendent, on the chance that this might be part of the string of attacks we've been investigating, would you mind if Detective Tofte stays on and liaises with your team?" Kari asked.

"No problem. We could use the extra help."

"Thank you. Jens, please work with one of Superintendent Rindahl's team to track down some information. Follow up on that license plate number. I want to know whose car that was and who the two people Bensen saw running from the church are. Also check with the airlines at the Harstad/Narvik Airport. Get passenger manifests of people arriving and departing over the past several days. Maybe whoever did this arrived or left on a flight into or out of that airport."

"Detective Tofte, I'll pair you up with one of my investigators and help get you set up with a hotel near our station," Rindahl said, then looked at Kari. "Anything else you need from me?"

"No, thank you for your time, Superintendent. We'll take a quick look around and then get out of your way." Kari pulled Jens to the side and said, "I hope you don't mind being volunteered to stick around and follow up on this."

"Not a problem. If you hadn't volunteered me, I probably would have suggested it myself."

Kari walked to the front of the church, stopping at the statue she had seen in the photo gallery during her online search. "Huh."

"Something wrong?" Jens asked.

"Two things. The expression on the face of the statue is exquisitely detailed. Notice any similarities?"

"You mean, like with the victims here in the church?" Jens turned to look at the expression of the pastor whose body was partially in the aisle.

"Exactly," Kari said. "The faces of the victims have exactly the same expression as the statue. It's an incredibly odd coincidence. Don't you think?"

"Yes, it is. What's the second thing?" Jens asked.

"In every picture of the statue I saw online, it had an orb in its hand. But the orb's missing."

Kari turned and walked back toward Rindahl. "Superintendent, how long has the orb been missing from the statue?"

Rindahl pursed his lips, "Sorry, forgot to mention that. The caretaker noticed it was missing when he was in here waiting for the police. He was here earlier in the day clearing the steps and walkway for the people coming this afternoon. He said the orb was still here when he left shortly before noon."

CHAPTER 12

The Lofoten Islands, Norway, Evening

"Who are you and what do you want?"

Not the greeting David Skye was expecting, nor was the shotgun aimed at his chest. David was cold, tired, and hungry. It had been a long day, and he didn't have the energy, physically or mentally, to deal with the agitated, nervous man aiming a loaded weapon at him. He and Epiphany needed to know if Johannes Stinar was in possession of the last remaining Ebony Sphere. It looked like it was going to be a much more difficult task than they had anticipated.

David steadied his nerves as he stared into the eyes of the man standing at the corner of the wraparound porch. He was maybe all of five feet seven inches tall. His gray sweatpants were tucked into his winter hiking boots. The large navy blue parka he wore seemed to be a size or two too big. His short brown hair was ruffled, looking as if he had just gotten out of bed. Boyish facial features belied his true age, which David guessed was probably early forties.

"Both of you, keep your distance," the man demanded.

"Whoa! Please take it easy." Staring down the barrel of a shotgun heightened David's need to focus his thoughts. His body temperature was rising from the stress. He glanced at Epiphany, who appeared equally nervous. "I'm David Skye, and this is Epiphany. Are you Johannes Stinar?"

"What the hell kind of name is Epiphany?" the man asked.

"It's a nickname my sister gave me. My given name is Jade Hendrix."

The man holding the gun tilted his head. It appeared as if he was concentrating on something. "Both of you. You're like me. You have two souls."

David sensed a soft, gentle hum emanating from the man's second soul. This had to be Johannes. Before he could say anything, Epiphany jumped in.

"You sense our second souls, don't you?"

"I do," the man said. "That doesn't mean I'm happy about you being here."

"So you are Johannes Stinar, right?" David asked again.

The man lowered the shotgun. "Yes, I am."

David's shoulders dropped as the tension melted away. *Safe for now,* he thought.

"We'd like to talk to you about something called the Ebony Spheres of Vayla Isarrus. Have you heard of them?" Epiphany asked.

"I recently learned about them. They're not my primary concern at the moment." Johannes shook his head in disgust. "I didn't ask you to come here. I've got work to do. I'm at a critical point in my studies, and I have a monumental task ahead of me. You can't just show up like this unannounced. I don't have time for interruptions."

"We apologize for the inconvenience, Johannes, but we really need to talk to you." David was willing to press a little harder now that the gun had been lowered. "Can we go inside to talk?"

Johannes motioned to the front door. "It's unlocked." David and Epiphany entered the one-story house. Johannes removed his boots and put his parka on the coat rack in the hallway. He leaned the shotgun against the wall. "Please remove your shoes and leave them on the rubber mat by the door. I don't want snow melting all over my floor."

David and Epiphany removed their shoes and hung up their coats. They followed Johannes into the living room and took a seat on the sofa. Johannes grunted as he sat down in a large, cushioned arm chair. A pleasant smell of burning wood wafted from the stone, raised-hearth fireplace. Several eight-by-ten pictures rested on the thick oak mantel. David recognized the pictures of Isaac Newton and the iconic Albert Einstein. He was unfamiliar with the other two men, presumably scientists. Johannes's house resembled an arts-and-crafts style on the interior. The white walls were simply decorated with several pictures of forest scenes and Norwegian fjords. Natural oak baseboard trim and window molding appeared to be a common feature used throughout the house. To David, it felt very much like he was sitting in the house he grew up in. The memory helped to settle his nerves after having had a shotgun aimed at him.

"I need to know who I'm dealing with before we go any further. Tell me about yourselves," Johannes insisted.

Epiphany started by providing a brief history of her efforts in starting the Samantha Foundation to help people who had emigrated from their homeland to adjust to life in a new country. David followed with a background on his efforts in starting Blue

Skye Technologies. He told Johannes about the technologies his company was developing for cleaning up the oceans and atmosphere.

Satisfied with the information they provided, Johannes asked, "Why are you here?"

Epiphany started in on the reason she and David came to Stamsund. "We tracked the only surviving Ebony Sphere created by Vayla Isarrus to a church in Tjeldsund. But as of this afternoon, it has gone missing. Other than David and me, only two people would have the ability to activate and use the sphere: you and Demetrius Wolffe."

Johannes's face drifted into an expression of anger. The heated tone of his voice quickly confirmed his emotional state. "And you two are here because you think I have it?"

"Do you?" David pressed.

"No, I don't." Johannes got up out of his chair and paced in front of the fireplace. "Why do you think I have it and not Demetrius Wolffe?" he demanded.

"We've tried calling Demetrius multiple times, and he doesn't answer," Epiphany said.

"Well, that should tell you something, shouldn't it?" Johannes shot back. "He probably has it."

"We know his business is struggling, and he's focusing on keeping it from going under," David interjected. "We didn't think he would be the one to take it. And we didn't know about you until today."

"So naturally you accuse me of taking it. I'm in the middle of a breakthrough on a new technology. That's what I need to be focusing on," Johannes stated emphatically. "Not on being accused of doing something I haven't done."

David kept watching Johannes. The man was agitated again, and David worried that he might make a move for his shotgun. "We're just trying to cover our bases."

"The sphere has been activated, Johannes," Epiphany stated bluntly. "Fourteen people were killed in the church in Tjeldsund. Now we think whoever has it will use it again—to change all of humanity."

"And to do that will require the sacrifice of tens of thousands of people to power the sphere. That's how many people are going to die if we don't do something," David stated. "We have to move fast to stop the person who controls the sphere."

"I'll say it again: I do not have the sphere." Johannes emphasized each of the words as he said them. "You can search every square centimeter of my house and property if you want."

"Johannes, would you mind if I speak to Epiphany in private?"

Johannes pointed to the adjoining room and said, "Use my study if you like. Don't touch anything!"

David followed Epiphany into the study. It was like stepping into another world. Flip chart paper covered the walls. Exotic mathematics seemed to fill every amount of available space on the paper.

"Have you ever seen anything like this before?" Epiphany asked.

"No, this is a first," David replied. "What do you think? Is this guy telling the truth?"

"I think I can read people pretty well. It seems to me that he is being truthful. I don't think he has the sphere."

"There are a couple of other things that I think support that notion," David said. "If he did take the orb from the statue in the church, that would have put him in Tjeldsund when we were there. When we pulled into his driveway, there were no tire tracks in the fresh snow. And did you notice that big black Range Rover parked alongside the house when we pulled up?"

"Yeah, I did. It was covered in snow as well. Hasn't moved at all today."

"That logic is pretty sound. It couldn't have been me, could it?" Johannes said, standing in the doorway between the living room and study. His voice startled David and Epiphany.

"And the only footprints in the snow around the house were yours. So I didn't wander out to the road and get picked up by someone either," Johannes added.

David looked at Epiphany. "I guess that leaves Demetrius."

"Let's contact Citizens for a Peaceful Planet first thing tomorrow morning during business hours. Maybe we can find another way to get in touch with Demetrius or at least find out where he is," Epiphany said.

"I like that idea." David leaned against the desk and then remembered Johannes's instruction to not touch anything. He moved away from it and added, "Johannes, we've inconvenienced you enough. Can you recommend a hotel around here where we can stay tonight?"

Johannes rolled his eyes. "Really? It's pretty late. You'll never find something at this hour of the night. Not around here anyway. I have a spare bedroom you can use if you don't mind sharing the room."

"That works for me," Epiphany said.

"Me too." David welcomed the idea of not having to hunt for a place to stay.

"So tell me more about this sphere. What is it the two of you hope to achieve?"

"We've been asked to find and destroy the last remaining sphere," Epiphany said. "I know you're busy with your work, but is there any way you can help us do that?"

"I'm not offering to help you find the damn thing, but I might be able to help destroy it."

David pointed to the wall behind the desk. "Sorry to interrupt, Johannes, but I see this written on several of the flip chart pages. 'Quinta Essentia.' What does that mean?"

"It's Latin for the Fifth Essence. The Quintessence." Johannes walked up to one of the flip chart sheets pasted to the wall. "Among all of these equations, I found an answer—one that will unlock the doors to the deepest mysteries of physics. Ever hear of a Theory of Everything?"

David nodded. "I've read a little about it. One overarching formula that unites the four fundamental forces in the known universe. Is that what all of these calculations on the wall are? Do you think you can actually solve it?"

"I believe I already have," Johannes said with a noticeable air of confidence. "These calculations you see, the mathematics involved is something I had to develop to make the theory work in eleven dimensions. During the earliest stages of our universe, the four fundamental forces that we know of existed as one unified super-force in an eleven-dimensional space. As the cosmos cooled and expanded, seven of those dimensions curled out of existence, leaving behind our three dimensions of length, width, and height, plus the fourth dimension of time."

"What happened to those hidden dimensions?" Epiphany asked. "Do they still exist?"

"An astute question." Johannes admired her insight. "They do still exist in the form of what we know as the Otherworlds. You've both experienced the Black Void, right?" Not expecting an answer to his rhetorical question, Johannes continued. "It's the boundary wall that separates our four-dimensional view of reality from the seven remaining dimensions of the Otherworlds."

"I wouldn't have guessed there was an answer in physics for what we actually experience when we cross the void," David said.

"I'd like to think physics has an answer for pretty much everything. The mathematics are revealing something very interesting. An ancient energy, the Quintessence, courses through the seven hidden dimensions and our four-dimensional reality. It's the fundamental energy from which everything is created, including our souls. Its influence on the physical world is like hidden currents surging deep below in the depths of the ocean, or like forces that alter the direction of the wind. We cannot see them or be aware of how they really move, but we can observe the effects of their actions. An example would be the dark energy physicists believe is causing our universe to expand at an accelerated pace."

"Going back to my earlier question, Johannes, you indicated you might be able to help us destroy this last remaining Ebony Sphere. How would you do that?" Epiphany asked.

"I've developed and have been testing something I call a quantum-well device. It can tear a hole in the fabric of reality and expose all eleven dimensions. Essentially it creates a well from which I can tap into the Quintessence. Through the quantum well I could provide an infinite source of energy capable of powering entire cities and enabling spacecraft to travel at light speed to the most distant stars."

"That's amazing, Johannes," Epiphany said. "And would this quantum well be capable of destroying the Ebony Sphere?"

"I think it can. The quantum well is a two-way street. We can extract energy from the well, and we can push energy into it. If you find the sphere, we can inject it into the quantum well, where it will be torn apart, never to be seen again."

"So will you help us?" Epiphany asked.

"Well, I think I kind of have to now," he said.

"What does that mean?" David asked.

"Because I think we have another problem—one that maybe you can help me solve."

"What problem?" David wasn't happy with the worried sound of Johannes's voice.

"I tested my quantum-well device in a remote area of Gimsøya, about an hour north of here. There were some anomalies during the trial run, so I double-checked the equations."

Epiphany was growing impatient and wanted Johannes to get to the point. "And what did you find?"

"As I said, my device creates a fissure that opens all eleven dimensions. The equations, under certain conditions, allow for aftershocks, not unlike those of an earthquake. I calculated there would be several over the next two days. The first one has already taken place. When that happened, it briefly reopened a rift, and something from the Otherworlds crossed over to our world."

"How do you know something crossed over?" David asked. "And what exactly was it that made the crossing?"

"A little over an hour ago I ventured into the Otherworlds to look at the trial run, to see what might be revealed about these future aftershocks.

It's how I learned about Vayla Isarrus and her last remaining Ebony Sphere. I witnessed the first aftershock from my device. It opened a pathway into the celestial prison in which Vayla Isarrus and her followers had been banished. Essentially, I'm responsible for freeing her last surviving follower."

David was quiet for a moment, while trying to absorb the magnitude of the problem. His thoughts quickly sidetracked to the conversation he had with Epiphany at Aidan's house, regarding whether or not they were equipped to undertake the task of finding the Ebony Sphere. Epiphany had voiced the concern of not knowing what risks they might face. This was shaping up to be one of those risks—a monumental one. "One of her followers is here now? What do you think it will do?" David asked.

"It will follow the beacon from the sphere to the location of whoever has it—most likely Demetrius Wolffe. The spirit will help him master the use of the Ebony Sphere for its intended purpose."

"How much time do we have, Johannes?" Epiphany asked. "How long will it take for Demetrius to master the use of the sphere to the point where he can use it to change eight billion souls?"

"That's been difficult to determine, and I didn't follow the timelines of this spirit to any great extent, but I'd say we are days away. Probably no more than five or six," Johannes suggested.

"Jesus," Epiphany uttered.

"There is another thing you should know," Johannes said.

"Oh, this just keeps getting better," Epiphany said sarcastically.

"This spirit will stop at nothing to protect Demetrius and to help him achieve the deployment of the sphere. If we're hunting the sphere, it will be hunting us, and it has the ability to take the souls of the living. It can rip a soul from a person's body."

"Can this spirit be killed?" David asked.

Johannes looked at him and stated in a blunt, matter-of-fact tone, "I don't know. That's the problem I'm hoping you can help me solve. How do you kill something that can't be killed?"

CHAPTER 13

Lyfjord, Norway, Late evening

The drive from the church to Lyfjord, a small village on the island adjacent to the western shores of Tromsøya, had been a tiring one. Demetrius Wolffe caressed his sore legs; they were stiff from sitting in the car for well over four hours. He took in the view of the harbor through the picture window in the living room. The glow of lights from a few houses scattered along the shoreline reflected off the water. The long, shimmering, green cords of the aurora arced across a clear night sky. The quiet solitude would do him good. A friend of Christian Slagg's owned the bungalow, and Demetrius was fortunate that it had been available for a few weeks. He made arrangements to snap it up throughout the rest of December and figured he'd use the time to lay out a path forward for whatever few months he had left. Hopefully Gerd Schumann would come through with the donation they had discussed. At the moment, it was the only viable option for keeping Citizens for a Peaceful Planet going beyond his lifetime.

Demetrius sat alone in the dark, sipping his bourbon. The smooth, sweet taste as it first entered his mouth was followed by a spicy finish. The alcohol eased his nerves, but it wasn't solving his problems.

Misery can eat a person away from the inside, and Demetrius felt as if he had more than his share of misfortunes: a failing business, recently learning that he had an inoperable form of cancer, and now the incident at the church. Fourteen deaths plagued his thoughts. He couldn't stop thinking about those innocent people, all dead on his account. It was an accident, completely and utterly unintentional. How could he have known they'd die like that? If he was going to save the Oslo office of Citizens for a Peaceful Planet, he'd have to find a way to move past the suffocating problems weighing him down.

As Demetrius sat quietly, gazing at the view outside, the sound of an approaching vehicle caught his attention. Its headlights illuminated the trees as it got closer. He placed his glass of bourbon on the side table, got his coat, and descended the stairs to the bonus room on the ground level. A dissonant hum filled his ears. Its complex resonance echoed deep inside his head. The source of the sound felt as if it was coming from somewhere nearby, outside the house. Eddies of static charge crept through the air. The shrill dissonance had gotten louder.

Goosebumps rippled across Demetrius's skin as he reached for the door knob. Whatever this was, it was close. He slowly opened the door. A white van was parked in the driveway in front of the bungalow. The driver got out of the vehicle, closed the door, and walked toward him. Demetrius wasn't expecting anyone and was shocked when he realized the dissonance was emanating from the approaching figure. The stranger stopped at the doorway. A man at least six feet tall with a muscular build stared into Demetrius's eyes. The light from the bonus room illuminated his long, brown hair. He had a thick beard and was dressed in jeans and a red-and-black plaid overcoat. To Demetrius, it looked like the guy had just wandered away from a logging camp. The stranger said nothing.

Demetrius stumbled backward. His voice quivered. "Who the hell are you?"

"My name is Asgeir." His gravelly voice was low and deep. "I am one of the Moirae, the last of the faithful followers of Vayla Isarrus."

"Asgeir, the Spear of the Gods," Demetrius said. The ability of his second soul to translate multiple languages had given Demetrius the meaning of the old Norse name. "You expect me to believe you're a spirit from the Otherworlds?"

Asgeir moved past him and entered the room. Demetrius moved aside and closed the door.

"I'll prove it to you," Asgeir said. His body slowly morphed into the shimmering wisps of a human figure.

Demetrius stepped back and bumped into the door as he watched in shock as the hazy humanlike figure faded in and out like a mirage. Asgeir was translucent and barely visible, appearing like heat waves rising off hot asphalt on a blistering summer day. Demetrius gasped as he watched Asgeir shed his gauzy veil and reappear in human form. "I didn't think spirits from the Otherworlds could cross into our world."

"A tear in the fabric of space and time was created by a man of science on your side of reality. He opened a gateway through which I could pass. The journey was not without its sacrifices. There is no going back, and I've had to forsake many of the powers that I once enjoyed in the Otherworlds. Nevertheless, the trek was worth the sacrifice. The song of the only surviving Ebony Sphere of the great Vayla Isarrus has guided me here to you."

Demetrius trembled, almost too distraught to speak. "I didn't mean to kill all of those people. That was never my intent."

"It was not you who killed them. You might have been the conduit that brought it to life, but it was the Ebony Sphere that took the souls of those people."

"Why did they have to die?"

"It's an unfortunate consequence. Sometimes innocent souls must be sacrificed for a greater good."

"What do you want from me?" Demetrius asked.

"It's not what I want from you that matters, Demetrius. It's what the people of your planet need from you that's important. I feel the torment that burdens your soul. You've tried to change this world for the better, but it hasn't been enough to make a difference. Your world should never have been allowed to progress to this point in its evolution. The people of your planet have become all too adept at finding ways to kill each other. They excel at it. Your society has been spiraling out of control for entirely too long. With my help, you can change that."

"I don't think I have it in me to use the sphere as it was intended," Demetrius said.

"If your life were to end tomorrow, would you be happy with the state of the world as you are leaving it?"

"No. Definitely not. There's so much more to be done."

Asgeir approached Demetrius. "Do you not wish to see the changes you're attempting to make come to fruition?"

"I'd love to see my aspirations become reality. But I knew going into this that changing the culture of society would take more than my lifetime."

"It doesn't have to be that way, Demetrius. You have an opportunity to save this world, but you don't have much time. The cancer that eats away at your flesh is spreading."

"How'd you know about my cancer?"

"The discordant harmonies of the disease fill my ears. If we act now, you will have time to change this world in the ways that you have envisioned and still live long enough to witness the fruits of your labor."

Demetrius felt tired and worn down. Although the past twenty-five years had been replete with joyous successes, they had also been grueling. The most recent several years had exacted a punishing toll. He was intrigued by what Asgeir was proposing. *What harm could there be in at least progressing to the next steps?* he thought, then he asked Asgeir, "How would this work? What would we have to do?"

"Tonight you need to rest. I will return tomorrow to show you the way."

CHAPTER 14

Tromsø, Norway

Kari Salversen was baffled by what she had seen in the church, and it was unclear at this point if the incident was connected to the others. Chief Nord was pushing hard to solve the string of attacks over the past several months, and the situation at the Tjeldsund Church added an unwelcomed wrinkle. Whatever pressure Nord was feeling from above was flowing downhill to her, with the added weight of his expectations. For now, she'd treat what happened in Tjeldsund as if it was related to the Trondheim attack and the ones that preceded it.

The sound of the pilot's deep voice resonated through Kari's headphones. "We'll be landing at Tromsø Airport in twenty minutes."

"Thanks," she replied.

Kari ran through a mental checklist. First, text Martin Kolbeck to let him know she was twenty minutes out. She smiled at the thought that Martin had advanced through the ranks to become the chief of police at the Tromsø district. He was an outstanding officer who possessed a natural inclination for the job. She couldn't have been happier when she had learned about his promotion to chief. Martin responded quickly, indicating he'd pick her up at the hangar area that had been preapproved for the chopper landing.

Martin was the officer who had mentored Kari early in her career. The man had great instincts and a keen sense when it came to deciphering disparate clues to a crime. He had provided her with an excellent foundation of analytical skills from which to craft her own methods. What she admired most about him was his patience and willingness to teach others. She had adopted those traits in her own approach to helping younger officers develop their abilities. Unfortunately, she had not maintained contact with Martin for some time now. He had taken a position in Tromsø, and Kari had remained in Oslo. She had gotten her law degree and went on to become one of the best detectives and police attorneys in the Norwegian Police Service. She looked forward to seeing him again.

Kari moved on to the second item on her mental list: checking her service weapon. She had the necessary approval to carry the weapon on her person. The standard-issue H&K P30 pistol was safely holstered under her coat. The magazine in the gun was fully loaded, and she had brought three more magazines with her. Given what had just happened in Tjeldsund, she wasn't going to take any chances.

The follow-up work at the church was left in Jens Tofte's capable hands. He'd coordinate the investigation in Tjeldsund and keep her up to speed. Anders Gustason going on the run was a setback, but they'd eventually find him, and when they did, she'd want to be in Tromsø when he was arrested because she would be the one leading the interrogation. As Kari stared out the window of the helicopter and scanned the horizon, her mind was filled with unanswered questions. The horrified expression on the faces of the victims who died in the church had etched a seemingly permanent imprint in her brain. There had been no evidence of foul play and no plausible explanation for what killed those fourteen people. She'd have to wait for the medical examiner's results to hopefully shed some light on the situation.

The pilot lowered the helicopter onto the tarmac. His voice came in over her headphones, "Detective Salversen, you're good to go."

"Thanks for the lift," she said into the mouthpiece. Kari removed her headset, opened the exit door from the passenger's compartment, and stepped out onto the ground. A wave of cold air crashed down over her body from the whirring props overhead. She slung her backpack over her shoulder, lowered her rolling luggage bag onto the tarmac, and closed the doors to the chopper. A gust of wind whipped through the landing area. She turned and moved quickly toward the building where Martin Kolbeck was waiting.

Martin smiled as she approached him. His stout body stood like an immovable object against the cold, gusting wind. Kari noticed that his dark brown hair was starting to show signs of graying. He reached out with a large, thick hand. "Good to see you again, Kari," he said in a mellow voice.

His strong grip enveloped Kari's hand as she answered, "Nice to see you as well. What's it been, a couple of years?"

"Sounds about right. Come on. Let's get out of the cold." Kolbeck led Kari to an unmarked police vehicle. "I thought Jens was joining us."

"He's staying behind to coordinate and supervise the investigation of the crime scene in Tjeldsund,"

Kari said. "Where do you stand on the arrest of Anders Gustason?"

"Whereabouts still unknown. He'll turn up, and we'll be there when he does."

Kari loaded her luggage bag into the trunk of the car. She climbed into the passenger's seat and buckled up. Martin started the engine and pulled out onto an access road. They headed for the Route 862 entrance to the tunnel system under the central portion of the island.

"Do your aunt and uncle still have that vacation house in Tromsø on the mainland? Is that where you're staying?" Martin asked.

"Good memory, Martin, and yes, that's where I'm staying."

A call came through on the police radio. "Hello Chief, there's been another suspicious death," the dispatcher on the other end of the line reported. "On the art center grounds across from the Polaria Aquarium. Forensics and an officer are there now."

"We'll be there in ten minutes," Martin responded.

During their brief jaunt through the tunnels, Kari and Martin discussed what needed to be done to locate and apprehend Gustason. Kari also provided a quick update on the Trondheim and Tjeldsund crime scenes. When they arrived at the art center, Martin parked the car. He and Kari hurried across the grounds to find the officer in charge.

The patrol officer, a man in his mid-thirties, led Kari and Martin to the body. He had cordoned off the area while the forensics team gathered and documented evidence. "How'd the victim die?" Martin asked.

"Not really sure about that, Sir," the officer replied.

Martin squatted and shined his flashlight into the face of the victim, a man dressed in winter jogging apparel. He was in his mid-fifties and had the physique of an avid runner. "Jesus," Martin exclaimed. "This is the third one like this today." He stood and handed Kari the flashlight.

Kari leaned in to get a closer look. "The expression on his face is identical to the victims in the church. It looks like he had been frightened to death," she said, parroting Superintendent Rindahl's words. "Were the other two like this?"

"Exactly. Same expression, no signs of what killed them," Martin said.

"Where and when did they happen?" Kari asked.

"The one before this happened earlier this evening, not far from here near the lake at the top of the island. The first incident occurred on Gimsøya in the Lofoten Islands. That's a six-hour drive from here. Local police found the body of a deliveryman off to the side of the road. Same characteristics: no sign of what killed him and the same horrified look on his face."

Kari nodded, her mind frantically trying to pull together all of the pieces of these crimes.

"What in hell is going on here, Kari?" Martin said as he took another look at the man's face.

CHAPTER 15

Lyfjord, Norway, Next day

A cool breeze drifted over the calm water of the harbor and made its way up the hillside on which the bungalow had been built. Demetrius Wolffe stood on the porch, admiring the beauty of the landscape when the wave of air washed over him. He had never experienced the "blue hour" before, which usually occurred between 1:00 and 2:00 in the afternoon this time of year. Even though the sun never rose above the horizon, its residual light reflected off the sea and the white snow, bathing the landscape in a rich, deep blue. He found the blue tint to be eerily beautiful. It helped put his mind at peace, a brief and welcomed counterpoint to the stress he had been experiencing almost daily over the past few months. Citizens for a Peaceful Planet would never achieve the goals he strived to attain in his lifetime. Time was slipping away, and there was nothing he could do to change that.

Demetrius's train of thought was disrupted by the sound of a vehicle driving along the four-hundred-meter stretch of winding road leading to the bungalow. He recognized the white van that Asgeir was driving and walked down to the driveway to greet him. After brief salutations, they entered the house from the ground level and walked up the stairs to the living room. Demetrius sat down on the couch and said, "I have the same question as last night. How do we proceed, assuming that I'm going to go through with this?"

Asgeir sat in a chair facing Demetrius. "I want to know what your vision of the future would look like if you had the power to change this world for the better. The most important thing you need to do is to have an absolutely clear picture of what that looks like."

Asgeir's response was expected to some extent. It was a good portion of what Demetrius's racing mind had thought about during the restless bouts that interrupted his sleep last night. "I've considered so many things." The details of the mission statement for Citizens for a Peaceful Planet came to mind. "We should have a society that revels in and embraces the things that make us different. Every person on this planet should feel like he or she has something vital to contribute to the greater whole. No matter how big or small the contribution, we're all important. I'd eliminate the ability to kill each other. That would put an end to all future wars, terrorist attacks, and deaths from gun violence or by any other means. I'd want to end the petty prejudices of the human mind that foster distrust in anything that's different. No more hate, no more racism."

"Everything you mentioned is what we envisioned the Ebony Spheres should make possible when Vayla Isarrus first created them," Asgeir said. "Is there anything else?"

"I'd like to see a world population that focuses on eliminating hunger and poverty. We need to do more to save our environment, not just for our generation, but for all of those that follow."

"These things are admirable ambitions, and how much progress has been made in solving these problems?"

"I think you already know the answer to that. Not enough!"

"You didn't mention technological advancement. How does that fit into your vision?"

Demetrius took a moment to think about his answer. "I probably haven't given that the consideration it's due. Technological advancement needs to be a vital piece of the puzzle in solving the problems the world faces. I'd like to see science focus more on solving issues with pollution, agriculture to feed the hungry, and sustainable energy. We also need to understand the downsides of technology and the harm it could do if misused, like nuclear technology and AI for example."

"Misusing technology has been a huge problem for your people. It's like putting loaded weapons in the hands of children."

Demetrius nodded; it was a sentiment he shared at times. "I think I've covered the full list as I see it. If I could only achieve one of these wishes, the most important thing would be to put an end to the ability to kill one another. There should never be a problem so big that the only solution is killing each other." Demetrius was hitting his stride. Talking about these things with someone else was cathartic. "This morning, I did a little research. In the last two hundred years, the number of people killed as a result of direct armed conflict is in the range of thirty to fifty million. And the people compiling these numbers believe their estimates are low. Even if I use the low end of that range, that's an average of one-hundred-fifty thousand people a year for two hundred years."

"You live on a bloody planet, Demetrius. This is why Vayla Isarrus and the others created the Ebony Spheres, to enable people like you to do something about these types of problems."

"Here's the thing that I found the most shocking. In recent years, the average annual global homicide rate is on the order of several hundred thousand people killed each year." Demetrius leaned back and looked upward at the ceiling. He let out a deep breath. His rant had been both exhausting and cleansing.

Asgeir stood. "You have an excellent grasp on what an idealized future should look like, Demetrius. I need you to focus on these ideals while I take care of a few things. When I return later tonight, we will discuss the details and preparation necessary to make your vision a reality. I hope you realize the magnitude of the opportunity being presented to you. You alone are in a position to craft the future of this civilization."

Demetrius watched Asgeir drive away. The tail lights of the van disappeared around the bend in the road. The magnitude of the responsibility that Asgeir was placing on him was starting to sink in.

CHAPTER 16

Tromsø, Norway

Epiphany stopped at an intersection along School Street to admire the scenery. From her vantage point, the view east opened up to downtown Tromsøya, the island portion of Tromsø municipality. The soft glow of street lights illuminated store fronts, residences, and office buildings. Light flurries drifted through the air in diaphanous veils. Large, puffy clouds hung over the city. The entire scene looked like something out of a fable. "Over there, on the opposite side of the water, you can see the Arctic Cathedral."

David stopped to look in the direction she was pointing. "It looks pretty cool lit up at night like that. I'm glad we came out for an after-dinner stroll. The cold air is waking me up. How long were we on the road?"

"With stops, about eight hours."

"It feels good to be out of that damn car and walking around." David reached down to massage the front of his legs. "Now that we're here, we can concentrate on finding Demetrius. It's too bad we don't know where he's staying."

"Yeah, when I called his Oslo office this morning, no one picked up, so I tried one of his staff. I had Hanna Ortiz's number in my cell. I've dealt with her a few times over the past several years. I was amazed she remembered me; otherwise, I don't think I would have gotten any details as to his whereabouts."

David crossed the street to the sidewalk bordering a small park. The grounds were lined with trees, and there was a seating area at its center. He moved to the side to allow a young couple walking their chocolate Lab to pass by. The dog looked up at him and wagged his tail. The woman gave a light tug on the leash and said, "Come on, Mack. You don't have to greet every single person you see," and led him into the park. David waited until they were sufficiently far enough away, and asked, "All we really know is that he came here to meet with some businessman. Any thoughts on how we find him?"

"That's all Hanna felt comfortable telling me. It would have been nice to get the name of the guy he's meeting with. But I understand; she didn't feel right about giving out too much information regarding Demetrius's business without his approval. I guess we keep calling him and hope he answers. Other than that, we keep trying to find his timeline in the Otherworlds, but so far, I haven't had much luck with that," Epiphany said. "Everything about his timeline after the Trondheim attack is blurry and inconclusive."

"It's funny how that works," David said. "Finding information in the Otherworlds is never a sure bet."

"Uncovering stuff about past events is hard enough given the vast troves of historical information that exists: every event, every person, every thought. It's all there." Epiphany paused to get one last glimpse of the Arctic Cathedral before moving on.

"Finding information about future events is even harder. I had an interesting conversation about that with Johannes yesterday. He told me that reality at the quantum level is probabilistic in nature. That notion goes back to the early 1900s when physicists were developing quantum mechanics."

"Okay, I'm bored already. But you're going to keep talking about this, aren't you?" Epiphany didn't have to wait long for an answer.

"All of the possible outcomes of an event exist all at once, and it's not until a specific event is actually observed that one of those outcomes becomes reality. It really helped me appreciate what happens when we search for future events in the Otherworlds. It's really fascinating."

"If you say so." Epiphany realized he wasn't going to let go of this train of thought.

"Each time we search for something about Demetrius Wolffe's future actions, the possible results are based on his thinking at that specific moment in time. Is he going to use the sphere tonight, tomorrow afternoon, or three days from now? Is he going to use it here in Tromsø or somewhere ten miles away? When we go to the Otherworlds, we see all of these possible paths, but they are in a constant state of flux as his thoughts change and evolve. It's going to take a lot of luck and one hell of an educated guess to find the right path to follow."

Epiphany had to admit it did make sense, and it explained why she was having difficulty determining what Demetrius was going to do next. He was probably trying to figure that out as well. Halfway into the next block, Epiphany stopped and grabbed David by the arm. "Do you hear that? That dissonant humming sound."

David stopped and concentrated. "It's really faint, but I do hear it. Which way is it coming from?"

Epiphany pointed in the direction from which the sound was emanating. "If it's the spirit that Johannes warned us about, at least it confirms we're in the right place." She picked up her pace from a fast walk to a light jog. David followed behind her.

She sped down the next block and crossed the intersection. Steel, chest-high barriers ran the length of the street. She gripped the top rail and hopped over a barrier. David ducked between the top two rails and followed after her.

After speeding by several more homes, she passed a quaint bed-and-breakfast and stopped at a fenced-off parking area in front of a secondary school. David came to a stop next to her.

"He's here. I can feel his presence," Epiphany whispered to David.

"Do you see him?" he asked.

"Somewhere in there." She pointed to King's Park in front of the school grounds. The park was crisscrossed with walking paths. Trees and small shrubs were scattered throughout the property. The statues of a man and a young child, ringed by park benches, were visible at the lower end of the park. "It's tough to see anything through the snow flurries."

"Was that a scream I just heard?" David said.

"Over there, at the base of those steps." Epiphany raced across the park and descended the hill to the base of the stairs. David ran along a path and sped down the steps to meet her at the bottom. A young woman in her early thirties was lying in the snow. A passerby stood over her. Epiphany blurted out, "Is she okay?"

The man leaning over the body stuttered, "I think she's dead."

"Did you see what happened?" David asked.

"No, but I did see a pretty big guy run from this area." He pointed to the downtown area of the island. "He went that way toward the shopping district."

"Call the police," Epiphany said. She surveyed the park grounds. "There he is! At the lower entrance to the park." She took off after him.

At the bottom of the grounds, Epiphany sped by the park benches and crossed between the two statues. Icy patches of packed snow made the chase treacherous. She nearly lost her footing as she bounded down the steps leading to the street. Epiphany glanced over her shoulder to see David was close behind.

The man she was chasing collided with a pedestrian on the sidewalk. It slowed him down, allowing her to close the gap. He was no more than twenty feet ahead as she sprinted down the road in the next block. The traffic light at the corner turned red. Cross traffic started moving in both directions.

Epiphany saw the man turn right at the next intersection. The first thing she felt when she rounded the corner was a pair of massive hands grab her by the coat and whip her around. Her momentum lifted her feet off the ground. He flung her through the air, and she tumbled and rolled off the edge of the sidewalk into the roadway. The headlights of an approaching car lit up her face as she sat up. The car swerved left. Epiphany cringed when she looked down at her right hand, watching the car's tires come within inches of her fingertips. The man moved toward her as she struggled to get back to her feet. David sped around the corner and tackled the man to the ground before he could reach her.

The attacker got up quickly and threw a punch that glanced off David's right shoulder. It knocked him backward against the large window of the corner store. The man reached out and grabbed

David's face with his right hand, pushing his head up against the glass. David's body stiffened as the man attempted to rip his soul away.

Epiphany came up from behind and rammed her right thigh into the back of the man's left leg. The impact brought him down, and David stumbled forward, landing on his hands and knees. The man got up quickly and turned to face her. Epiphany experienced that moment where time seems to slow down, where both opponents get the full measure of the person standing across from them. Where every detail is garnered. She stared into his black eyes. In his face she saw the young kid who shot her sister. She saw the faces of every assailant about to take a life. Her anger and adrenaline surged. Epiphany assessed her foe and then unleashed a right jab that hit the man in the left cheekbone below his eye. His head snapped back. His face contorted. Her martial arts training kicked in. She countered his attempted punches with several body blows and another shot to the face that rocked him backward. Epiphany moved in for another right jab to the man's head. He ducked her punch and hit her in the lower abdomen just below the ribs. She stumbled backward and landed on the ground in a sitting position. The sirens of an approaching police car caught her attacker's attention. He turned and sprinted away.

Epiphany got to her feet. "God damn, that fucking hurt!" The punch had winded her. She massaged her side and glanced at David.

"I'll be okay," he yelled. "Go! I'll catch up."

Epiphany raced down Green Street after him.

CHAPTER 17

Tromsø Center for Contemporary Art

Kari Salversen's phone rang. "Where are you? Are you at the art center?" the voice on the other end of the call asked.

"Martin. Yes, I got here about fifteen minutes ago." Kari had mentioned she was going to take another look at the crime scene this evening. When she was a young officer, Martin Kolbeck had taught her to examine a crime scene from every angle. Take in every detail. On occasion, some of the most important leads can be gleaned from things that aren't there. She had asked Martin if he wanted to go with her, but he was tied up with other work and had opted out. "Why?"

"There's been another killing. On the grounds in front of the secondary school. Same as the others. A witness said a large man with long hair and a beard was seen running from the site of the attack. He's dressed in jeans, wearing a red-and-black plaid overcoat. Apparently two civilians are chasing after him. They're reported to be heading your way, running down Green Street. A patrol car is on the way."

"Got it. I'll move in their direction."

"Be careful," Martin said and ended the call.

Kari put her cellphone in her coat pocket. The man she had been warned about was running toward her.

"Police," Kari yelled. "Stop!" She crossed in front of the man's path and raised both arms in the air, palms out as a signal to stop.

The man moved toward her and grabbed her by the coat sleeve as she attempted to stop him. He managed to fling her to the ground. She got up quickly and dodged his first punch. She countered with two of her own, landing both to his midsection. He reached for her face with his hand and latched on. Shock, pain, and confusion hit all at once. It felt as if her life's energy was being drained from her body. Before Kari could react, a tall, athletic woman charged into the man's side, taking him to the ground. Kari stumbled backward and lost her footing, landing on her back in the snow. When the man got to his feet, the woman swung at him twice, hitting him in the chest with the first punch and missing with her second.

Then something happened that left Kari in a state of disbelief. The big man just disappeared. It looked as if he vaporized into the falling snow. When she landed on her back, her head hit the ground pretty hard, but not so hard that she'd be hallucinating. She knew what she saw, dizzy or not. The man vanished. "What the fuck," she said out loud.

The woman who had charged into the man knelt down to check on her. "Are you okay?" she asked. Her words sounded muffled and distant.

Kari mumbled, "He disappeared." Then she managed to say, "I'll be alright."

The woman turned and sped off across the grounds.

Kari stood, trying to maintain her balance and clear her head. She swore the man who attacked her was the physical embodiment of the marble statue in the church in Tjeldsund.

CHAPTER 18

Tromsø Cemetery

Epiphany chased the shadowy spirit from the Otherworlds for several blocks, but ultimately she lost him as he disappeared into the wooded cemetery near the middle of the island. She bent over, placed her hands on her knees, and desperately tried to catch her breath. She must have covered a good half-mile, at least half of which was in an all-out sprint. The frigid air bit at her lungs with every deep breath. Her leg muscles ached. The pain from the blow to her lower abdomen intensified. She lowered herself to a seated position on the ground and leaned her back against a stone pillar at one of the entrance roads into the cemetery. A few moments later, David Skye jogged up the road. He kneeled down next to her.

"I lost him in the woods," she said dejectedly, still attempting to catch her breath.

"I don't think that's the last we'll see of that guy. The way he cloaked himself like that was unnerving, weaving in and out of people walking by. They didn't know he was there. I've never seen anything like that."

"I need to walk; otherwise, I'm going to stiffen up," Epiphany said as she extended her hand toward David. He grasped her hand and helped her up. Epiphany rubbed her lower abdomen. "Hurts like a son-of-a-bitch. He can really throw a punch." She turned and started down the entrance road toward the center of the graveyard. David walked alongside her.

"Where'd you learn to fight like that?" he asked.

"After Samantha was killed, I dove headlong into martial arts of all types. Couldn't get enough of it. I even studied a deadly form of silat, a style of street fighting, in Indonesia for a year after college. I swore I was never going to let myself become a willing victim and that I'd fight like hell to prevent someone else from becoming one."

"Well, whatever style of martial arts you used, it saved my life back there in town. When he grabbed onto my face with that massive hand of his, I felt my soul being torn away." David shivered as he said the words, reliving the experience in his head. "Imagine the most intense migraine headache magnified a hundred times."

"Judging by the look on that woman's face in the park, it must have been a painful experience." Epiphany stopped for a breather in front of the chapel. She gazed up at the cross mounted on the peak of the gabled roof, wondering what kind of God would allow a creature like that to exist. "What do we know about that spirit, or demon, or whatever the hell he or it is?"

David leaned against the waist-high stone wall bordering the grounds in front of the church. "He can cloak himself. When he's cloaked, people with a single soul can't see him. Apparently, our second souls give us the ability to see through the veils of his shroud. He kind of looked like a mirage."

"That's how he looked to me as well. I keep thinking about what Johannes asked: How do you kill something that can't be killed? When he's in human form, he can feel pain. I landed several punches that caused him to wince. He can be hurt and slowed down. But can we actually kill him? Who knows?"

"If Johannes is right about the reason he's here, Demetrius can't be that far away," David said.

"That thing, whatever it is, knows we are here, and the police know it's here as well—at least one of them does anyway."

David gave her a bewildered look. "What are you saying?"

"When I chased him across the grounds in front of the art center building, he attacked a woman who identified herself as a police officer. She saw him vanish right in front of her. There was no mistaking the fact that he disappeared like that."

"Well, then he isn't playing by the same rules we are if he doesn't care who knows about him," David said.

"I agree. The aphasia we've been given at birth that prevents us from revealing we have a second soul other than to someone else who has one doesn't seem to apply to him."

"Let's say that Demetrius still hasn't made contact with that thing. And maybe he doesn't have the Ebony Sphere of Vayla Isarrus. I mean, we didn't know Johannes existed until the other day. There could be another apostle out there who we don't know about. We should probably alert Demetrius to the fact that thing is here," David suggested.

"Or the reason he hasn't responded to any of your texts and phone calls is because he's already dead."

David grimaced at the thought. He reached into his pocket, pulled out his cellphone, and made another phone call to Demetrius.

CHAPTER 19

Lyfjord, Norway

"We have to move more quickly than I would have liked."

Demetrius Wolffe stood on the porch, gazing at the smattering of light from a few distant stars that had managed to make themselves visible through the cloud cover. Asgeir's words joined the clutter of random thoughts that filled Demetrius's head. The approaching finality of his life had a way of bringing order to the chaos that had been consuming him. It became easier to focus on the critical items that mattered most and to push those of lesser importance out of the way.

"Demetrius, did you hear what I said? I need you to focus!"

Asgeir made no attempt to hide his frustration at Demetrius's apparent lack of concentration. It didn't bother Demetrius in the least. He'd operate at the speed that suited himself. He turned to face the otherworldly creature standing next to him—so human-looking in every way. Even the deep, gravelly voice seemed to have softened. He wondered if that was how Asgeir made it so easy to talk to him in such a relaxed, conversational way, like catching up with an old friend. Demetrius cautioned himself to tread with care, to question everything. Don't let Asgeir's disarming ways move him to a decision he might not otherwise have made.

"Why do we have to move more quickly?" Demetrius asked.

"I encountered two apostles in Tromsø tonight. They are going to be more of a problem than I would have thought. I fear they will try to prevent you from bringing about the future we are trying to realize. When I stepped through the rift to come into this world, I had taken some precautions to ensure this location would not be accessible by anyone's attempts to find it in the Otherworlds."

"How did you manage to do that?"

"I disrupted the timelines that have anything to do with you bringing the sphere to this place. It should buy us some time to finish our preparations."

Demetrius thought about the multiple phone calls and texts he had been receiving from David Skye. They were part of the frenzied haze encircling his life. He didn't have time for the distraction that David Skye and Jade Hendrix would bring with them. It was just as well that Asgeir made it harder for them to find him. "If I'm going to deploy the Ebony Sphere, I need to know the details of exactly how this is going to work."

"You'll need to accomplish several things: imbed your view of the future behavior that you'd like to bring about into the Ebony Sphere, and then infuse it with the amount of primordial energy needed to change every soul on the planet. To achieve both of these goals involves one more critical step."

"What would that be?" Demetrius asked.

"You will need to infuse your second soul with the Quintessence, and that does not come without risk."

"I'm struggling with how these things all tie together," Demetrius admitted. "It feels like I have all of the pieces of a jigsaw puzzle but don't know what the final picture is supposed to look like."

"Let me try to paint that picture in terms of an Earth-based analogy. If the Ebony Sphere is an automobile, it will need fuel to run to change eight billion souls. The source of that fuel is the ancient energy from the Quintessence, and you are the conduit through which that energy will flow. That's why you will need to infuse your second soul. A battery is needed to start the engine. The source of power for the battery will come from the souls that will be sacrificed. They are the ignition system."

"That's a good analogy, Asgeir. It helps me understand this better. How exactly do I infuse my second soul with the ancient energy of the Quintessence?"

"You need to understand a few things. The Quintessence flows through every dimension of the universe in veins that continuously branch off into smaller and smaller tributaries and eventually into micro-filaments to form a universal, interconnected web of energy."

"In all of my travels to the Otherworlds, I have never seen these veins that you talk about," Demetrius said.

"The veins of the Quintessence cannot be detected until you learn how to hear the fundamental frequency at which it resonates, and that takes time. Once you do, the primary veins of the Quintessence appear as luminescent vapor trails. Fortunately, there is another way to find them. Look for the *whispering sage* plant. Its luminescent purple flowers emit light when near the flow of the Quintessence. The closer you are to a large vein, the more brilliant the light."

"When I find one of these veins, then what?"

"You'll need to step into the flow just long enough to let it wash over your second soul. We have to do this in smaller, discrete steps. Otherwise, you could easily be overpowered by the strength of the Quintessence. If that happens, your second soul will be decimated, and you will cease to exist," Asgeir cautioned. "That's why we need to find one of the smaller tributaries that branch off of the larger veins. To lessen the risk to you."

Demetrius turned to face the sky; his thoughts drifted out to the distant stars once more.

"Is there anything else?" Asgeir asked.

"Will this work? How do I know the sphere will make the changes I intend?"

"Vayla Isarrus went to great lengths to infuse the Ebony Spheres with her knowledge. They will work as she intended. In order to use them, to make them do what you want them to do, your thoughts must be pure like hers were."

"Is there a way to test this on a small scale without killing anyone?"

"The sphere that you retrieved contains enough residual energy from the souls of the people who had been in the church when it was first activated. You should be able to affect a small number of people without having to take their souls to ignite the sphere."

Demetrius immediately thought about the upcoming northern lights trip with his prospective donor. It would be in the mountains. There'd be no one else around. "When the time comes, how would I actually activate the Ebony Sphere?"

"Raise the sphere up to the sky, connect to the Quintessence and funnel its energy into the sphere to charge it, and then focus your mind on the behaviors you'd like to instill. Once that happens, the Ebony Sphere will make the changes."

"One last question," Demetrius said. "What happens when I do this on a grand scale, to affect every person on this planet? Exactly how many lives will be sacrificed?"

"You ask a lot of questions, Demetrius. Why is it so important to know these things?"

Demetrius glared at Asgeir. He took a step closer to him. The tone of his voice was forceful when he spoke. "If I'm going to do something of this magnitude, I want to go into it with my eyes wide open. Answer my question."

Asgeir did not react to the anger in Demetrius's voice. His answer was calm and direct. "To power the Ebony Sphere will require the souls from a thousandth of a percent of the population to be affected. Vayla Isarrus did everything in her power to minimize the size of the sacrifice to be made."

Demetrius took his cellphone from his pocket and opened the calculator app. "Eight billion souls times one percent equals eighty million. Eighty million divided by a thousand is a thousandth of one percent, which equals," he paused and entered the numbers, "eighty thousand." Demetrius paused again as the magnitude of that number sunk in. "Shit!" he exclaimed.

Asgeir remained composed in his reply. "How many people did you say die in armed conflict on this world?"

"On average, over one-hundred-fifty thousand people have been killed every year for the last two-hundred-plus years," Demetrius answered.

"You would sacrifice eighty thousand souls to make the world better for eight billion. In the first ten years after this change to humanity is made, you would save the lives of well over a million people. Certainly, that is a trade-off worth making," Asgeir stated.

Demetrius walked back inside the house. "Eighty thousand people is still a lot no matter how you cut it."

"I'm not arguing that. But the lives that will be saved will be orders of magnitude larger after the change is made. There is one more thing I can show you that will eliminate any doubts that this path is the only one that's right for the people of Earth. But that must wait until after you've taken the steps to infuse your second soul with the Quintessence. Right now, however, I need to address another urgent matter regarding our two apostles. I came across the name of a man who fits the profile I am looking for—one whose mind can be altered to carry out my wishes. I will meet him tomorrow morning." Asgeir motioned for Demetrius to take a seat.

Demetrius sat on the sofa, and Asgeir sat down beside him. "There's something I need you to do." He grasped Demetrius's left forearm. Demetrius stiffened. His senses became hazy. Asgeir's thoughts entered Demetrius's head and provided detailed instructions about a phone call that needed to be made. A few seconds later, Asgeir released his grip, and Demetrius fell into a deep sleep.

CHAPTER 20

The Lost Fjord Café, Tromsø

Anders Gustason sat alone at a booth, keeping a watchful eye on the window. The Lost Fjord Café was bustling with businesspeople stopping in for their morning jolt of caffeine before heading to work and with tourists looking to get a cup of coffee before starting their busy day of sightseeing. Anders sat back in the cushioned seat and studied the interior décor. High ceilings, exposed brick walls, and colorful tile flooring, while aesthetically pleasing to most of the patrons, amplified the noise too much for his liking. He pulled back his left sleeve to reveal his watch, just below a tattoo of Earth with a dagger through it: 7:15 am. He had taken a risk by stopping in here, but he figured the police wouldn't expect him to be hanging out in a busy coffee shop. Anders stopped in to enjoy a strong cup of coffee before getting the hell off the island and heading north. He had made arrangements with a local fisherman to ferry him around the coast, and then he'd slip across the border into Finland. It had taken time to gather some clothing and the money needed to pay for the trip; otherwise, he would have left sooner than this. The police watching his house didn't help matters. *Life is never fucking easy,* he thought.

Anders nervously tapped his right foot on the tile floor while he sipped his coffee. The sound of the soft rubber soles of his work boots was inaudible over the loud din. He'd never been in this café before. Three baristas were busy behind the counter serving their customers. A quarter of the patrons didn't appear to be Norwegian. They were a mix of nonnative nationalities, Asian, central-European, and some that appeared to be from Middle Eastern countries. Anders felt the temperature in his face rise as his anger increased. *The foreigners who work in my country don't belong here,* he thought. *They're taking our jobs, work that should rightly be the privilege of Norwegian-born citizens like me.* It's the reason he joined the Brotherhood, the shorter name his comrades adopted over the wordier Daggers of a New Dawn. The purity of the nation was being diluted, and the Brotherhood was doing something about that. His anger was swelling. His left hand clenched into a fist so tight that his fingertips began to ache.

Anders noticed a big man with a beard and long hair enter the café. He looked like some kind of lumberjack. The guy had a backpack slung over his shoulder and was walking toward the booth in which Anders was sitting.

The lumberjack stopped next to his booth. His physical size and muscular build presented an imposing figure. When the man sat down across the table from Anders, it surprised the hell out of him. There was something about his dark, penetrating eyes, the way they locked onto his. Anders tried to look away, to break the stare, but he couldn't.

"We have important things to discuss, Anders," the man said.

"How do you know my name?" Anders asked curtly. He leaned forward and whispered, "Are you with the Brotherhood?"

"I knew you'd be here this morning, and I also know the police have a warrant for your arrest. They don't like what you and your Brotherhood stand for."

"Who are you? What do you want from me?" Anders asked gruffly.

"My name is Asgeir. I have a mission for you—one that will raise your standing within the ranks of your Brotherhood. You do something for me, and I'll keep the police away from you." Asgeir reached his right hand across the table.

Anders felt the warmth of the man's hand as it gripped his left forearm. But no, it wasn't warmth. It was something different, like electricity almost, a sensation that flowed into the base of his skull and permeated his thoughts. It felt as if the inside of his head was charged with a pulsing electrical current. A normal Anders Gustason would never have allowed a complete stranger to get this familiar, to invade his personal space, to make physical contact. Ever! He wanted to do something about it. His blood was beginning to boil. The muscles in his arms tensed. But all he could manage was to sit there—quiet, motionless.

The electric sensation at the base of Anders's skull intensified. His thoughts were slowly blanketed in a silky haze. The noise in the café—the sound of espresso machines, clanking coffee cups, people's idle chatter—became a dull blur of indiscernible background noise. Anders stared into the eyes of the man sitting across the table from him. Never once did the man move his lips, yet Anders heard the man's words inside his head loudly and clearly.

"I have a mission for you. Two people will come in here later today. They represent the things you hate the most about the direction this country is taking. I am giving you the chance to stand up and take your country back from the hands of people like this, Anders. This is your chance to be a hero, to be the spear of the Gods." A deluge of hatred and violence flooded the inner reaches of Anders's mind like a tidal surge, latching on to his darkest of thoughts, the kind that are buried deep, never to be entertained.

Anders slowly came out of the fog that had clouded his mind. He looked down at the table. Various nicks, scratches, and coffee stains all blurred into an obscure collage. The words that had filled his head stayed with him for a moment. They were all he could focus on, resonant, deep, and so very clear. The cloudy rumble of background noise came whooshing back to crystal clarity, the clanking of coffee cups, the sound of espresso machines, the idle chatter. The miasma that had clouded his thoughts receded. Anders looked up. The seat across from him was empty. He didn't remember seeing the big man leave. What was his name? He couldn't remember it. The electric hum that filled his head had dissipated.

Anders looked at the backpack on the seat next to him. The man had left it for him with specific instructions on what to do with it. Anders stood, hefted the backpack over his right shoulder, and exited the coffee shop. He paused to breathe in the cold morning air. The names and images of the two people he'd come back for were etched into his brain. Anders Gustason had clarity. He knew exactly what he needed to do.

CHAPTER 21

Tromsø Police Station

The computer monitor flickered to life in the makeshift work area that had been set up for Kari Salversen, basically an unused desk and workstation tucked away in the back corner of the Tromsø Police Station on the second floor. The fact that she had a window overlooking the street was an added bonus. There had been a constant buzz of activity from the moment she arrived in the office this morning. Kari didn't mind the noise level. The energy in the office was contagious. She took a sip of coffee and checked her watch: 7:30 am. When Kari signed into the video conference, a familiar face appeared on the screen. Jens Tofte was calling from the Harstad Police Station. After a brief exchange of pleasantries, Kari got right to work. "What have you gotten on the car?"

"The car was a rental. It was picked up at the Hertz Rental Agency at the Harstad/Narvik Airport in Evenes." Jens expressed the time using standard military convention, "Between 1315 and 1330, according to their records. It was paid for by a man named David Skye. The clerk at the rental desk remembered that a woman was traveling with him.

Both fit the age range provided by the caretaker for the church."

"Did you get anything interesting from the flight manifests?" Kari asked.

"Yes. David Skye was on the noon arrival out of Trondheim. He was traveling with a woman named Jade Hendrix. Both are American. We're running background checks on them. You should be seeing their pictures on the screen now."

Kari watched the images of a male and female fill the monitor. "Oh my God," Kari exclaimed. "The woman, Jade Hendrix, she's here in Tromsø. Hendrix was pursuing a man suspected of killing a woman in King's Park. She chased him through the grounds of the art center when I was there, revisiting an earlier crime scene. The guy attacked me, and she helped to fight him off. They both ran off into the surrounding neighborhood." Kari elected not to mention that she saw the man vanish. She still wasn't convinced that it was anything more than her eyes playing tricks on her.

"Are you okay?" Jens asked, his voice tinged with concern.

"I'll be fine. Was just shaken up a little," she said. "Here's the other interesting thing that's transpired on this end. There have been four attacks on individuals in the past two days. Each of the four victims was murdered in a way that resembles the killings at the church in Tjeldsund, and each of them had the same look of horror on their faces."

"That is really odd," Jens said. "Which reminds me, we've gotten preliminary findings for the victims from the church attack. It really has the medical examiners perplexed. They're unable to provide any type of rational explanation for it. The tox reports came back negative, no signs of foreign chemical agents that could have killed these people. That rules out some kind of mass suicide by ingesting poison. The initial indication at this point is simultaneous heart failure."

"What on Earth could possibly have done that, Jens?" Kari asked incredulously.

"That's what has the medical examiners mystified. Before I forget, I did one extra check. I cross-referenced Skye and Hendrix against the list of witnesses who came forward at the Trondheim attack. Both of them gave formal statements to the police. They indicated they had come to Trondheim to meet a friend at one of the outdoor restaurants along the mall. And here's another interesting bit. They came to meet Aidan McCallum, who was killed by the blast. He was the man the news team captured on video chasing Lars Bohle. I also double-checked the video footage of the Solsiden Mall bombing. The film footage captured someone that looks very much like David Skye leaning over the bodies of Aidan McCallum and Lars Bohle."

"These two were in Trondheim at the time of the attack, they were seen two days later leaving the church where fourteen people were found dead, and now I see her in Tromsø, where we've had several murders resembling the attack at the Tjeldsund Church. That's enough to put out a warrant for their arrest."

"Sounds like it to me," Jens said. "These two are moving around a lot. We need to get them into custody before they move on."

"Get their pictures out to all of our police districts and indicate they are to be brought in for questioning. I'll get started on a warrant for their arrest. Have you traced the use of their credit cards? Do we know where they're staying?"

"Skye used his card to pay for the rental car. If they are staying in a hotel or rental property, she must have paid for it. Nothing since the rental car charge has shown up on his card. We're waiting for the credit card information used to pay for their flights to travel into Harstad/Narvik Airport. Apparently, there's some computer glitch with the airline. We'll track it down ASAP, and I'll get back to you."

"Great. Let me know as soon as you have something," Kari said.

"Will do. Any news on the Anders Gustason arrest?" Jens asked.

"His whereabouts are still unknown. He hasn't shown up for work and hasn't been to his house. We have an officer watching his residence. Once we have him in custody, I'll let you know. Thanks for the updates. Good work, Jens. Talk soon." Kari signed off.

She glanced out the window at the gray sky. A light snow was falling. It was shaping up to be a snowier winter than usual. It was on a day much like this one, during her early teens, when she read about a ruthless attack at a railway station in northern France. Innocent lives were lost, and for what reason? The people who died were just going about their day like any other day. The cold-blooded, senseless nature of that incident was the trigger that sent her down the path of becoming a police officer. Life was a precious thing, a brilliant light to be nourished during our all-too-brief time on this planet. To extinguish that flame before it ever has a chance to shine was incomprehensible to her. To quash the lives of the next Beethoven or Galileo, the likes of Isaac Newton or Madame Curie was not something she could bear the thought of. Kari was committed to her cause. Her personal life would always come second to protecting the innocent, to giving humankind a fighting chance to fulfill its greatest potential. Bringing the people behind these killings to justice was her singular focus.

The reminder for her call with Chief Nord brought her out of her thoughts. She called into his office, and his administrative assistant put her call through. Andreas Nord had pretty much done it all over the course of his career. He had earned the respect of his direct reports, his peers, and the upper echelons of the command structure within the National Police Service. Kari had learned from years of dealing with him that he'd want concise information based on facts—not supposition.

Nord skipped any opening pleasantries and jumped into the conversation, "Salversen, what do you have for me on Trondheim and this church thing in Tjeldsund?"

"On the Trondheim front, we have a connection between Lars Bohle, the man who planted the bombs at the Solsiden Mall in Trondheim, and Rutger Solberg, who committed the attack in Bergen. Both men had the same tattoo on their wrists. We have people canvassing tattoo parlors where these men lived, but so far none of them remember doing that type of tattoo. As you already know, we also found some email correspondence between Bohle and an associate of his here in Tromsø, a man by the name of Anders Gustason. We have a warrant out for his arrest."

"How about counterintelligence? Anything on right-wing conservative groups?" Nord asked.

"I talked with them. None of the known fringe groups are taking credit for any of these attacks. We don't have any information on a group whose members have this tattoo," Kari noted.

"Updates on Tjeldsund?" Nord asked.

"Fourteen dead. Preliminary cause of death is simultaneous heart failure and no evidence of poisons or other foreign agents that could have killed them."

"Jesus Christ. What was used to kill them?" Nord growled.

"We're still trying to figure that out. Subsequent to the incident at the church, we've had four more individual attacks, each of which looks like the same cause of death as seen in Tjeldsund," Kari added.

"Please tell me you have something to go on here, Kari," Nord said as a hint of frustration crept into his voice.

"Well, in fact we do. We have a connection between all of these recent attacks. A pair of Americans, a man and a woman, David Skye and Jade Hendrix, were present at the Trondheim attack, they were seen at the church incident, and now they're here in Tromsø at the sight of one of the recent murders. We have a warrant for their arrest and are in the process of finding where they are staying."

"Okay, keep at it, Kari. Keep me posted on this." Chief Nord ended the call.

Nord sounded satisfied that some progress was being made. Kari knew that if things didn't progress quickly, she'd be feeling his wrath in short order.

CHAPTER 22

Tromsø, Norway

David Skye finished off the last of his breakfast and took a sip of his coffee. His eyes wandered to the long wall of windows in the hotel dining area. It was shaping up to be a cloudy day with more snow. Light flurries had been falling for the past twenty minutes. A few people he noticed walking by outside were bundled up in heavy coats with scarves, hats, and gloves. He shifted his gaze to the dining area. About a quarter of the tables were occupied. Quiet conversation drifted through the large, open room. David looked across the table at Epiphany. "I'm not feeling good about our chances of finding Demetrius Wolffe and that damn sphere. I keep visualizing an hourglass, and the last grains of sand are about to drop to the bottom."

Epiphany set her coffee cup on the table and folded her napkin. "It's worrying me too. We've been able to find information in the Otherworlds about other facets of this mission fairly quickly. Why are we having so much trouble locating Demetrius?"

"I'm wondering if the follower of Vayla Isarrus who came through the Black Void to help Demetrius has some ability to obfuscate current and future information about him."

"I wouldn't have thought that's possible, but I don't know anymore. If he does have that ability, we might never find Demetrius. I'm not ready to give up, though. I'd like to head up to my room to keep trying."

David agreed. "I think that's our only option right now."

They got off the elevator at the third floor and walked to their rooms. David's cellphone rang when he was halfway through the doorway. He stepped into the hallway. Epiphany was about to enter her room. "Epiphany," he waved for her to come to his room. "It's Demetrius."

Epiphany hurried into David's room while he answered the phone. "Demetrius, it's David. I've got Epiphany here with me. I'm putting you on speaker." He set the phone on the long counter at the base of the windows. His eyes drifted to the docks below where several boats were moored. The downtown area of Tromsøya was waking up.

"Are you okay, Demetrius?" Epiphany asked. "We've been trying to reach you."

"Sorry about that. I've been distracted by recent events. I found the sphere we were contacted about. It was in a church in Tjeldsund." Demetrius sounded tired. His words were drawn out, with a few long pauses in between them.

"We were there, Demetrius, at the church," David interjected. "What happened? All those people were dead."

"I know. It was my fault. When I touched the sphere, I somehow activated it. Those people were killed instantly. I think the sphere took their souls. You've got to believe me when I tell you that I didn't know that would happen." Demetrius paused for a few seconds. The sound of a deep inhale and exhale came across the phone. "I was scared. I didn't know what to do. Something came over me. I grabbed the sphere and ran."

"Where are you now?" Epiphany asked.

"I'm on a small island near Tromsø."

"We're at a hotel on Tromsøya," David said.

"I'm worried, David. I think something is following me. I've seen it twice now. It moves like a mirage. I don't know if I'm hallucinating or if the sphere is playing games with my head."

"We've seen it too, Demetrius. We've encountered it here. You're not hallucinating." David looked over at Epiphany to gauge her reaction to what they were hearing.

"I need to get rid of this damn sphere."

"We can take it. We know someone who might have a way to destroy it," Epiphany said. "We can come to you and pick it up."

"No. No, don't do that. I don't think it's safe here. I'm packing my things and getting the hell out of here. Meet me at the Lost Fjord Café in Tromsø, today, at 4." The line went dead.

"Damn it," David said.

"He sounded scared. I say we meet at that café, get the sphere, and get out of here as well. We should call Johannes. Let him know we talked to Demetrius and will have the sphere later today."

David gave Epiphany a thumbs-up signal. "I agree. Let's pack our things and be ready to leave. We get the sphere at 4 and drive to Stamsund to deliver it to Johannes."

Epiphany nodded in agreement. "He can fire up his quantum-well device, and we can rid ourselves of this Ebony Sphere once and for all."

CHAPTER 23

Lyfjord, Norway

Demetrius Wolffe woke from a deep sleep. He looked down and realized he must have dozed off with his cellphone in his hand. He swiped his right thumb across the screen. A list of calls filled the display, the most recent of which was from this morning. It was an outgoing call to David Skye—one that he didn't remember making. He deleted the record of the call.

Something he did remember, however, was the monumental crossroads awaiting his decision. Which direction he should take would be the most important choice he'd ever make. He could continue down his original path and maybe secure enough funding to keep Citizens for a Peaceful Planet alive. There would always be that hope of steering the world in a better direction. His circumstances, however, meant he'd never get to revel in any longer-term successes that might be realized. Or he could use the Ebony Sphere of Vayla Isarrus and live to see the impact of his changes—a world free of war and hate. In business terms, the risk versus reward of the latter choice was huge, not one that could be quantified in dollars and cents. The toll would be exacted in lives—tens of thousands of them. Those things aside, he was still committed to at least testing the sphere.

The ticking clock in his head was counting down the little amount of time he'd have left in this life. Months at best. Asgeir had insisted that Demetrius wait for his return before attempting a journey into the Otherworlds to search for the Quintessence. Demetrius was tired of waiting—tired of scheduling his life around the timelines of others. He stretched out on the sofa, relaxed his mind, and journeyed into the Black Void.

Demetrius stepped across the dark divide into the Realm of the Forever Sun. Its sheer brilliance and majesty were immediately overwhelming. Ethereal landscapes beyond anything Earth had to offer were on full display. Colors brandished vivid, lush hues. Sounds were silky and alive, steeped in rich complexity. But Demetrius had not made this passage to admire the beauty of the Otherworlds. He came for a specific purpose—to find the Quintessence and harness its energy.

His second soul followed a circuitous pathway across a meadow. The Forever Sun glistened as it hovered just above the horizon. A warm breeze moved over the tall grass, causing it to sway like the rolling waves of an ocean. Specs of purple light flickered in the shadows cast off by several trees in a nearby grove. Demetrius picked up his pace and ventured into the woods. At the center of the grove, he came upon several *whispering sage* plants. The tips of the spiky, waist-high stems were covered with vibrant, luminescent purple flowers. Demetrius broke off the top six inches of one of the stems. The ancient energy that caused them to glow tingled his fingertips as he held it in his hand. He walked in the direction in which the luminosity of the flowers increased.

Demetrius crossed over a rise in the landscape and descended into a long, narrow valley. The glow of the purple flowers became intense. He stopped, closed his eyes, and concentrated, listening for the fundamental resonance of the Quintessence. The passage of time was always difficult to determine in the Otherworlds. He couldn't say for sure how long he had stopped. When he opened his eyes, the long, shimmering vapor trails of primordial energy came into view. A thick, central vein ran through the valley. Smaller tributaries branched off into progressively smaller and smaller threads.

Asgeir had warned him to take it slow, to step into a smaller tributary to become accustomed to the sheer force of the flow. Demetrius was determined to do this his way. He ignored the cautions that Asgeir had provided and stepped into the large central vein of the Quintessence. The full brunt of the ancient energy swept through his second soul, overpowering him instantly. His thoughts became jumbled. His ability to concentrate and focus was almost nonexistent. Demetrius panicked. He was carried along in the turbulent flow as the vein swept through the valley. If he didn't regain control, he'd be lost. His second soul would be decimated—broken down into its constituent subatomic pieces and scattered throughout the universe like dust. Demetrius was face-to-face with his own mortality, with no more than a few seconds separating life from eternal darkness. Somewhere from deep inside, he mustered the will to right himself against the raging currents and stepped out of the chaotic maelstrom of energy.

The ceiling of the living room was the first thing to come into view when Demetrius came out of his trance. His head felt as if it was on fire. The chill of cold, damp air was exacerbated by his perspiration-soaked clothing. He sat up and stared out the window overlooking the inlet in Lyfjord. He was lucky to be alive. It took a few minutes to slow his racing mind and steady his heart rate.

He leaned forward and removed the Ebony Sphere from his backpack. He held it in his right hand at eye level. His fingertips grasped the smooth outer surface of the orb. He had absorbed enough energy from the Quintessence to reveal the holographic image of Vayla Isarrus that had been encoded deep inside the sphere. The vivid imagery played back inside his head. Her beauty was unbounded. Eyes greener than a field of grass. Long, thick braids of blonde hair draped over her shoulders. Her voice sounded like a melody drifting in the breeze, "Our thoughts are one, Demetrius. The way of the Ebony Sphere is your only path."

CHAPTER 24

The Lost Fjord Café, Tromsø

The bite of cold winter air nipped at the back of Epiphany's neck when the door opened and a man walked in. He stopped near the ledge along the window and scanned the café. She glanced over her right shoulder. He appeared to be in his late thirties. *Must be meeting someone*, she thought. Epiphany was waiting at the counter near the entrance to the Lost Fjord Café. A young female barista was finishing the second of the two lattes she had ordered. Epiphany made another quick glance over her shoulder. Something didn't seem right. Maybe it was the way the man carried himself. Could have been the angry scowl chiseled into his face. The guy appeared to be focusing his gaze in David Skye's direction. The pistol coming out of his pocket in his left hand changed everything.

Some things are so painful that even twenty-four years can't erase the anguish left in their wake. It had been that many years since that dreadful day when Epiphany's sister, Samantha, was shot dead on the school grounds. The feelings of fright, anger, and despair came rushing back at the sight of the pistol. The gun was now completely out of the man's pocket. He was raising it upward at David.

Experiencing someone close to her getting gunned down had been bad enough. She wasn't about to go through that a second time if she could help it.

Of the emotions that came flooding back, anger was front and center, driving her actions. Three steps between the shooter and her, she figured. Just three steps. As little as a second of indecision could be something that changes a person's life forever or possibly ends it. The shooter was reaching for the pistol grip with his other hand for a two-handed shooting stance to steady his aim. Epiphany shouted at him as she took her first step, hoping it would distract him just long enough. It was a gamble. She hoped she'd be lucky enough to have it pay off.

He maintained his shooting stance and looked over his shoulder at her. She took her second step. A look of recognition flashed across his face, like he knew her somehow. His torso twisted to change his firing position so she'd become his first target. The third step closed the gap between them as she dropped her shoulder and lunged into him like a battering ram. She slammed into his ribs just under his left arm. The gun went off. The impact drove him into the ledge along the front window. He grunted in pain as his body dropped to the ground.

The sound of the gun going off was quickly followed by the sound of screeching chairs sliding backward on the tile floor as people stood to flee for safety. The café was filled with screams and shouting. Epiphany had been cognizant of people running by her after the gun had been fired. She still didn't know if anyone had been hit. Her focus had remained unwavering as she concentrated on the man with the gun. He was on his hands and knees, reaching for the pistol. It had dropped out of his hands when he hit the ledge. Epiphany threw a punch that hit the shooter just above the left ear. The crack of her knuckles slamming into the side of his skull was quickly followed by the sound of his voice crying out in pain. He fell onto his right side.

The moment Epiphany had driven the shooter into the ledge, David had gotten up from the table and started running toward her. He picked up the pistol, grabbed her by the left arm, and shouted, "Come on! Let's get out of here."

They bolted out of the café and sprinted through the parking lot toward the 4Runner. As Epiphany got in on the driver's side, she saw the shooter get into a large pickup truck. "Ah fuck! I think he's going to follow us."

She fired up the engine and pulled out quickly. "Was anyone hit when the gun went off?" she hurriedly asked.

"No, the shot hit the floor."

"Good!" Epiphany sped away. After two quick turns, she raced down Beach Road. A car ahead of her had come to a stop when the light turned red. A quick glance in the rearview mirror indicated no one else but the shooter was behind her, about a half-block away. She swerved into the left-turn lane and sped around the stopped car. Her body strained against the seat belt from the momentum of the hard right turn. The 4Runner's tires screeched as she steered the vehicle into the Route 862 tunnel entrance.

David kept an eye on the pickup truck. "He matched our turn. He's closing in!"

Epiphany glanced in her rearview mirror to assess how close their pursuer was. She pressed on the accelerator, but it wasn't enough. The pickup accelerated and nudged the rear bumper of their

4Runner. The impact lurched them forward in their seats. "Fuck," she blurted out.

David muttered, "Oh Christ, a roundabout."

Epiphany fought with the steering wheel to keep the vehicle steady, then accelerated toward the first roundabout. The cross street was the road connecting the airport to the east side of the island. Headlights from a car approaching the intersection from her right illuminated the center pillar. "Hang on!" *And hope for the best,* she thought.

They made it through the first roundabout without incident and were traveling northbound, just seconds away from the next traffic circle. "I have no idea where I'm going," Epiphany yelled.

"Neither do I. Just keep going straight across. At this speed, we'll never be able to make a right turn out of these circles."

At the next traffic circle, the road split into two. One split veered off east, and the other northwest. The pickup truck sped up and pulled alongside them. Epiphany was startled by the move. "What the fuck is this guy doing?"

"He's going to hit the goddamn concrete pillar in the middle of the circle," David yelled.

Epiphany accelerated into the circle, fighting with every ounce of strength to keep the big vehicle on the road.

The pickup veered quickly to the left and went around the pillar against oncoming traffic.

David shouted, "That guy's really rolling the dice." The sound of screeching tires drew his attention to the connecting lanes on their right. A black sedan was attempting to enter the circle at the moment they crossed into it. Its headlights lit up the front compartment of the 4Runner. The black sedan made a glancing blow off the rear quarter-panel of the 4Runner and sent it spinning hard to the left. Epiphany wrestled with the steering wheel, but there wasn't much she could do. The black sedan skidded sideways into the concrete pillar at the center of the circle.

The pickup truck came out of the circle at about the same time as Epiphany and David did and immediately glanced off the driver's side doors of a vehicle coming from the opposite direction. The scraping of metal on metal sounded like a banshee fleeing hell. The impact of a three-axled dump truck hitting the pickup head-on was worse. The 4Runner spun around and hit the wall in the opposite lane.

Epiphany looked over at David. "You okay?"

"Yeah, so far," he said. "My heart is pounding through my chest, but I'm okay."

"Shit, this can't be good," Epiphany said as two patrol cars, lights flashing, came to an abrupt stop in front of them.

David looked over at Epiphany, "Hey, we're alive and uninjured. What's the worst that could happen now?"

CHAPTER 25

Tromsø Police Station

Martin Kolbeck finished making a few keystrokes on his computer keyboard and then leaned back in his chair. "How hard are you going to push on these two?"

Kari Salversen was seated in front of his desk. This was the first time she had been in his office since he had been promoted to chief of police. She glanced around the room. A large topographical map of Tromsø and the mountainous areas surrounding it was mounted on the wall behind his desk. He had two windows in his office, both of which offered a partial view of the waterway separating the island of Tromsøya from the mainland portion of the municipality. "Now that we have David Skye and Jade Hendrix in custody, I am going to lean in pretty hard. They're the only link we have to what looks like a connected series of attacks with the more recent spate that started with the Tjeldsund Church."

Martin shuffled through a few papers on his desk to find a note he had made earlier. "Here it is. We have David Skye in Interrogation Room 1 and Jade Hendrix in Room 2."

"Have they been examined by a doctor? Are we okay to interview them this close to the crash in the tunnel?" Kari asked.

"A team of EMTs examined both of them at the crash site. They checked out okay. You're good to go," Martin said, nodding his approval.

"Can't say as much for Anders Gustason." Kari paged through several printouts of photos from the tunnel accident scene. "He might have had half a chance of surviving if he had been wearing a seat belt. The steering wheel was bent from his body when he was thrown through the front windshield of the pickup. We'll have to wait for the medical examiner to tell us if it was the impact with the steering wheel or slamming into the grill of the dump truck that killed him."

"Probably a little of both," Martin surmised.

"We have two different types of attacks," Kari said as she closed the folder containing the crash scene photos and put it on the chair next to her. "The killing sprees, the most recent of which was in Trondheim, were carried out by what looks like a right-wing, radical group targeting non-Norwegian-born citizens. Their weapons of choice have been guns and explosives. The only link we have connecting all of those attacks is the tattoo on the wrists of two of the attackers."

"Anders Gustason had the same tattoo on his wrist," Martin noted.

"Right. Rutger Solberg from the Bergen attack, Lars Bohle in Trondheim, and now Anders Gustason here in Tromsø." At this juncture, Kari was willing to bet the perpetrators of the earlier attacks, who hadn't been apprehended yet, probably had the same tattoos.

"We'll work the tattoo angle from this end for Gustason. We've executed the search warrant for his residence. He had a laptop, and we've gotten some burner phones. Our tech guys are going through that stuff now. Hopefully, we get a few leads on the organization behind this," Martin said.

Kari nodded. "Then there's the attack in the Tjeldsund Church, followed by four individual assaults. The method of killing is still unknown, but conventional weapons and poisons have been ruled out."

"Yeah, we're in a whole other league when it comes to those killings," Martin said.

"What we do have is a possible connection. David Skye and Jade Hendrix were at the Solsiden Mall during the time of the bombings. A vehicle they had rented was seen leaving the Tjeldsund Church within minutes of the attack, and now they show up here in Tromsø where we've seen several more murders that mirror what we saw in Tjeldsund."

"I was reading Jens Tofte's update from the church attack. The caretaker could not definitively say it was them he saw. The sky was dark, and squalls were whipping the snow around pretty heavily," Martin added.

"But the Toyota 4Runner was definitely rented by David Skye," Kari stated. "Hendrix and Skye are a link between the early attacks and these more recent ones. And now, Anders Gustason, who has a connection to the earlier attacks, was chasing after those two with intent to kill."

"You've seen the background information on Hendrix and Skye?" Martin asked.

"I have. On the surface, they seem like fairly decent people, pursuing noble causes."

"How do two people like that get mixed up in a string of bizarre, unsolved murders?"

"That's what we're going to find out."

Martin leaned forward and rested his arms on his desktop. "We can keep them in our holding cells for a day or two. But we will need to get them in front of a magistrate at the district court within three days of the arrest. If you want to remand them in custody, after two or three days they'll have to be placed in Tromsø jail or one of our designated municipal residential units."

"We're definitely going to hold them in custody. I'm going to ask for four weeks. If we need more, I'll request an extension," Kari said.

"Who are you going to start with first?"

"Jade Hendrix."

CHAPTER 26

Tromsø Police Station

Giving in to a profound sense of helplessness was not an option. However, there wasn't much that Epiphany could do at the moment—not while sitting in an interrogation room in the middle of a police station with an officer standing outside the door. If she and David didn't find a way out of this, Demetrius Wolffe would succeed. She wondered what that would feel like. Would she know that her soul had been changed? Would she be the same person she is now? Her thoughts wandered to the phone call that put them in this mess. Demetrius had been more than convincing. It sure as hell sounded as if he was genuinely distraught and wanted to free himself of the Ebony Sphere. Instead, it was a trap to lure them into the snare of an armed attacker. The conclusions she drew from this were clear: Demetrius has the sphere, and he plans to use it.

In moments like this, Epiphany frequently looked for inspiration from Samantha. Her sister had been an outstanding softball player, who instilled the notion to always go down swinging. Epiphany embraced that idea. Just because she was trapped in this room didn't mean her second soul had to be. Epiphany leaned back in her chair, closed her eyes, and focused her thoughts on finding Demetrius. *Where is he? What's he going to do next, and when is he going to do it?* Her second soul crossed the Black Void into the depths of the Otherworlds.

———

Epiphany's second soul stood motionless on the shoreline of a lake. Its smooth surface shimmered in the brilliant light of a faraway sun. A breathtaking mountain peak rose skyward on the far side of the still water. Steep, vertical cliffs disappeared among billowing clouds. A waterfall spilled over a rocky ledge several hundred yards up on the side of the cliffs. The soft hues of a rainbow hung in the water vapor floating through the air.

Epiphany turned and followed a footpath that took her deeper into the heart of the forest. Broad trunks of massive maple trees lined the pathway. Leaves rustled in a gentle breeze; their song drifted peacefully in the wind. She stopped to absorb the tranquility of the ancient woods. Several salient glimmers of information, remnant echoes of Demetrius's thoughts, spilled over into the Mesh. Epiphany managed to penetrate the blurry shroud that had been clouding earlier attempts to find Demetrius's whereabouts. She locked onto the unique sonority of his second soul.

The landscape around Epiphany shifted. She stepped out of the forest and found herself standing in a field. The dark sky was clear and rich with stars. Epiphany turned through a complete circle. The field was in a valley surrounded by tall mountains on all sides. *What is going to happen here?* she wondered. A vision materialized. The image was blurry, as if viewed through a sheer veil. A dozen or more people exited a small tour bus. They milled about in the field. It appeared to be a social gathering. Epiphany turned to see Demetrius standing next to the tour bus. He reached into a backpack to retrieve the Ebony Sphere but then decided to put it back. The vision fast-forwarded. Everyone who had been in the field boarded the bus, and it drove away. *Did he change his mind and decide not to use the orb?* she wondered. *Is that the only possible outcome?*

A second vision appeared, identical to the first except this time there was no backpack. Like the first vision, this one was also blurry. Epiphany was beginning to get her hopes up. Maybe he won't do this after all.

The third vision eradicated that notion. The same busload of people was milling about, talking to each other, in the middle of the field. The imagery was crystal clear this time. Demetrius removed the sphere from his backpack and raised it skyward. The sphere erupted into a magnificent display of light. A few seconds passed, and then the sphere went dark as if a switch had been flipped. Demetrius dropped to the ground. The lifeless bodies of the people who had made the trip with him were scattered throughout the field. A van pulled up alongside the tour bus. The man Epiphany had chased through the streets of Tromsø got out and helped Demetrius into the vehicle—very much still alive.

Where will this take place? When will it happen? Epiphany wondered, though she had a strong sense that the event was going to take place tonight. It might already be underway. Epiphany knelt down to feel the ground beneath her feet. The location was uncertain. Either Demetrius hasn't decided on a specific location yet, or maybe several different locations were being considered. The closest she could get to a specific place was in the mountains east of Tromsø.

————

Epiphany's eyes fluttered open to view the emptiness of the cold interrogation room. *Is that intentional to make me feel uncomfortable?* she wondered. She thought about the visions and the three possible outcomes. The difference was that one of the three, the one in which Demetrius used the sphere, was the clearest, and therefore the most probable. *People are going to die sometime tonight.*

The door to the interrogation room swung open; a man and a woman walked in. Epiphany recognized the woman—the police officer she met on the art center grounds. Epiphany quickly sized her up—tall, maybe five feet nine, possibly a little taller. Her casual clothes fit loosely but didn't hide the fact that she was fit. She moved across the room in even, flowing strides with an air of confidence. The man who entered the room with her walked around the table and sat in the chair on Epiphany's right.

The woman took a seat across the table from Epiphany and then introduced herself. "I'm Detective Kari Salversen with the National Police Service. I'm the police attorney leading this case and will be conducting the interview."

Is that what this is going to be? Epiphany thought. *An interview? Not likely.*

With a gesture of her hand, Detective Salversen pointed to the man sitting next to Epiphany. "This is Isak Westrum, the public defender who will be representing you and David Skye, as you both agreed."

Detective Salversen looked directly at Epiphany when she spoke. "You have been arrested under suspicion of involvement in several major crimes, which include the bombing attack in Trondheim, an attack in the Tjeldsund Church that left fourteen people dead, and a string of individual attacks similar in nature to the church incident. These are extremely serious crimes, and we are here today to understand your role in them."

Epiphany looked at her attorney, then back at the detective, electing not to respond to the charges for now.

"Did you and David Skye kill those people at the church in Tjeldsund?" Detective Salversen asked.

Epiphany looked directly at the detective. "Absolutely not!" *This woman is going for the jugular right out of the blocks.*

"Why did you go to the church?"

Epiphany had no plausible answer for that. To recover an ancient artifact that could change every soul on the planet probably wouldn't fly. Never having been under arrest and interviewed by a police officer before, Epiphany felt the best approach would be to keep her answers short and not offer any more information than necessary. The last thing she wanted was to get caught in a lie that could be turned against her, so she replied, "No comment." However, she worried she might be digging a hole for herself.

"What brings you to Tromsø, Miss Hendrix?" the detective asked.

"We were attempting to locate Demetrius Wolffe."

"And by we, you mean you and David Skye?"

"Yes."

"Why were you trying to find him?"

Now Epiphany was faced with a decision. How much of the truth does she tell the police?

"Miss Hendrix, why were you attempting to locate Demetrius Wolffe?" the detective asked again.

Apparently, she had taken too long to decide which way to answer. *Be careful where you go with this,* Epiphany thought. "Both David and I know Demetrius through our respective work. His foundation has been struggling, and he sounded a bit despondent about it the last time we talked. We were concerned and wanted to talk to him face-to-face to better assess how he was doing."

"You said you were trying to locate him. Couldn't you just call him? You have his number, I presume."

This detective was sharp. Epiphany felt like she was being drawn closer and closer to a giant drain. If she wasn't careful, she'd get sucked in with no way to escape. "We did try calling him, but he never answered, hence our concern for his well-being."

"So how did you know he was here in Tromsø?"

"I got his itinerary from his office. They know me there because we've collaborated on things in the past. They told me he was in Tromsø, only he never told his office staff exactly where in Tromsø he was staying." Epiphany noticed the detective making a few notes while she talked about calling Demetrius's staff. She could feel her body temperature starting to rise. *What is the detective jotting down? Did I give away something of importance?*

"Have you found him?" the detective asked.

"No."

The detective shifted gears. "Let's talk about the confrontation on Green Street. You got into a physical altercation with a man, who was described as being a little under two meters tall, muscular, long brown hair and a thick beard."

"I'd never seen him before that night or since," Epiphany answered. Finally, a question she didn't have to think about.

"Why did you and David Skye get into a fight with that man?" the detective asked.

"We heard a scream and went to see if we could help. Apparently, he attacked a woman. Another man who was nearby also heard the scream and was checking on the woman when David and I arrived. The bystander told us that he saw the man you just described running away."

"So you and David, not knowing anything about this guy, whether or not he was carrying a gun or some other weapon, just decided to chase after him, instead of contacting the police."

Epiphany's body temperature was rising more, and it felt as if she was getting closer to the drain she had been circling. "I wanted to see where he was heading. If he had a car nearby, I thought I might have been able to get a license plate number that would help the police. Right?" Frustration was beginning to become evident in her voice.

"Did you get a license plate number?"

"No."

"When that man crossed into the property in front of the art center, he attacked me. I know how to defend myself, Miss Hendrix. I've been trained in self-defense. He was bigger and stronger than me. I was fortunate you were chasing after him. I don't know if I would have been able to overtake him had you not been there to help fend him off. Thank you for that."

The detective paused. Epiphany wasn't sure where she was going with the thank you.

"But still, most women would not have done what you did. Why did you attack him?"

"I've been trained in self-defense as well. I'm pretty confident with my abilities. If I can help someone who is being attacked, you better believe I'm going to try to do that."

"Why did Anders Gustason attempt to shoot you and David Skye in the café and then chase after you in the tunnels under the downtown area?" the detective asked.

"Was that his name? I'd never seen the man before in my life. You'll need to ask him why he wanted to kill us," Epiphany said.

"That's going to be hard to do. He was killed in the collision with the truck. So you have no idea why Anders Gustason wanted to kill the two of you?"

"No. I was hoping you'd be able to tell me that."

"Trouble seems to follow you and David Skye, doesn't it, Miss Hendrix?"

Epiphany wasn't about to respond to that question.

"Okay, let's review the events of the past several days. You and David Skye meet in Trondheim, where a bombing attack kills twenty-three people. Then the vehicle the two of you were traveling in is seen fleeing a church where fourteen more people had been killed, and you're refusing to tell me why you just happened to be at that church. You wind up in Tromsø, where four more people are killed in a manner consistent with the attack in the church."

"Four? I only know about the one we stumbled upon. And I was chasing after the man who was seen at the site of the attack. That's the guy you should be looking for." The tone in Epiphany's voice was beginning to move from frustration to anger.

"In addition to the attack you happened upon, three more people were killed, and as I just mentioned, in the same manner that was used in the church."

"I don't know anything about that."

The detective continued with the summary she had started before Epiphany had interrupted her. "And finally, you are chased through the tunnels of Tromsø by a man who has connections to the bomber in Trondheim and to another man involved in an earlier attack in Bergen." The detective slammed her fist on the table. "You can see how this looks from my perspective. You know something, and you're holding back on me. I'm going to find out what that is. Better get comfortable because we're just getting started."

Fuck it! Epiphany thought. *I'm tired of being pushed around by this woman. I'm going to go down swinging. Cop or no cop.* In a low voice, not much above a whisper, Epiphany said, "I heard what you said when that big guy attacked you on the art center grounds. I saw what you saw. He did vanish into thin air."

The detective looked at Epiphany strangely, like she wasn't sure what to say next. *Good,* Epiphany thought. *I put her on the defensive.* Epiphany leaned in closer across the table. "Demetrius Wolffe is the one you need to find. He's planning an attack similar to the one in Tjeldsund. Tonight! Somewhere in the mountains around here. And I don't fucking know where; otherwise, Detective, I'd fucking tell you. It's probably a trial run for something bigger than anything you could ever imagine. I'm talking 'change the world' bigger. And the only two people who can stop it are sitting here in a police station wasting valuable time answering your fucking questions!"

CHAPTER 27

Office of Chief Martin Kolbeck, Tromsø Police Station

Kari Salversen left Jade Hendrix in Interrogation Room 2 and walked through the police station to Martin Kolbeck's office. The comment about the man running through the art center grounds stuck with her. Hendrix saw it too. She acknowledged seeing the man vanish. Kari had blocked that event out of her mind, chalked it up to being dizzy as a result of the fight with the big man who had accosted her. It was probably her eyes playing tricks on her. *There has to be some logical reason for what happened. People don't just vanish into thin air,* she thought. When she reached Martin's office, she knocked, entered, and sat in one of the chairs in front of his desk.

"So how'd it go?" Martin asked.

"She's definitely hiding something, and I need to figure out what that is. I took a slow, methodical approach, the way you taught me all those years ago." Kari noticed the slight smile on Martin's face. She was thankful for the guidance he had provided through his mentorship earlier in her career, and he appeared to be appreciative of the fact that she acknowledged it.

"I kept reeling her in, but she kept her cool. Then I lost mine and snapped at her. She snapped back at me. Threw a man named Demetrius Wolffe under the bus."

"Has his name come up in this investigation?" Martin asked.

"Only in a marginal way," Kari said. "Demetrius Wolffe is the founder of Citizens for a Peaceful Planet. They organized the cultural event that was the target of the bomber in Trondheim. I find it hard to believe that he would have something to do with all of this."

"These cases of yours are taking on the form of a giant tapestry with all of these interwoven threads," Martin suggested.

Kari appreciated the analogy. "Yeah, only we don't know what the tapestry looks like."

"You'll get there," Martin said confidently. "What did Hendrix say about Demetrius Wolffe?"

"She said he was planning an attack somewhere in the mountains near Tromsø and that it's going to happen tonight."

"Not much to go on." Martin turned around and glanced at the topographical map on the wall behind him. "There are a lot of mountains around Tromsø. Did she say how she knows this? Do you believe what she said is credible?"

Kari smiled. Martin was asking all of the questions she was asking herself. "She was very emphatic about it. Is she credible? I can't be certain, but everywhere Skye and Hendrix show up, something bad happens. So, yeah, I think there could be a modicum of truth to what she said."

"We need to find Demetrius Wolffe," Martin said. "Did Hendrix offer up his location?"

"She said she doesn't know where he is, and said she'd tell us if she did."

"Right, but somehow, she suspected he was here in Tromsø. She had to come by that information somehow," Martin suggested.

"Correct. She said she called one of the people who works for him. I'd like to check in with Jens, see if he can get more information from Wolffe's staff. Do you mind if I call him now?"

"Go ahead."

Jens Tofte answered on the third ring.

"Hi Jens, this is Kari. I've got you on speaker phone. I'm here with Chief Kolbeck in his office." Kari set her cellphone down on the edge of Martin's desk.

"Hi Kari. Chief."

"I know it's late. Are you back at your hotel room?" Kari asked.

"No, just got back from dinner. I'm at the Harstad office. Wanted to follow up on a few things."

"We have an update. We've taken David Skye and Jade Hendrix into custody."

"That's great news. Have you had a chance to talk to them?"

"I just finished interrogating Hendrix. Skye will be next. There's something I need you to check for me. Hendrix has implicated Demetrius Wolffe in the Tjeldsund case."

"Really? The Citizens for a Peaceful Planet guy?" Jens's voice sounded noticeably skeptical.

"Can you check something for me?" Kari asked. "You have the flight manifests, right? Was Demetrius Wolffe on an incoming flight to the Harstad/Narvik Airport during the timeframe preceding the church attack?"

"I have those here. The airline printed them out for me," Jens replied. "Hang on a sec."

Kari heard Jens rifling through papers.

"Here we go. I don't see him on the flight that arrived the morning of the attack. Let me check the day before." Jens took a moment to review the next list. "Shit. He flew into Harstad/Narvik the day before the attack. The flight arrived in the evening."

Kari glanced at Martin, who nodded at her.

"Jens, Jade Hendrix mentioned that Wolffe's staff told her he was in Tromsø, but he didn't give his staff any information as to where he was staying. I don't care who you have to call or wake up. Contact someone on Demetrius Wolffe's staff and find out where he is staying and who he might be meeting here. This is urgent, Jens. Hendrix indicated that Demetrius Wolffe is planning another attack, somewhere in the mountains near Tromsø. Tonight!"

"Got it. I'll get on it now and get back to you as soon as I have something."

"One more thing, Jens. The techs here examined incoming and outgoing phone calls over the past few days on Jade Hendrix's and David Skye's cellphones. Both of them have had short calls with a Johannes Stinar in the village of Stamsund. I'd like you to visit Mr. Stinar and see what his connection to these two is. Don't be afraid to tell him we have them in police custody. I'd be curious to hear about his reaction to that."

"I will do that," Jens said.

"Thanks," Kari said and then ended the call.

"Maybe she's telling the truth," Martin suggested.

"Could be. Demetrius Wolffe flew into the same airport that Skye and Hendrix came into. He was there the day before the attack."

"I've been reviewing the reports that Jens has been preparing regarding the Tjeldsund incident," Martin said. "By the way, he's a very detailed guy. Anyway, what if we're coming about this from the wrong direction?"

"What do you mean?"

"What if the deaths of those fourteen people weren't the focus of what happened in that church? We could be glossing over a salient point."

Kari leaned back in her chair and glanced out the window. She played back the crime scene at the church in her head. She had noticed the orb was missing from the statue's hand. "Do you mean the statue?"

"Yes. I've been reading about it," Martin said. "*The Angel and the Orb*. Jens's reports mentioned the orb had been taken the day of the attack. The caretaker said he was in the church that morning, and the orb had still been there. What if the main intent was to steal the orb, and somewhere during that crime, those people were killed?"

Kari thought about what Martin had just said. It was an interesting insight. "So Demetrius Wolffe gets to the church before Skye and Hendrix, takes the orb, and through some means we have yet to determine, kills fourteen people to cover his tracks."

"Yeah, I know. It's a little out there."

There's a disturbing air of mysticism about this case, Kari thought. She was accosted by a man who has a striking resemblance to a five-hundred-year-old statue. That same man vanished before her very eyes, and she wasn't the only one to acknowledge seeing it. And a mysterious orb was taken from the statue. For a person who believed in cold, hard facts, she was struggling with this notion, but she couldn't dismiss it either. "If it's one thing I learned from you,

Martin, it was to look at things from every possible angle, including the improbable. I just wish I knew what a five-hundred-year-old orb has to do with any of this?"

"That's the question of the day," Martin said.

CHAPTER 28

Tromsø Police Station

David Skye sat impatiently at the table in the center of Interrogation Room 1. He'd been waiting entirely too long, and the futility of being trapped in this room was depressing him. Demetrius Wolffe had set them up to be killed. He had the Ebony Sphere of Vayla Isarrus and seemed intent on using it, and there wasn't much that he and Epiphany could do about it while in police custody. An obvious way out of this predicament hadn't presented itself as of yet. The sound of the door opening jarred him from his thoughts. Finally, something was going to happen.

A policewoman and a man dressed in a suit entered the room. She introduced herself and the public defender who had been assigned to his case. Detective Salversen sat across from David, and the attorney, Isak Westrum, sat to his right. She informed him again of the reasons for which he and Epiphany were being detained and then began with her line of questioning.

"What brought you to Trondheim, Mr. Skye?" Her tone was soft and nonconfrontational.

"I traveled to Trondheim to meet two people: Aidan McCallum and Epiphany. Sorry," David apologized. "Jade Hendrix, but she prefers her nickname."

"Why were you meeting them?" Salversen asked.

"We were meeting to discuss possible collaborations between our respective organizations."

"How long have you known Aidan McCallum and Jade Hendrix?"

"Probably four or five years. We've met occasionally over that time period."

"Would you say you know Aidan McCallum well enough to judge his character, to understand his motivations?" Salversen prodded.

David shrugged slightly, not yet understanding where she was going with this. "Yeah, I think so."

"We have video coverage from a news crew showing Aidan McCallum chasing after the man who set the explosives in place. Why would he do that? Did he know this was going to happen?"

"I don't know how Aidan would have suspected that. If he saw something suspicious, if he sensed something bad was going to take place, then yes, I think he would have tried to stop it," David said.

"Did you know the attack in Trondheim was going to happen?" Salversen asked pointedly.

"No! Not at all. I was shocked by it," David exclaimed.

"How did you know Lars Bohle?"

"I've never heard that name before in my life. Who is he?" David was getting angry with the questioning. He knew he had to keep that in check. It would not be good to blurt something out that could be misconstrued and get himself into trouble later on.

"Then why were you leaning over his body at the site of the first explosion?" Salversen asked.

"What are you talking about?" David asked, in an agitated way. *So much for keeping my cool,* he thought.

"Lars Bohle is the man who detonated the bombs at the Solsiden Mall in Trondheim. He's the man that your associate, Aidan McCallum, was chasing before he died. We have video footage of you kneeling over Bohle's body."

David leaned back and took a deep breath. "I never heard his name before you mentioned it just now. I never saw the man before that day in Trondheim."

The detective opened a file folder, took out a photo, then laid it on the table in front of David. "Recognize this?"

David looked down and studied the image. It was a picture of Earth with a dagger through it with a rising sun in the background. He looked up at the detective. "I saw that on the wrist of the man you said Aidan was chasing."

The detective laid out two more photos of the same tattoo. She pointed to the first one. "This same tattoo was on the wrist of Rutger Solberg, who initiated a violent, armed attack in Bergen, and this second one was on the wrist of Anders Gustason. How do you know Anders Gustason, Mr. Skye?"

By the tone of her voice, it sounded like she was getting impatient with him. "I don't know Anders Gustason. Who the hell is he?" David snapped back.

"Then why was he trying to kill you in the Lost Fjord Café this afternoon, and why'd he chase you and Jade Hendrix through the tunnels of Tromsø?" she demanded.

David leaned forward and rubbed his head. This was now getting infuriating. And she wasn't letting up.

"Do you know Demetrius Wolffe? What is your relationship with him?" she asked.

"We've talked a few times here and there," David replied.

"The recent calls on your cellphone indicate you've tried to reach out to him quite a few times. In fact, he called you this morning before the attempt on your life this afternoon. What did you talk about?"

"He was feeling down about what happened in Trondheim. That coupled with the fact that his organization is struggling had made him really depressed. Epiphany... excuse me, Jade and I were concerned, so we reached out to him."

"What do you know about *The Angel and the Orb*, Mr. Skye?" She continued on, pushing even harder.

"Not much," he responded curtly.

"We have records showing that Demetrius Wolffe flew into the Harstad/Narvik Airport the day before you. What business did he have on Tjeldøya Island, and why did you and Jade Hendrix go to the church there?"

David didn't answer.

Salversen slammed her fist on the table. It startled David. "Why?" she demanded again. "Why would Demetrius Wolffe take the orb from the statue? Did you know he was going to do that? Is that why you were there? Were you and Jade Hendrix trying to get to it before he did?"

David was quickly losing his ability to concentrate and focus. She was pushing more intensely now.

"Why is Wolffe planning another attack like the one in Tjeldsund?" Salversen asked. "Is he going to use the orb in some way?"

"What are you talking about?" David asked.

"Your associate, Miss Hendrix, was adamant that Demetrius Wolffe is going to initiate another attack like the one in Tjeldsund. She seems to think it's going to happen somewhere in the mountains nearby. Tonight!" Salversen said.

David paused. Was she lying to trap him in some way? Did Epiphany really tell her that?

"I don't know anything about that attack."

A knock on the door interrupted the interrogation. An officer stepped inside and said, "Detective Salversen, Chief Kolbeck would like to speak with you. He said it's urgent."

CHAPTER 29

In the mountains near Overgård, Norway

Demetrius Wolffe exited the bus along with all of the other passengers. They had gathered in an open field situated in a valley surrounded by mountain ranges in the remote village of Overgård. The upper atmosphere was crystal clear and laden with stars. Long coils of green light slowly snaked through the sky. He had seen the northern lights before but never as vivid as this. As beautiful as the aurora was, it wasn't the reason he was here. An ample donation from Gerd Schumann, the owner of Alfheim Shipping, was what he had come for.

The trip had taken an hour and twenty minutes. Every minute of that time seemed to tick away at an interminably slow pace. Gerd had been sitting in one of the two seats directly behind the driver. Henrik Lorensen, the chief financial officer of Gerd's company, was sitting in the seat to his left. For most of the trip, the two of them were in the weeds on the current financial situation of the company. From what Demetrius could make of it, the conversation didn't sound all that happy. Revenues and profits were down, and short-term headwinds did not bode well for an improvement in their current financial situation. Demetrius was sitting in the front seat on the other side of the aisle to Gerd's right. The seat to Demetrius's right had been empty, so other than an occasional comment from Gerd about the scenery and what a good night it was shaping up to be for viewing the lights, Demetrius had a lot of time to get lost in his own thoughts. The future of Citizens for a Peaceful Planet was riding on the outcome of this escapade.

Demetrius adjusted the backpack over his right shoulder. The gentle hum from the sphere filled his head with a harmonious resonance. Ever since he first touched the sphere in the church at Tjeldsund, his connection to it was growing stronger. A driving need to hold it in his hand consumed his thoughts. It felt as if an essential part of him had been forcibly separated. He was desperate to feel its power surging through his fingertips.

Gerd addressed the passengers, all of whom were his direct reports. This tour was meant to be a celebration of their hard work over the past fiscal year. He made a short thank you speech as they set up several collapsible tables with brandy, wine, and an assortment of cheeses. While Gerd spoke to his employees, Demetrius thought about his own troubles. His foundation was going under, and his pancreatic cancer would limit the number of days he'd have left on the planet. Unfortunately for him, his future did not look as bright as the one Gerd had just promised his direct reports.

The intensity of the resonant hum from the Ebony Sphere had increased slightly. Asgeir said there'd be ebbs and flows and indicated that the bond he'd feel with the sphere would grow stronger. Prior to coming on this trip, Demetrius suggested that he might try the sphere tonight. He told Asgeir that he had ventured into the Otherworlds and had entered the flow of the Quintessence. What he did not reveal was the fact that he had almost perished in the attempt.

Asgeir had been upset that Demetrius attempted it on his own and reiterated that any future attempts needed to be made with the proper guidance. Nevertheless, Asgeir assured him that his second soul would have been infused with enough of the ancient flow of energy to activate the Ebony Sphere without taking the lives of the people around him. But that came with a strong condition—provided that Demetrius kept his thoughts pure and concentrate only on the desired picture of humanity that he wished to create. As a precaution, Asgeir had decided that he'd follow behind the tour bus at a safe distance should something go wrong. With all those considerations, Demetrius was still unsure if he would attempt the trial run tonight. Things could go wrong, and he wasn't sure he could live with another catastrophe similar to the one in the Tjeldsund Church.

"Demetrius," Gerd Schumann called to him as he approached. Gerd was fifty-five years old. He was a man whose physical stature seemed to command respect—two meters tall, with a lean, muscular build. His deep voice projected an air of confidence and authority. His predominantly gray hair lent a sense of wisdom that comes with age. "Have a drink. I hope you're enjoying the night."

Demetrius nodded and took the glass of blackberry brandy being offered to him. The syrupy sweet warmth of the alcohol seemed to stave off the cold bite of the night air.

"Listen, I don't know how much of my conversation with Henrik you overheard," Gerd said.

Demetrius was weary of the uneasy tone in Gerd's voice. He had heard enough of the conversation between Gerd and Henrik Lorensen that he suspected what was surely going to follow would not be good.

Gerd shifted his drink to his left hand and put his right hand on Demetrius's shoulder, as if the human touch would soften the blow that was about to come. "I know I just spoke of a promising future to my direct reports here, but the truth of the matter is that our financials over the past quarter and a half have started to slide. We've hit some rough patches financially. I'm confident we'll come out of this, and we will see the good times I mentioned to my people. But it will take a little time to turn things around. I'm afraid we are going to have to postpone that donation we talked about. Believe me when I tell you, Demetrius, I am sincerely unhappy about this. Your organization is doing great things for society and I … we at Alfheim would like to be a part of that. If things start to turn around by the end of the second quarter of this current fiscal year, I'm confident we will be standing here this time next year celebrating a healthy donation to Citizens for a Peaceful Planet." Gerd squeezed Demetrius's shoulder and walked back to talk with his employees.

Christ, Demetrius thought, *the guy didn't even give me a chance to say anything. He just walked away.* "Screw you, Gerd," is what he would have liked to have said. His better sense prevented that from happening. The letdown was yet another emotional trauma Demetrius felt he had to accept. By this time next year, he'd be dead. The cancer will have overtaken his body's best efforts to fend it off. Without the two-million-dollar donation, Citizens for a Peaceful Planet will be just as dead. He and his organization could be buried in the ground together.

Gerd's decision to hold off on the donation was the impetus Demetrius needed. If he had been uncertain about his path forward before tonight, he no longer had any doubts. Demetrius walked over to the back of the tour bus while the Alfheim people enjoyed their evening celebration under the glow of the northern lights. He lowered the backpack to the ground and unzipped it. Gerd's pronouncement about the donation brought him to a decision. He would not be denied the success he had dedicated his entire life to achieve. If there was a chance to see the world as he dreamed it could be, he was going to take it. Dying alone in a hospital bed, another also-ran with good intent who didn't quite make it to the finish line, was not an option.

He reached into the backpack with his right hand and grasped the Ebony Sphere of Vayla Isarrus. It felt cool, almost weightless—its color deep and rich. Energy from the sphere radiated into his fingers and through the palm of his hand. A soft, orange haze roiled like boiling water as it enveloped the entire surface of the otherworldly orb.

A sudden rush of energy surged through Demetrius's body. His consciousness transcended its physical Earth-bound existence. An image of Vayla Isarrus filled his head. Her voice called out to him, "We will make this journey together." His second soul summoned the flow of the Quintessence. Its ancient energy swelled through his body and into the sphere like a tsunami. The images of the people around him came into view one by one, but it wasn't their physical human form that he saw, it was the wispy spiritual aura of each soul. Vayla Isarrus spoke again, "Raise the sphere skyward. Fill it with your vision of what this world shall be."

Demetrius raised the glowing orb; it felt as if he was staring into the vast reaches of eternity. A burst of energy erupted from the sphere, sending long, swirling streamers of light arcing across the sky. In the time it took to inhale a breath of cold air, everything went black, the souls around him evaporated, the sphere went dark, and as Demetrius's body dropped to the ground, a troubling notion ran through his head: His thoughts had not been pure.

CHAPTER 30

Office of Chief Martin Kolbeck, Tromsø Police Station

When Kari Salversen walked into Martin Kolbeck's office, he was on the phone. He motioned for her to come in and take a seat. Martin finished the call and hung up. "Kari, Jens got back to me. The man is efficient as well as detailed. He managed to contact Demetrius Wolffe's assistant. Didn't get an address, but he did get the name of the person Wolffe is meeting with. Ever hear of Gerd Schumann?"

"No. Who is he?"

"He owns a large regional company called Alfheim Shipping. He's a pretty big name in this part of the country. Does a lot of domestic and international shipping. Mostly larger cargo. One of our officers has been trying to reach him, but with no luck, I'm afraid. He's also been trying to reach Demetrius Wolffe using the phone number on David Skye's cellphone. No luck there either."

Kari stood and walked over to the window. Her adrenaline was pumping from the interrogation, and she needed to move to burn off some of the excess energy. "Well, if Hendrix is right, and if they're in the mountains somewhere, cell reception is probably bad or nonexistent."

Martin nodded in agreement. "That's what I thought. So it got me thinking. What would be going on in the mountains this time of year?"

Kari looked at him but didn't answer. Her mind was focused on the two suspects she had in Interrogation Rooms 1 and 2.

"Northern lights tours," Martin said. "They're busy as hell this time of year. I had one of my guys check with the local outfits. We got a hit—a trip was chartered on behalf of Gerd Schumann by Alfheim."

That got Kari's attention. "When and where?" she asked, as she walked back to take a seat in front of Martin's desk.

"A company called Arctic Aurora Tours took a small bus of sixteen people on a lights tour. They have three standard viewing areas that they use, depending on weather conditions. Tonight, they're out past a little village called Overgård. It's about eighty kilometers southeast of here. An hour-and-ten-minute drive on a good day. Based on the timetable we were given by the tour company, the group has probably been at the site for at least an hour."

"Can we get a car out there to check on them?" Kari asked.

"That's who I was on the phone with when you walked in. We have a station in Nordkjosbotn. They'll have a patrol car there within fifteen minutes. I told them to bring Demetrius Wolffe back to their station and hold him for questioning, assuming Wolffe is with them. Care to wait?"

Kari answered with an enthusiastic yes. She was anxious to see how this played out. She and Martin passed the time by discussing the details of both interrogations. Twenty minutes had passed when Martin's phone rang. "I'm putting you on speaker phone, with Detective Kari Salversen in the room."

"This is Officer Finn Risberg, with the Nordkjosbotn station. They're all dead sir, fifteen bodies lying in the snow and the driver inside the van. Sixteen total."

Kari moved her chair closer to the phone on Martin's desk. Officer Risberg paused for a moment, and when he spoke again his voice wavered. "Their faces … they look like they're contorted in pain."

Martin jumped in, "Officer, secure the site. We're going to send a forensics team out there." Martin glanced up at Kari, who nodded. "Detective Salversen and I are heading there now. We'll probably be there in a little over an hour." He thanked the officer and ended the call.

"I'm going to have Skye and Hendrix taken to holding cells. I'll tell their public defender we'll start again sometime tomorrow morning," Kari said.

"Okay. Meet me in the parking lot. We'll take my car."

Kari met the public defender, apprised him of the situation, and asked him to come back the next morning. She had the officer standing guard escort David Skye into Interrogation Room 2 with Jade Hendrix. "Well, it looks like your premonition came true, Miss Hendrix. I think I'm beginning to understand how you got the nickname Epiphany. There was an incident in the mountains to the southeast, near Overgård, eighty kilometers from here."

Kari watched the reaction from both suspects. David Skye glanced at Jade Hendrix with a rather perplexed look on his face. Hendrix pursed her lips with what looked like disappointment. "Sixteen people were killed in what appears to be an attack that mirrors what happened at the Tjeldsund Church. You'll be spending the night in holding cells here. We'll resume our discussions tomorrow." Kari instructed the officer to take them to their cells, then hurried to meet Martin at his car.

The drive to Overgård took an hour and five minutes. When they arrived, Martin drove along a narrow lane and came to a stop. A second patrol car had already arrived, and two more officers were cordoning off the area. Officer Risberg walked up to Chief Kolbeck and Detective Salversen. "We have the area secured, Chief," the officer said.

"Good," Martin replied. "The forensics team will be here within the next twenty or thirty minutes."

"What can you tell us, Officer?" Kari asked.

The officer led them to a spot in the open field where Arctic Aurora Tours brought their customers. He was careful to lead them into an area where there weren't any footprints in the snow to protect the integrity of the crime scene. As Kari surveyed the area, she could see why they brought their customers here. It was remote, away from any light pollution. The sky was clear, and the mountains that surrounded the valley in which they stood were spectacular. For early December, the outside temperature was somewhat mild, with little to no wind.

Officer Risberg shined a large, powerful flashlight at the bus. Its doors were closed, and the beam illuminated the driver's seat. "The driver is still inside, so whatever killed all of those people appears to have killed the driver from outside the bus." Officer Risberg looked at Detective Salversen and Chief Kolbeck. "What could do that?" he asked.

"That's what we're trying to figure out," Martin said.

"There's the bus driver, and I counted fifteen passengers in the field. They're all dead, and they all look like this." Officer Risberg shined his flashlight on the two closest victims, lying in the snow about four meters from where they stood.

"Jesus," Martin exclaimed.

"This looks exactly like what we saw at the church in Tjeldsund, Martin," Kari said.

"There is one more thing." Officer Risberg aimed the beam of the flashlight to the area by the side of the van. "Tire tracks from a second vehicle. The indentations in the snow where the vehicle pulled up look like something big was on the ground. Maybe another body. You can see the tire tracks where the vehicle turned around and left."

"Nice observations, Officer," Martin said. "We've got a few minutes until the forensics team gets here. I'm going to wait in the car."

Kari and Martin sat in the car until the forensics team and medical examiner showed up fifteen minutes later, a little earlier than expected. It took an hour to photograph the crime scene and collect evidence. They had opened the doors to the bus and confirmed that only the driver was inside.

The forensics lead and a medical examiner came up to Kari and Martin, who were now standing outside Martin's sedan. "It's okay to look around," the forensics lead said.

"What can you tell us about the cause of death?" Martin asked.

"That's a tough one to answer right now," the medical examiner replied. "No signs of physical trauma, bruising, or wounds from a gun or a knife. They all just dropped where they were standing. The looks of pain on the faces of the victims are unsettling. I hope I never see anything like this again." She looked at Kari, "Officer Risberg told me you've seen this before, at a church somewhere."

"Yes, that's right," Kari said. "In Tjeldsund. Fourteen killed in a manner that closely resembles what we see here. The medical examiner indicated heart failure was the cause of death. Their bodily functions stopped like someone flipped a switch and turned them all off."

"I'll contact the examiner for that case and look at similarities here. Based on what you've just said, I'd say we're looking at the same thing. Simultaneous heart failure if you could believe that. Based on their body temperatures and adjusting for the cold outdoor temperature, these people haven't been dead very long—between two and three hours max."

Kari looked over at the forensics lead. "What can you tell us about the tire tracks near the bus? Were they made tonight or were they already here?"

The man walked them over to the bus and shined his flashlight at the tracks. "I'd say they were made tonight. You can see by the well-defined tread marks in the snow that these must be fresh. There was a light dusting of snow this morning out here, so had these tracks been made before today, these indentations from the knobby tire treads would have been filled in."

"Okay, so someone else might have come and left when this attack happened," Martin said.

"Looks that way," he said. "Also, we recovered a clipboard inside the van. It has a passenger list. It's on the table we set up over there."

"Thanks for the update," Martin said. He watched the forensics lead and medical examiner walk away and then turned to Kari. "Take a look around. All of these people killed at a remote site set up for viewing the northern lights. How did Jade

Hendrix suspect this was going to happen if she wasn't involved?"

"Exactly. It's uncanny how she and David Skye have been in the locations where these attacks have happened," Kari said. "They were in our custody in Tromsø when this occurred out here. No way it was them who killed these people, but Hendrix knew about it in advance."

"I've never believed in psychics," Martin stated firmly. "But this is starting to change my mind. Let's go take a look at that clipboard."

Kari followed him over to the evidence table. He picked up the clipboard, which was sealed in a clear plastic evidence bag. "Not counting the driver, there's sixteen people listed here, but only fifteen passengers and the bus driver are here at the site. We're missing one body. Take a look at the name for passenger sixteen." He handed the clipboard to Kari.

Kari read the name out loud, "Demetrius Wolffe."

CHAPTER 31

Vestpollen, Norway, Next day

Johannes Stinar drove his Land Rover on a deserted stretch of Midnattsolveien, southwest of the village of Vestpollen in the northern Lofoten Islands. He brought his SUV to a stop on the side of the road at the spot where he'd make his hike into the woods. Johannes listened to the end of Brandenburg Concerto No. 3, by Johann Sebastian Bach, before turning off the engine. There was a reason the great composer's music had survived more than three centuries. In Johannes's opinion, the sheer splendor and precision of the music was unmatched. He found it amazing that the human mind was capable of creating such beauty and hoped the inspirational music would motivate him for the work he needed to complete. Tens of thousands of lives depended on it.

As Johannes gazed out the front windshield, he thought about the name *Midnattsolveien*, the "midnight sun road." However, during this time of year, there'd be no sun. The morning sky had shifted to something a little darker than twilight. There'd be just enough light to hike into the valley between the two mountain ridges and set up his next trial run.

Using the quantum-well device to destroy the Ebony Sphere of Vayla Isarrus was something he had never foreseen, but technically it should work. To test that theory, he brought a ball with him that was close in size to his estimated diameter of the Ebony Sphere. There were several variables at play: the size and weight of the ball, the velocity with which the ball is tossed, the manner in which it is thrown, and the angle of impact. During his trial run, he planned to toss the ball at the quantum well to ensure that it would in fact break the plane and pass through.

Composing his thoughts for a few minutes helped to steady his nerves. Johannes opened the SUV door and stepped into the snow. A blast of arctic air reminded him of just how far north he was. He pulled the hood of his parka over his head and walked to the back of the Range Rover to remove his gear from the trunk. In addition to the weight of the gear he'd be lugging through the woods, he'd be carrying the burden of ensuring his quantum-well device would work. Warm, steamy breath billowed from Johannes's mouth as he began his trek through the trees.

He followed a mountain stream, over a long, gradual incline between two ridges. His journey ended at a depression in the landscape. Beads of sweat trickled down his back. The moisture-wicking inner layer of his clothing managed to keep him drier than he had expected. According to his fitness watch, he had hiked 1.33 kilometers from the road. It had taken him forty minutes to hike the rough, snow-covered terrain. His legs felt like rubber, and his heart rate was elevated, nearly in his aerobic zone. This was far enough.

As Johannes had done with his previous trial, he had chosen this area with careful deliberation. It was far enough away from homes and businesses that no one would see what he was doing, and if a catastrophic failure were to happen, no one would be close enough to get injured or killed. Johannes removed his backpack and set it down in the snow. He shrugged and rotated his shoulders to relieve some of the strain from carrying the heavy pack. It took twenty minutes to get the quantum-well device set up the way he wanted. He double-checked the notes and sketches in his lab journal to make sure everything was done correctly.

The quantum-well device was a stainless-steel cylinder measuring six inches in diameter and fourteen inches long. Johannes removed the outer stainless-steel shell, revealing the internal mechanisms, an array of wires and posts, microelectronics, a quantum gyroscope at its core, and an array of miniaturized magnetic toroids. Everything looked okay. The device had survived the jostling of the hike. He slid the outer cover back over the mechanisms.

Johannes stepped back and thought about the work that had brought him this far. His theories that made what he was about to do possible had led him to an interesting discovery. He had managed to delve into the myriad veils of the Quintessence and map out the single underlying, fundamental waveform from which all other vibrational states exist, as part of a complex, cosmic overtone series. He had discovered the God Frequency, the single, most fundamental building block of everything that exists. It was the key that unlocked the hidden dimensions to reveal the ancient energy of the Quintessence. Johannes smiled at that thought and continued with the work at hand.

A few more things needed to be done. He set up a tripod and mounted his video camera to it. During the hike to this point in the mountains, the morning sky had transitioned from a medium level of darkness to a modest twilight sky—the lightest the sky would be for about four to five hours. It wasn't ideal lighting, but it would suffice for making a recording. He concluded his preparations and made a few notes about the ambient conditions in his lab notebook.

The quantum-well device was rigged to stand at an angle rather than upright. Johannes had calculated that a twelve-degree angle from grade would be needed to cast the initial bead the desired distance and height above the ground. Johannes fired up the unit and tapped the ignition button on his remote. It took forty-two seconds for two entangled, tiny beads of pure energy, about the size of golf balls, to form. The first bead was twenty meters from the quantum-well device and about five meters above the ground. The second bead formed within an intense magnetic field within the device itself. Ten seconds later, the first bead erupted into a ten-meter-diameter sphere of twisting and turning energy tearing at the fabric of space-time. This was one of the modifications he had made. The outer shell was larger than what the previous version of his device could generate. There'd be more surface area available to push both the spirit working with Demetrius and the Ebony Sphere through.

Johannes extracted the ball from the backpack and moved in closer. He ran through his options: throw the ball underhand, throw it overhand, toss it lightly, or throw it as hard as he could. He opted for what he considered a worst-case scenario: throw the ball underhand with as little velocity as possible. Johannes tossed the ball into the rotating sphere of primordial energy. Its outer surface swallowed the ball and immediately lit up in shades of yellow and green. Success. He smiled.

Then something unanticipated happened. The outer shell started expanding, possibly from the sudden influx of energy due to the matter-to-energy conversion of the ball once it penetrated the quantum well. Johannes turned and started running away from the sphere, looking over his shoulder as he moved over the uneven terrain. If he had been any slower, the outer shell would have overtaken him. He stumbled over a snow-covered rock and lost his footing. His momentum carried him forward as he tumbled head over heels. Johannes landed on his back and quickly rolled over to his hands and knees. When he lifted his head, the outer shell of the sphere was a few centimeters from his face. *It's going to swallow me up,* he thought. A second later, the sphere collapsed in on itself and disappeared. The air where the sphere had once been was swirling. It picked up snow from the ground and tossed it around—like a giant snow globe. Several seconds later everything went still.

Johannes's heart was pounding a staccato rhythm inside his chest, but at least he was still alive. He sat back on his legs and stared at the empty space where the quantum well had formed. This trial was better in some ways than the first one had been. The diameter of the sphere was larger, and it stabilized for a longer period of time. It felt like it was on the order of three to five minutes. On the downside, the sphere had expanded suddenly. He'd have to spend more time to analyze the data along with his calculations to understand why that happened. The window of opportunity was still too small. There would be very little time to take the Ebony Sphere from Demetrius Wolffe and toss it into the quantum well before it snapped shut.

Johannes took his time gathering and packing up the equipment. He was rattled by how quickly the outer shell of the quantum well had expanded. Hopefully the data he gathered would give him insights into why that happened. As he walked back to the Range Rover, he figured he needed several weeks to work through the problem areas in the detail needed to adequately address them. The trouble was, he knew he probably had no more than four or five days if he was lucky.

CHAPTER 32

Tromsø Police Station

David and Epiphany walked side by side in silence while a tall, thin police officer escorted them to Interrogation Room 1. The officer opened the door and motioned for them to enter. "Your breakfast is on the table. I'll be outside the door," he said in a low, monotone voice.

They walked to the table and sat down. The food and coffee smelled great. One Styrofoam container had been placed in front of David's chair and another one in front of Epiphany's. When David opened his container, his face lit up with about as much joy as he could muster given where they were at the moment. He was staring at a sausage, egg, and cheese breakfast sandwich on grilled rye. Several other breakfast options were laid out on the table: jars of plain and flavored French-style yogurt, toast, and pitchers of orange juice and coffee and a stack of cups. He poured a cup of hot coffee and took a sip. The rich flavor lingered in his mouth.

Epiphany sat, grabbed a yogurt, and looked at David. Her hair was a tangled mess, from what must have been a lot of tossing and turning during sleep last night. She poured a glass of orange juice and took a long gulp. "Do you remember sitting in the

4Runner yesterday, when the two police cars were rolling up on us?"

David had already started devouring his sausage, egg, and cheese sandwich. He was famished and was concerned he might bite off one of his fingers if he wasn't careful how he attacked the sandwich. He nodded yes to her question.

She asked, "Do you remember what you said?"

He shook his head "no" as he took another massive bite. Both cheeks were puffed out as far as they could possibly stretch, looking like a squirrel gathering nuts in the forest in anticipation of a long, cold winter.

"You said, and I quote," she made air quotes with her right hand as she said the next bit, "'What's the worst that could happen now?'" Epiphany paused and then leaned in close to David. "Well take a fucking look around!" After another short pause, she blurted out "Numb-nuts," for further effect.

David was unfazed as he continued hammering his sandwich.

Epiphany took a sip of orange juice and leaned back. She was on a roll; David let her run with it.

"Did that blonde cop, Salversen, interview you yesterday?" she asked, speaking as if saying the woman's name aloud was like a caustic chemical eating through her lips.

David was slamming through the last bits of sandwich. He nodded "yes."

"I wanted to clock that fucking bitch!"

David laughed uncontrollably. He hadn't expected that phrase to come out of Epiphany's mouth. Unfortunately, when the laughing was about to start, he had been at an awkward tipping point. Should he spit the food out or swallow it? He opted for the latter and started gagging on a piece of sausage that would have choked a rhino. Somehow, he managed to swallow all of it.

Realizing how funny her words had sounded and seeing David laughing uncontrollably made Epiphany burst into laughter. "Jesus Christ, you're eating like a goddamn animal. We should be feeding you from a fucking trough."

David started laughing so hard his sides were aching. Epiphany was laughing along with him. Their situation was dire. He knew it. She knew it. *It's good that she got to vent a little steam,* David thought. They both were frustrated. The laughter did them good.

Eventually they settled down and finished eating in silence. The magnitude of the problems they were facing had regained its grip on their demeanors. David took another sip of coffee. "Tell me what happened yesterday with the interrogation."

"I was fuming. We've had no involvement in any of the attacks. Yet, we're being treated as if we were the masterminds behind them."

"Yeah, we're in a tough position here," David admitted. And at the moment, he was starting to doubt they'd be cleared and released in time to stop Demetrius Wolffe.

"Then I started thinking about that bastard, Wolffe. He lured us into a trap at the café, with the intent to have us murdered. Why protect him? So, I threw him to the wolves. If we're stuck in here, maybe this cop can get to him before we do. Either way he is stopped."

"Was it through a journey to the Otherworlds with your second soul that you were able to see he was planning to use the sphere again?" David asked.

"Yes. Right before Salversen came in to interrogate me, I had been drifting through the Otherworlds looking for answers."

"Well, you've made a connection to one of the threads of Wolffe's timelines. That's a good thing. Can you continue to follow those threads and maybe figure out when and where his big attack is going to happen?"

Epiphany thought about it. "Yeah, I can do that. If we're stuck in here, maybe I can find something of use that I can give to Salversen to help her find Demetrius."

"Good. I've been thinking about an approach for getting out of here. Salversen showed me pictures of the tattoo that several of the attackers had on their wrists. Last night, I traveled into the Otherworlds to see what I could find out about it."

"Any luck?" Epiphany asked.

"I found something about the organization the men belong to. If I offer it up and it puts Salversen in a position to arrest this gang, maybe we can exchange that for our freedom—even if it means surrendering our passports and promising to stay in the area until this is all over."

"I think it's worth a try," Epiphany said. "We don't really have many options."

"Here's the other thing I've been considering: bring Detective Salversen into the fold, so to speak."

"Into the fold? What do you mean?"

"Eventually, that detective is going to push really hard to find out how we know these things. I'm suggesting I take her on a journey through the Otherworlds. She will see what I see as if she were actually there."

"I've never heard of something like that being done before."

"There's a first time for everything."

CHAPTER 33

Lyfjord, Norway

Floor-to-ceiling windows in Demetrius Wolffe's master bedroom provided a panoramic view of the mountains on the western side of the fjord. The snow-covered ridges were the first thing that came into view when he awoke. His head and neck ached and his focus drifted in and out between various degrees of blurriness. He had no recollection of how he wound up in his bungalow in Lyfjord, let alone how he got in his bed. Demetrius managed to sit up. He swung his legs out over the edge of the bed and planted his feet on the carpet. Asgeir was sitting in his armchair gazing at the mountains.

"How long have I been out?" Demetrius asked in a tired, weak voice.

Asgeir did not answer immediately. "Close to twelve hours," he eventually replied.

"What happened last night?"

"You weren't ready to use the sphere," Asgeir said. "Everyone on the tour bus was killed."

Demetrius was quiet as he let Asgeir's words sink in. "Gerd Schumann too?"

"Everyone means everyone," Asgeir said bluntly, without turning around to face him.

Hearing that news didn't have the impact that Demetrius thought it would. The Tjeldsund Church deaths had left him numb, but this was different. To his surprise, he was beginning to embrace the use of the Ebony Sphere, despite the ramifications. His connection to the sphere and its influence over him were strengthening. "I thought this was supposed to work, that no one would be killed."

"It would have, had you been properly prepared. What happened when you went to the Otherworlds?"

"I found a branch of the Quintessence as you instructed and stepped into its flow."

"Why did you go without me?"

Demetrius noticed the aggravation in Asgeir's voice. "I couldn't wait any longer. Time is slipping away for me. You know that as well as I do. I was ready to try, and that's what I did."

Asgeir stood and repositioned the armchair to face Demetrius. "Do not lie to me. What happened in the Otherworlds?"

Demetrius pulled the blanket from the bed and wrapped it around his shoulders. The chills coursing through his body were getting worse. "My own arrogance got in the way. I stepped into a vein of the Quintessence that was too large. Its raging currents overtook my body. Somehow, I regained my composure and stepped out of the flow. A few seconds longer and I would have been killed."

"You're lucky to be alive." Anger consumed Asgeir's voice. "You needed to do this in smaller doses to acclimate your second soul to the primordial energy."

"I know that now." Demetrius massaged the back of his neck, which did little to relieve the stabbing pain. Memories of last night slowly meandered back to him. "When I held the sphere in my hand, images of Vayla Isarrus came to me."

"When the Ebony Spheres were created, Vayla Isarrus encoded her essence into them to help those who would eventually use them."

"She instructed me on what to do. My second soul connected with the Quintessence. I felt its energy flowing through me into the Ebony Sphere. I concentrated on the characteristics of the future I wanted to bring about, and ..." Demetrius's words tailed off. He paused as he recalled the last thing he remembered before passing out last night. "I was so angry at Schumann. He was delaying the donation to my organization."

"That's why those people died. The sphere responded to your anger," Asgeir said. "You haven't truly mastered the ancient power that flows through the Quintessence, and you haven't learned how to control the purity of your thoughts."

"My attempt last night was an utter failure. Can I really do this?" Demetrius asked.

"I cannot make this more clear: The only way you will succeed is with my guidance and the help of Vayla Isarrus. We will make you ready! No more distractions. You are the last hope for humanity. Don't you see that? The people of your planet have started down a path from which there is no turning back. They are being carried forward by an inexorable momentum that will bring about their demise long before your sun eventually burns out and turns this planet into a charred cinder. Demetrius, we have to keep pushing forward."

"What will they feel?" Demetrius asked.

"What will who feel?"

"Everyone. Everyone whose souls have been changed. Eight billion people will be different after

I use the Ebony Sphere. What will they feel once it's been done? Will they know they've changed?"

Asgeir paused to think about his reply. "We've never done this before, Demetrius. We have to put our trust in Vayla Isarrus. I believe she got this right. If it works as planned, people might sense slight differences in their views of the world and their ideals. But they should still have the same basic interests as they had before the change was made."

"So there's no guarantee? We have to rely on faith?"

"I wish I could tell you otherwise."

The reality of the situation hit Demetrius hard. He quietly contemplated what Asgeir had said. Demetrius stood and walked to the windows. The view of the mountains was truly beautiful. This is how God must have wanted it to be. "What do we do next?" he asked.

"Tonight, we will enter the Otherworlds together and step into the great flow of the Quintessence. When we return, you will see firsthand how your soul will be different. What you will experience from that moment forward is what everyone will experience after you use the Ebony Sphere. It will be a rebirth, and your connection to the planet will be alive in ways you could never have thought possible."

CHAPTER 34

Stamsund, Norway

Johannes Stinar turned off of the main road onto the long driveway to his house. He had spent the hour-and-a-half drive from Vestpollen running through the results of the trial in his head—what went well and, more importantly, what did not. He stopped at the beginning of the driveway and turned off the Bach piece playing on the car stereo. The way Bach intertwined melodies and countermelodies between the stringed instruments must have required a mind capable of working on multiple levels at the same time. To solve the work ahead of him would require the same type of multi-level thinking.

He navigated the winding driveway to his house and was startled as he made the last hard-right turn past a row of fir trees. The headlights of his Range Rover illuminated a police car. Two officers stood next to the vehicle, watching him as he drove up to his house. He came to a stop and turned off the engine. Unhappy about the unwanted intrusion, he shook his head in disgust and got out of the car to see what they wanted.

"Johannes Stinar?" the older of the two officers asked.

"Yes," Johannes said. He was not comfortable around people he didn't know. Meeting someone for the first time always made him anxious. When those people were police officers, it heightened his level of anxiety.

"I'm Detective Jens Tofte, and this is Officer Heija Schal." Both officers showed their identification.

Johannes didn't say anything.

"We'd like to talk to you about a case we're investigating. Can we go inside?" Detective Tofte requested.

"What case?" Johannes asked, although it almost came out as a demand. He realized that, but only after the words had left his mouth. *Don't make yourself sound suspicious,* he told himself.

"It's a serious case, Mr. Stinar. It involves some people you might know."

Large gray clouds rambled through the twilight sky. Johannes bristled at a spray of icy snow particles kicked up by a gust of wind. "Okay," he said, having resolved himself to get this over with and move on with the work that needed to be done.

Johannes walked by the two officers, stepped up onto the porch, and opened the front door. He led the men to the living room. The lamp on the end table was still on from this morning when he left. The smell of recently burnt wood from the fireplace filled the room. Johannes sat in a wingback chair, and the two officers sat on the sofa. Johannes didn't bother with any pleasantries, like offering them coffee or something to eat. *Ask your questions and get out of my house* was the only thought running through his head at the moment.

"How do you know David Skye and Jade Hendrix?" Detective Tofte asked.

It appeared as if the detective was going to do all of the talking. The other officer seemed content to sit and listen. *The detective asked how I know David*

Skye and Jade Hendrix—not if I know them. "What police districts did you say you were from?"

"I'm with Kripos from the Oslo office, and Officer Schal is from the Harstad police station."

They traveled a long way to talk to me, Johannes thought. He was working through his response to the previous question as his mind processed his options. *Can't tell them about the Ebony Sphere of Vayla Isarrus or say anything about the quantum-well device. Maybe a mutual acquaintance. Demetrius Wolffe.*

"Mr. Stinar. David Skye and Jade Hendrix. How do you know them?" the detective prodded him.

"I never met them until the day they showed up at my front door. They were here about a man named Demetrius Wolffe." Johannes watched Detective Tofte write something in his notebook at the mention of Wolffe's name.

"When were they here?"

Johannes ran through the calendar in his head. "Four days ago, I believe it was."

"What did they want to know about Demetrius Wolffe?" the detective asked.

"He's a mutual acquaintance of theirs. Apparently, his business is struggling, and they were concerned about his well-being," Johannes said. Now he was regretting his journey down this path as he anticipated the next question.

"Why did they think you could help with the problems Demetrius Wolffe was facing? How do you know him?"

Johannes figured the detective was going to ask that question. *Don't have a great answer for that one,* he thought. "Demetrius Wolffe was familiar with my work in physics. He approached me about being part of an international gathering of scientists and engineers who are working on projects having a global reach—part of Wolffe's Citizens for a Peaceful Planet initiative. If I remember correctly, David Skye was asked to participate in that as well. So Skye must have thought I might have dealings with Demetrius Wolffe." Up until now, his answers to the detective had been rooted in some modicum of truth and were therefore somewhat defensible. However, he was worried the lying would have to start.

"On the day you indicated that David Skye and Jade Hendrix came to your residence, they had left from Tjeldsund. That's a four-hour drive—a pretty long way to come on the hope you might be able to help with a mutual friend of theirs, don't you think, Mr. Stinar?" the detective asked.

The "Mr. Stinar" bit was beginning to wear thin on Johannes. He looked the detective in the eyes, trying not to explode. "I don't know the details pertaining to whatever kind of problems Demetrius Wolffe is having, Detective. They must be pretty big, or Demetrius Wolffe must be in a worrisome state to prompt them to drive all that way to see me."

"Were you able to help them?"

"No. I really haven't been in touch with Demetrius Wolffe, so unfortunately, I wasn't of much help to David Skye and Jade Hendrix."

"How long were they here?" the detective asked.

"They showed up at my place pretty late in the evening. They stayed here that night and then got on the road early the next morning."

"They stayed here overnight?" Detective Tofte made a few more notations in his notebook as he spoke. "I did a background check on you, Mr. Stinar. It seems you are one of the brightest physicists of your time. I also read that you are a bit of a recluse.

So why would you let two people you've never met before stay in your house overnight?"

"I checked their backgrounds online while they were here," Johannes lied. "They seemed to be nice people, who according to their online profiles are doing good things for the world. So I let them stay. They got here late that night and wouldn't have had much luck finding a hotel at that hour. I was busy with my research in my lab all week, so as long as they weren't bothering me, I didn't care if they were here an extra day."

"Can we see your lab?" the detective asked.

"No," Johannes said.

"Why not?"

"The work I'm doing is proprietary. It cannot be shared with anyone other than the people who commissioned me. I have too many important documents, drawings and sketches, and prototypes lying around, and you're not cleared to see any of it."

"What kind of prototypes?" the detective asked.

"Again, I can't share that with you," Johannes stated as firmly as he could without losing his temper. "Why did you come all this way to talk to me? What have David Skye and Jade Hendrix done that warrants a long drive from Harstad to talk to me?"

"I can't divulge the details of the case, Mr. Stinar. I can tell you that we have David Skye and Jade Hendrix in police custody in Tromsø. They are being questioned regarding their involvement in a string of attacks in Norway that have resulted in over forty deaths. You wouldn't know anything about that, would you?"

Johannes slumped back in his chair and shook his head, "No."

The detective stood and offered a brief smile. "That'll be all for now, Mr. Stinar. If we have any more questions, we know where to find you. Thank you for your time."

Johannes stood and escorted both officers to the door. He watched them from the doorway as they got in their car and drove away. A chilling thought came over him: *If David and Epiphany are in police custody and not released anytime soon, I'll be the one who'll have to confront Demetrius Wolffe and the spirit who traveled across the Black Void to help him.*

CHAPTER 35

Tromsø Police Station

Kari Salversen glanced at the screen on her cellphone—an incoming call from Jens Tofte. "Hello, Jens. Before you get started, I need to inform you that we had an incident up here last night. Sixteen people were killed in a manner consistent with what we saw in Tjeldsund."

Jens paused for a moment and sounded a bit shocked. "Again? Where did it happen?"

"In the village of Overgård, about eighty kilometers southeast of Tromsø," Kari answered. "A bus driver and fifteen passengers of a privately chartered tour bus on a northern lights expedition were killed. A sixteenth passenger was not among the victims: Demetrius Wolffe."

"Looks like he gets added to the persons of interest list."

"He might have jumped to the top of the list." Kari shuffled through the preliminary forensics report. "The similarities to Tjeldsund were numerous: no bullet wounds, stab wounds, or bruising—and horrified looks on the faces of each of the deceased. We're still waiting for the final reports. I'll let you know if we learn anything more. Did you talk to Johannes Stinar?"

"Yes. Officer Schal and I just finished with the interview at his residence in Stamsund. I'm calling from a local diner down here. I wanted to give you an update now, while everything is fresh in my mind, rather than delaying it four hours until we get back to the Harstad office." Jens gave Kari a detailed summary of his discussion with Johannes Stinar, focusing on the man's relationship and interactions with David Skye, Jade Hendrix, and Demetrius Wolffe.

"Thanks for the update, Jens. What was your general impression of him?" she asked.

"Sometimes he seemed a little evasive, and other times he paused maybe a little too long before answering some of my questions. I wondered if he was conjuring up a believable lie as opposed to giving me straight answers. When I told him about having Skye and Hendrix in custody, he seemed unfazed. I didn't get the sense that they were collaborating in some way. His responses were logical, and I didn't see any evidence that he is involved in anything nefarious."

"Was there anything out of the ordinary or unusual?"

"Well, there was one thing. He mentioned his lab, and I asked if we could see it. He gave me a flat-out, hard no. Said most of the work was highly proprietary in nature and that he could not share what he was working on with me. He mentioned some prototypes, so my mind immediately went to something that could kill people in the manner we saw at the church in Tjeldsund. A brilliant mind like his would probably be capable of developing something like that."

"I'm not surprised he's working on proprietary projects. A man of his intellect is probably sought after by a lot of big tech companies and possibly the military. As for the prototypes, I'm not sure we have enough to get a search warrant."

"I agree," Jens said. "I've finished everything that needed to be done here. Superintendent Rindahl indicated that he can manage any follow-up that's needed out of the Harstad office, so I'll be leaving for Oslo later tonight."

"Okay, safe travels, Jens. We'll talk soon." Kari ended the call and walked into Chief Martin Kolbeck's office.

As Kolbeck looked up from his desk, a look of frustration filled his face. "Still nothing new from the forensics team and medical examiner as to what killed those people—multiple, simultaneous heart failure and cessation of all bodily functions." He pursed his lips and shook his head again. "How does that happen?"

"We seem to be no closer to an answer," Kari said as she took a seat opposite Martin. "Jens just called with an update on the Johannes Stinar interview. Not really much to go on there. We'll keep tabs on him."

"Jade Hendrix's tip on the Overgård attack turned out to be real," Martin said. "If she was involved in any of this, why would she tip us off?"

"Right, that's what I keep coming back to. She implicated Demetrius Wolffe, and his name appeared on the passenger lists for a flight into the Harstad/Narvik Airport and for a northern lights bus excursion to Overgård. How Hendrix knew Wolffe was planning something for Overgård and the fact that she wouldn't divulge it are problematic. She's withholding something, and I need to find out how she's getting her information."

Martin had been organizing several folders on his desk while listening to Kari. He finished and then looked up at her. "We can put Skye and Hendrix at the scenes of these incidents or in the vicinity of them, but we have no real evidence that they were involved. Everything is circumstantial so far. And I don't know what to make of Anders Gustason either. He's tied to the earlier attacks and for some reason wanted to kill Skye and Hendrix. Why would he want to do that if Skye and Hendrix were aiding and abetting those earlier crimes? How all of these things are related is still muddy."

"Too muddy for my liking," Kari said.

"So what about Skye and Hendrix? We're holding two US citizens in custody without any hard evidence against them. Do we release them? As an option, we could confiscate their passports and release them on their own recognizance with a long list of very specific requirements, such as staying in Tromsø, handing over their driver's licenses, and checking in on a routine basis."

"I'm still thinking I'd like to have Skye and Hendrix remanded in custody," Kari said. "I'm not quite ready to release them, even if it's on their own recognizance with the stipulations you noted. I need to talk to them about a few more things before we go that route."

"I can live with that," Martin said. "In the meantime, let's increase our focus on Demetrius Wolffe."

"That's the plan," Kari said as she stood to leave. "I'm going to have another chat with our two persons of interest."

Kari asked one of the officers to bring David Skye and Jade Hendrix from their holding cells to Interrogation Room 2. She was sitting at the table facing the door when the officer escorted Skye and Hendrix into the room. Kari stood and motioned to the two chairs on the other side of the table. "Have a seat."

Kari wasted no time in getting started. "Sixteen people were killed in Overgård last night, and you knew it was going to happen." She addressed her question to Jade Hendrix. "How did you know that?" She leaned back and waited for a response. Hendrix didn't answer, so Kari continued.

"Well, maybe this will help you to decide. Until you tell me how you knew this information, I'm going to have the two of you remanded in custody. You will appear before a magistrate at the district courthouse. I'm petitioning for a remand of four weeks, and if you still haven't told me by the end of that period, I'll get an extension for another four weeks." She delivered her message and then watched their expressions turn to disbelief.

"Do you know what you're doing here?" Jade Hendrix demanded. "In four weeks, it will be too late. It'll be over by then!"

"What will be over?" Kari shot back.

Hendrix gripped the table with both hands and leaned forward. "I told you yesterday. The incident in the mountains was a trial run. Demetrius Wolffe is planning something that will be life-changing. For everyone!"

"I need answers, details about what you know," Kari said, then added with emphasis, "and how you know it." Hendrix was clearly pissed off. Skye, on the other hand, seemed unusually calm.

Epiphany glanced at David. "How much do we tell her?"

David inhaled and then let out a long breath. "There are things we know, information we can," he paused and then stretched out the next word as he said it, "access."

"You mean like a hacker?" Kari asked. "Is that what you two are?"

"No, we're not hackers. We know things in ways you wouldn't have dreamt possible."

"David, are you sure you want to do this?" Epiphany asked in a low tone.

Kari detected the uneasiness in her voice. *Maybe now we start to get somewhere on this,* she thought.

David looked at Epiphany as he spoke, "Remember the two options I mentioned earlier this morning? I still want to pursue both."

Kari watched the back-and-forth conversation between them, wondering where this was going.

David returned his gaze to Kari. "How's that scar on your right calf? A mountain biking accident when you were seventeen, right?"

Kari instinctively reached for the scar on her leg. "How did you know that?" Kari asked. He spoke as if it was common knowledge. She was as much curious as she was angry at the invasion into her past by a man she had met just a day ago.

"Brand-new bike, wasn't it? You got a little reckless, took your eyes off of the terrain in front of you, and took a spill," David said.

Kari didn't respond. She was still trying to process how he could have known that. She was alone on that particular ride. The only one who knew about the mishap was her.

"What if I were to give you some information about these cases you've been working on? About the men with the tattoos on their wrists," David said. "If what I tell you pans out, will you release us, even if it has to be on our own recognizance?"

"What do you know about these men?" Kari asked. She was leery, watching for any telltale signs of lying—like looking away, avoiding eye contact, or wavering in his voice.

"If this information pans out, will you release us?" David insisted.

"If what you tell me leads to arrests, I'd at least consider releasing both of you with a very specific set of stipulations governing what you can and cannot do."

David looked over at Epiphany, who nodded okay.

"The people involved in the earlier attacks belong to a broad network of right-wing radicals. They have men in several major cities in Norway. They're planning a major attack at the Nobel Peace Prize Awards Ceremony in Oslo City Hall on December 10th. You don't have much time, Kari."

Kari looked at David Skye. She wasn't happy with the fact that he referred to her informally by her first name. It implied an air of familiarity that they didn't have. That aside, his story sounded a bit incredulous. If it was true, in the same way Hendrix's premonition was true, then he was right, she had very little time. The 10th was a few days away. The Nobel Peace Prize Ceremony is a big deal. An attack there would be unforgivable. "Who are these men?"

"They call themselves the Daggers of a New Dawn. The tattoos they wear are emblematic of their name: Earth with a dagger through it, and a sunrise coming up in the background represents the new dawn they want to bring about. You are looking for two men. Brothers. The older of the two, Stefan Balto, is their leader, a big, burly man, with short-cropped hair and a bushy beard. He's holed up at a small house not too far from here in a place called

Birtavarre. He's got a detached, red garage filled with more semiautomatic weapons and explosives than you've probably seen in one place in your life."

Kari was feverishly taking notes. "I don't suppose you have an address for him?"

"No, I don't," David replied. But he did proceed to give her a physical description of landmarks as references.

"Somewhere in that house is a list of the members of his organization. The other man you need to find is Stefan's brother, Jusse. He is a younger, spitting image of his older brother with a close-cropped, military-style haircut, a long, bushy beard, and pale green eyes. Jusse is a little bigger and definitely a lot meaner than his brother—not the type of person you'd want to run into in a dark alley. He is the mastermind of the attack being planned for City Hall in Oslo at the awards ceremony. He and the men working with him are in a renovated barn in the woods near a large lake directly north of the city." David Skye paused, then said, "That's all I know."

Kari finished making her notes. "That is really detailed information. How do you know this, and why didn't you tell me about this sooner?"

David stared intensely into her eyes. "Because I just found out about it last night in my cell."

"How is that possible? You were alone all night. No one came in or out of your cell during that time," Kari said. She was astonished and still skeptical that he could just know that information.

"I'll tell you how I know, but not here—somewhere more private, and only if you release us tonight. That's the deal. Oh, and there's something else. The deaths in the church and in the mountains last night will pale in comparison to what's being planned. The bigger event that Jade talked about is going to happen. Soon!"

Kari paused a moment to evaluate what he was asking. Myriad thoughts shot through her head. *How can I validate what Skye just said? Do Stefan and Jusse Balto really exist? I can't afford to go on wild goose chases that would tie up valuable time and resources.* "I am going to follow up on these details now. If what you've told me can be validated, I will consider your request. Now if you'll excuse me, I have some work to do. The officer outside the door will take you back to your holding cells." Kari left the room and hurried back to her desk.

CHAPTER 36

Tromsø Police Station

As soon as the door to Interrogation Room 2 slammed shut behind Detective Salversen, Epiphany blurted out, "How the hell did you find so much information about that radical group and its leaders that quickly?"

"I spent all night wandering the Otherworlds for it. The tattoo was the key. It's very unique. Once I locked onto that, information flowed pretty quickly."

Epiphany nodded. Searching for information in the Otherworlds was often a painstaking process. Having very specific and unique attributes was essential to finding something in an expeditious manner. "When we're taken back to our cells, I'm going to continue my search for Demetrius Wolffe. If I find him, we find the sphere."

"Yeah, I think that's a good plan. Somehow, you need to narrow your search. What are all of the moving parts?" David Skye asked.

"There's Demetrius obviously and the Ebony Sphere of Vayla Isarrus."

"There's *The Angel and the Orb* statue and the man who sculpted it. Do you remember his name?" David asked.

"Tiorvi Eiken. And there's that spirit who came through the void to presumably help Demetrius."

"I think those are the main facets. Somewhere there is a connection between all of them. Didn't Johannes say that his quantum-well device was responsible for freeing the last known surviving co-conspirator of Vayla Isarrus?"

"Yes, he did," Epiphany said. "I'll start my search by finding whatever I can about Vayla Isarrus's followers. If I can determine who that lone survivor is, I'll search his timeline for any intersection with Demetrius."

"I think that's your best bet," David said.

"How about you? What are you going to do?"

"I need to think through my approach with Detective Salversen. How do I get her to see what we see in the Otherworlds and accomplish it so she believes what I show and tell her?"

The door to the interrogation room opened, and the officer walked in. "Time to go," he said.

David looked at Epiphany and whispered, "Good luck."

"Likewise," she replied.

CHAPTER 37

Tromsø Police Station

"We got a hit," Markus Fiske blurted out. He was sitting at his computer workstation and had keyed in a search for Stefan Balto in the database of registered Norwegian drivers.

Kari Salversen moved in closer for a better look.

"We've got Stefan Balto's driver's license on file," Fiske said.

Kari recalled David Skye's description: a big, burly man, with short-cropped hair and a bushy beard. Although the driver's license was only a headshot, the short-cropped hair and bushy beard portion of Skye's description were on the mark. She read the street address. His residence was in Birtavarre, where Skye said it would be. "Bring up a map application, key in Balto's street address, and enter street-view mode. I want to see if we can get a shot of his property. My intel said there should be a large, detached garage on the site."

Markus entered street-view mode and navigated to the address for Stefan Balto. He rotated the image and zoomed in. "There's your big, detached garage," he said as he looked up at Kari over his left shoulder.

Kari took a seat to Fiske's left and mumbled, "How the hell did he know that?"

"What?" Markus asked.

"Nothing. Do we have anything on Stefan Balto in our criminal record database?"

Markus navigated through the records and found a file on Stefan Balto. "Here you go. It appears this guy likes to get into bar fights. He's got several misdemeanor charges for drunk and disorderly conduct. That's about it."

"Okay. Print copies of the street view, the driver's license information, and his criminal record."

Next Kari instructed Markus to check into Jusse Balto, Stefan's younger brother. Markus pulled up his driver's license and criminal record, which pretty much mirrored his older brother's.

"Bring up his address on the map," Kari instructed.

"It's on the southeast side of Oslo," Markus said.

"My informant said something about a property on or near a large lake north of Oslo. The first one that comes to mind is the lake in Maridalen. Check the property registers; see if we have anything owned by the Baltos."

Markus began searching. "Okay, here we go. A property transfer. Looks like the parents passed away, and the house was deeded to Stefan and Jusse Balto as joint owners."

"Print that information, along with Jusse's driver's license info and arrest record." Kari's next stop was Martin Kolbeck's office.

Kari met with Kolbeck and brought him up to speed on the information that David Skye had provided regarding the men involved in the attacks leading up to and including the Trondheim bombing.

"Daggers of a New Dawn. I've never come across that one before," Martin said.

"Neither have I. The members of that tribe all wear the same tattoo apparently. Skye indicated that the Balto brothers are the ring leaders." Kari handed him the printouts that Markus had given her. "Stefan Balto is the founder of the group, and his younger brother, Jusse, is planning some type of disruption and possibly an attack at the Nobel Peace Prize Ceremony in Oslo."

"Jesus, Kari, that's two days from now. How comfortable are you with this? Do you trust what he's telling you?"

"The information David Skye provided about the Balto brothers was on the money."

"We've got to get our arms around this—now!" Kolbeck exclaimed. "Under no circumstances can we let these guys go through with an attack on the Nobel Ceremony."

"I think we need to do one more thing to confirm the information that Skye provided," Kari said. "Stefan Balto has a place in Birtavarre. That's a two-and-a-half-hour drive from here. If we leave now, we'll get there by 5:00 pm. We search Balto's residence and bring him in for questioning."

"Okay, but let's call Nord and give him a heads-up. I'll suggest he put eyes on Jusse Balto until we can confirm all of this," Martin said. He placed the call and explained to Nord's assistant that this was an extremely urgent matter.

Chief Nord picked up the phone. "What's this emergency you've got, Martin?"

"I have you on speaker. Kari is here in the office with me. We brought two informants on the Tjeldsund and Overgård cases in for questioning. They've given us credible information into the men behind the Trondheim bombing and the attacks that preceded it. We believe one of the men might be planning an attack on the Nobel Peace Prize Ceremony in two days."

"And this is credible information?" Nord asked.

Martin looked up at Kari, who nodded. "Yes, we believe it is," Martin answered.

Kari chimed in quickly and added, "Two men have been implicated. Stefan Balto has been identified as the leader of a group called the Daggers of a New Dawn. Martin and I are going to his residence in Birtavarre as soon as we end this call. We should hopefully be able to confirm how real this threat is in the next four to five hours."

There was a brief moment of silence. Knowing how Chief Nord's mind worked, Kari suspected he was processing what he had heard and probably had already formulated what actions needed to be taken. "We need to move quickly and cautiously until we know for sure that this threat is real."

"We believe we will find evidence at Balto's residence confirming this group's involvement in the attacks. Jusse Balto is the man you're looking for on your end. He has a residence on the southeast side of Oslo, and we think the group's activity is being planned at his family's property near Maridalen Lake." Kari took her cellphone from her pants pocket. "I'm texting the address information for both locations now."

"I'll put surveillance teams on the Oslo and Maridalen residences and increase our police presence around City Hall," Nord said. "We'll be ready to act on this end. Call me as soon as you have an update. Is there anything else I need to know?"

"That's it, Chief," Martin said. "We'll call you later tonight." They ended the call.

Kari stood. "David Skye told me the garage on Balto's property has more weapons than we've ever seen in one place. We better be ready for some fireworks."

Martin started walking toward the door. "Oh, we will be!"

CHAPTER 38

Lyfjord, Norway / The Realm of the Forever Sun

Demetrius Wolffe sat patiently on the sofa in the living room of the bungalow. It felt as if he was about to embark on the last few legs of an incredible journey.

"There will be no turning back from this point forward. Are you ready to take this step?" Asgeir delivered his message to Demetrius, then sat down next to him.

"If I can do just one thing in the short time I have left, this would be it. I'm committed to this path."

"We will enter the Black Void together and make our way through the Realm of the Forever Sun."

"I didn't think you could return to the spirit realms."

"Once I stepped through the rift between our worlds, I became bound to yours. Now, I'm much like you. My human form will remain behind while my spiritual entity makes the passage to the Otherworlds."

Demetrius leaned forward and placed his hands on his knees. Tremors of pain filtered through his legs. "My body hasn't fully recovered from the previous trip. Will I survive a second journey? What if the same thing happens again and this time my second soul fails to master the energy of the Quintessence?"

"This time when you step into its flow, Vayla Isarrus will be there to shield you from the torrents that would otherwise tear you apart."

Demetrius closed his eyes and relaxed his mind. The warmth of Asgeir's grasp on his left forearm calmed his nerves. Together they crossed the Black Void into the Realm of the Forever Sun.

CHAPTER 39

Tromsø Police Station / The Realm of the Forever Sun

A subtle vibration in the Mesh reverberated through eleven dimensions and tinged Epiphany's second soul. The message it delivered was clear: Demetrius Wolffe had crossed the Black Void into the depths of the Otherworlds. Through her previous forays into the realms that lie beyond the physical reality of Earth, Epiphany had established a strong connection with the unique resonance of Demetrius's second soul. And now that link could be used to reveal his future pathways. Epiphany laid back on the cot in the holding cell and closed her eyes. She focused on the streamer of energy that resonated in her head as she sent her second soul into the Black Void.

Epiphany fell through an infinite darkness. There was no sense of time or direction, of motion or stillness. Her blood coursed through her body like a river about to overflow its banks. The Moirae who guided Epiphany across the dark expanse steadied her beating heart and with a gentle nudge sent her second soul through the barrier of the Black Void into the Realm of the Forever Sun.

Epiphany stood at the bank of a meandering stream. Enormous trees lined both sides of the water. The gnarled brown trunks, resembling multiple intertwined snakes, were speckled with splotchy white patches. Their reflections shimmered on the surface of the smooth-flowing currents. A soft breeze washed over the long, arching branches of the trees. Brilliant green leaves rustled throughout the dense forest cathedral. Sailing through the warm eddies of air was the subtle resonance Epiphany was looking for—the song of Demetrius Wolffe's second soul.

She moved in the direction of the harmonies that filled her head. Demetrius was close by. She veered off to her right into the depth of the woods, following the sound that would lead her to the man she desperately needed to find. The trees had gotten much taller, their trunks every bit of fifteen feet in diameter and reaching hundreds of feet into the sky above. Long rays of sunlight knifed through the outstretched branches above her head, speckling the ground ahead of her with drops of light. Wolffe's signal was getting stronger.

The light of the sun was dimming as she approached what appeared to be the edge of the forest. Another breeze, carrying much colder air, filtered through the trees. Epiphany increased her pace; the resonance in her head intensified. She stepped beyond the forest into an expansive valley. A second harmony drifted in the wind, a complex dissonance—counterpoint to the softer resonance of Demetrius's second soul. She had experienced this dissonance before, in King's Park in Tromsø.

Epiphany surveyed the lush, green landscape. The tributary she had been following crossed the valley and rejoined the main artery. If she could stop Demetrius's second soul here, she could end his plans once and for all. She sprinted through the valley toward a distant light at the edge of the horizon.

CHAPTER 40

The Quintessence

"We're being followed." Asgeir stopped, closed his eyes, and concentrated. He let his hands drop to his sides and raised his palms skyward. "I sense the rhythms of her soul. Our paths have crossed before. In Tromsø. We need to find a vein of the Quintessence. Soon."

Demetrius Wolffe followed Asgeir as they ran along a narrow mountain pass carved out of the rocky surface. They descended into an area of flat land that rimmed the base of the ridge. A grove of deciduous trees spread out ahead of them. A low-lying mist rolled over the path that disappeared into the thickly wooded forest.

When they reached the beginning of the woods, Asgeir stopped again. The tall trees cast long shadows across the ground. "Do you see them? The shimmering light of the *whispering sage* plants." Asgeir pointed into the forest. "They're hidden among the shadows of the trees."

It was an ethereal site. Demetrius darted into the woods and came to a stop at a clump of the glowing plants. He knelt down and gently broke off the top of the stem as he had done on his previous venture into the Otherworlds. The dozen or so purple flowers continued to glow. The portion of the stem that had been broken off immediately began to grow back. He held the flowers in the palm of his hand and let the subtle harmonies of the Quintessence resonate within his second soul. Demetrius turned and walked in the direction from which the song of the Quintessence was originating. He came to the edge of the woods and entered a meadow. The radiance of the *whispering sage* flowers intensified. Demetrius cleared his mind and concentrated. A long, flowing streamer of vapor materialized along the ground. The wispy coils of energy snaked across the meadow, shimmering in shades of violet light. Demetrius turned to Asgeir. "I see it. I see the flow of the Quintessence."

Asgeir placed his hand on Demetrius's shoulder. "Focus your thoughts and connect with Vayla Isarrus. She will guide you from here."

The excitement of the moment was abruptly interrupted. Demetrius and Asgeir turned to their right. Stepping out of the shadows of the tall trees, the second soul of a woman appeared.

CHAPTER 41

The Quintessence

Epiphany sprinted toward Demetrius Wolffe and the spirit standing by his side. As she approached, a magnificent glowing streamer of energy came into view. It was her strong connection to Demetrius's second soul that enabled her to see the Quintessence. She witnessed Demetrius take several steps forward and then disappear into the long vapor trail.

She ran to the spot where she saw Demetrius vanish. To her surprise, the spirit that was standing next to him didn't move. He was waiting for her.

"Know the name of the one who will end your existence," the spirit said. "My name is Asgeir, the Spear of the Gods."

This time Asgeir struck first. He grabbed Epiphany by the throat. Epiphany grabbed his wrist and attempted to break his vicelike grip, flailing at the large hand beneath her jaw. The tips of her feet were barely touching the ground. This was his domain. His strength was stronger here than on Earth.

Asgeir dragged her through the meadow and stopped at a point where two more vapor trails merged with the one that Demetrius had stepped into. He raised her up off the ground. "You're about to feel the full wrath of the Quintessence."

Epiphany struggled to free herself, but his grip was too strong.

"The ancient force is most violent at a nexus where two or more veins cross." He laughed at her while she struggled.

Her back was to the flow of energy that churned through the junction of the three veins. She struggled to grip her feet on the ground. He had lifted her too high to be able to push off and halt his progress. Epiphany tried to yell at him to stop, but she couldn't eke out the words. A sudden inrush of fear overwhelmed her as her sense of gravity gave way to weightlessness.

Asgeir released her into the turbulent flow of the nexus.

Epiphany tumbled through the powerful torrents. It felt like shards of glass stabbing at her second soul. Shadowy beams of light cut through the shimmering vapor. Its strong currents carried her toward oblivion.

CHAPTER 42

Birtavarre, Norway

"Stay alert, we're coming in unannounced," Martin Kolbeck warned, as he eased up slightly on the accelerator of the BMW command car. He and Kari Salversen had discussed their options, and both agreed that giving Stefan Balto any inclination that the police wanted to speak to him would give him time to hide evidence that might be invaluable to their investigation. And most likely, he'd disappear.

"That's it—up ahead on the right," Kari said. They were little more than a hundred meters away when Balto's house came into view. Kari noticed the detached garage, exactly as David Skye had said it would be. His information better turn out to be true—a lot was riding on it. Chief Nord had set the wheels in motion on his end, preparing for a possible attack at the Nobel Peace Prize Ceremony. She wasn't looking forward to facing Nord's wrath should this turn out to be a colossal waste of police resources.

Kari took a deep breath and glanced over at Martin. For the past two-and-a-half hours, they had been speeding along winding roads leading to Birtavarre. Now, no more than a hundred meters separated her from a major breakthrough or an enormous mistake. She took another deep breath to calm her nerves.

Headlights from the vehicles behind them reflected in the passenger's side mirror. Kari glanced back over her left shoulder at the second BMW command car and the Mercedes transport van following them—each with two armed police officers. Martin had instructed them to switch off the flashing lights on their vehicles once they entered Birtavarre. He wanted to come in as unannounced as possible.

When they arrived at Balto's residence, Martin turned onto a gravel area along the roadway and came to a stop. The other two vehicles pulled in behind him.

Kari got out of the BMW and reached under her coat for her shoulder holster. She touched her service weapon, hoping that it wouldn't be needed and that no one would get hurt. David Skye had warned her there'd be a lot of weapons here. Martin agreed with Kari's suggestion to go in armed. "Lights are on in the house," Kari said. "Be ready for anything."

Martin instructed one of the officers who had driven in the car behind them to keep watch at the vehicles, and he instructed the other officer to go to the back of the house in case Balto attempted to flee that way. The two men from the transport van went with Kari and Martin to the house.

The walkway to Balto's residence hadn't been shoveled in a while. Deep, frozen ruts from multiple footprints made the approach more difficult than it should have been. Kari constantly scanned the property in all directions to detect any unwanted approach.

Martin reached the residence first and rapped on the door with his large, heavily veined hand. "Police. We'd like to speak to Stefan Balto."

No answer. Martin rapped again and repeated his announcement. Still no answer.

Kari tried the front door. "It's locked," she said.

Martin looked over at one of the officers from the van. "Do it," he said.

The officer hefted the battering ram, and with a big backswing swung the heavy implement into the door. Kari and Martin stepped back while the first officer from the van entered Balto's house with his gun drawn and shouted, "Armed police." The second officer put the battering ram on the ground and followed behind him. Kari and Martin stepped through the doorway as the two officers fanned out in front of them.

"Shit!" Kari blurted out. She ran to her left into the living room, toward an open window. She saw Stefan Balto dropping to the ground outside. "He's running," she shouted.

Martin ran to the back of the house, announcing himself as he opened the door to avoid startling the officer stationed outside. By the time Kari dropped out the window and turned to face the direction in which Balto ran, she heard the loud roar of an engine. A four-wheel-drive pickup truck barreled around the back of the garage toward the road. Martin raced to the side of the house and met up with Kari. He instructed the two officers who came in the transport van to follow them. As they sprinted to their vehicles, Martin shouted orders to the remaining two officers to secure the house and garage.

Balto turned right onto the road in front of his house, heading away from Birtavarre.

Martin and Kari got in their car and were quickly in pursuit. The transport van was close behind them.

"Oh Christ," Martin blurted out. "He's heading toward Gorsa Bridge."

"What's wrong with that?" Kari asked.

"It's a nasty stretch of winding road up ahead. Hold on! This could get dicey."

Balto's brake lights came on as he slowed to enter a hairpin turn to the left.

Martin stayed close behind Balto on the partially snow-covered dirt-and-gravel road. He immediately entered another hairpin curve to the right. "Son of a bitch," he yelled.

Kari gripped the door handle with her right hand and found herself digging her right foot into the floor mat, reaching for an imaginary brake pedal. Martin sped through a series of sharp S-curves, fighting to keep the vehicle on the road as it fishtailed several times. Balto approached a narrow bridge spanning a shallow gorge. Martin was within one car length of the pickup truck.

Balto crossed the bridge, veered to his right, and then sped through a hard left bend in the road. "I don't know how this guy is keeping that damn truck on the road," Kari blurted out. They immediately entered into a series of switchback curves. Martin did his best to keep the vehicle under control, muttering expletives as he drove.

Balto sped up as he entered another hairpin turn to the left at the trailhead to the Gorsa Bridge. He misjudged his speed and the severe bend in the road. The pickup slid into a shallow culvert and dense underbrush.

Martin came to a sliding stop. The transport van was not far behind. Kari immediately jumped out of the BMW and sprinted toward Balto with her gun drawn. Balto was desperately trying to get the pickup out of the ditch. The whine of spinning tires filled the air, but the pickup didn't budge.

Kari ran up to the window. "Stefan Balto. Police. You're under arrest. Turn the vehicle off. Hands in the air. Now!"

By the time she was halfway through her declaration, Martin had arrived and aimed his pistol at Balto's head.

While the two officers from the transport van pulled Balto from the pickup and handcuffed him, Kari informed him of the charges he was facing. "Stefan Balto, you're being arrested for your involvement in the attacks in Oslo, Bergen, Drammen, and Trondheim."

"Take him back to his house," Martin instructed his two officers. He looked over at Kari and said coyly, "Well, that went smoothly."

She started walking back to the car. "Next time, I'm driving. Now let's go search his house."

CHAPTER 43

Residence of Stefan Balto, Birtavarre, Norway

Martin Kolbeck brought the BMW to a stop at Stefan Balto's house. He instructed the men in the transport van to take Balto inside and sit him down. "He doesn't go anywhere!" he added. His men acknowledged his orders and escorted the handcuffed Balto into the house.

Kari Salversen was barely out of the vehicle when one of the officers ran toward them. "You've got to see this," he said excitedly.

The officer escorted Kari and Martin into the high-bay garage. He led them into a rectangular room approximately five meters wide by eight meters long. "We found the keys in the main house. Otherwise, we would have had to break the door in with the battering ram," the officer noted.

"Oh my God," Kari exclaimed. "Skye was right. I've never seen this many weapons in one place." The walls were lined with semi-automatic and high-powered rifles, along with an assortment of shotguns. A work table in the corner of the room was completely covered with handguns. Boxes of ammunition were stacked under the table and next to it.

"Have you started cataloguing the armory here?" Martin asked the officer.

"Here's what I have so far," the officer said, handing his tally sheet to Martin.

Martin read through the list and handed it to Kari. "I'm going to call the Lyngen Police Station. It's about thirty minutes away. We'll get a few of their officers to come out here to help with cataloguing everything and getting the weapons and evidence to a secure location at the Tromsø office."

Kari took a photo of the weapons tally with her cellphone and handed the list back to the officer so he could continue with his work. When Martin finished his call to the Lyngen station, they walked back to Balto's house.

They entered the living room. "Look at this place," Kari said. She stepped over a pile of dirty laundry—a jumble of hooded sweatshirts, T-shirts, a pair of ratty jeans, and some overalls. The kitchen at the back of the house was visible from the living room in the front. What looked like two weeks of dirty dishware and drinking glasses was piled on the countertop and a small, round kitchen table. Several paint cans were stacked on the floor, along with a dried-out paint brush with an unattractive shade of yellow caking the bristles.

Kari glanced over at Balto. The large, burly man engulfed the small sofa on which he sat. His legs were outstretched, resting his clunky work boots on a coffee table that was littered with Styrofoam take-away containers and crushed beer cans, several of which had made their way to the floor. The entire house had a dank, musty odor. Kari had seen the inside of places worse than this, but this was easily in the top five. "It's like a pigsty in here," she said.

"He's not much on housekeeping. I don't think you'd find many pigs that would want to live in this squalor." Martin looked over at the officer guarding Balto. "Did he say anything while we were in the garage?"

"Not a word, sir."

"That's quite a weapons cache you have in your garage, Mr. Balto." Kari glanced at the photo of the weapons tally she had taken with her phone. "Forty-two pistols, thirty-one semi-automatic rifles, a healthy supply of shotguns, and what is in the neighborhood of twenty thousand rounds of ammunition. And that's just a partial list."

Kari observed Balto for his response. The big man smirked and nodded approvingly.

"Ever hear of the Firearms Weapons Act, Stefan?" Martin chimed in. "What do you think?" Martin asked as he looked over at Kari. "Is he in compliance?" Again, Balto smirked. "How many violations of the Firearms Weapons Act does Mr. Balto have?"

"Sixteen of the handguns are above the caliber restrictions. Eight of the rifles are fully automatic, which is illegal in this country, and three of the semi-automatic weapons have been converted to fully automatic rifles, which, if Mr. Balto cannot produce documented police consent for that conversion, is also illegal."

Martin stepped closer to the sofa, staring at Balto. "Do you have the proper paperwork for the conversions, Stefan?" Martin emphasized Balto's first name as he asked the question. Balto remained quiet. "We'll take that as a 'No,'" Martin said.

Kari smiled at Martin's comment. "None of the weapons were securely locked in an approved safe, and he is well over the limit for guns and ammunition that a private citizen is permitted to own."

"What do you have to say for yourself, Stefan?" Martin demanded.

"So I have a few extra guns. I'm a collector," Stefan replied and then offered a big ear-to-ear smile.

"That isn't a collection. It's a goddamn arsenal," Martin said angrily.

"We're just getting started, Stefan. The weapons charges alone mean serious jail time for you," Kari stated.

One of the officers on the scene came down the stairs. "Chief, there's an office in one of the rooms upstairs. There are some things you and Detective Salversen really need to see."

Martin instructed the officer standing next to Balto, "Don't let him get off of that sofa!"

Kari and Martin followed the officer up the stairs. She noticed several large fist-sized holes through the wallboard, presumably from Balto punching holes in the wall out of anger or, knowing the guy, just for the fun of it. She reached for the banister as they ascended the stairs, but immediately retracted her hand once she felt the sticky, grimy residue covering most of its surface. Taking a shower was going to be one of the first things she did once she knocked off from work tonight.

The officer led them into a small room at the back of the house. While Kari and Martin donned their rubber gloves, she surveyed what appeared to be Balto's office. It wasn't much more than three by four meters. The only furniture in the room was a desk, a desk chair, and a work table. A bare bulb in the middle of the ceiling illuminated the room. The light brown wall-to-wall carpet was well worn and splotchy with stains. The room smelled like the rest of the house—a nasty mix of unwashed clothing, stale sweat, and rancid food. The officer handed Kari an evidence bag containing a notebook page. "Looks like it could be a members list for Balto's gang."

Kari glanced at the paper and handed it to Martin, "Rutger Solberg, Lars Bohle, and Anders Gustason are on the list."

Martin nodded. "What else did you find?" he asked his officer, who handed him another clear plastic evidence pouch with multiple typed pages in it. At the top of the first page, "The Daggers of a New Dawn" had been typed. Martin scanned the first paragraph. Many of the words had been misspelled. He handed it to Kari. "Appears to be their manifesto."

"But here's the big thing," the officer stated. He led them to the work table. None of that evidence had been bagged yet. "There are plans for each of the recent attacks in Oslo, Bergen, Drammen, and Trondheim." Then he pointed to a stack of papers and maps of downtown Oslo on the corner of the table.

Kari leaned in closer and read through the handwritten notes. She looked over her shoulder at Martin. "These are plans for an attack at Oslo City Hall at the Nobel Peace Prize Ceremony."

"We're taking Balto back to Tromsø and placing him in custody," Martin said. He instructed the officer to stay at the house and continue collecting evidence with his partner. "When the officers from the Lyngen station arrive, work with them to gather the weapons and arrange to have them transported to a secure evidence locker at the Tromsø station."

Kari photographed the front and back of the member list and emailed it to Jens and Chief Nord from her phone. She called Nord at his work number and was not surprised that he was in the office at this hour.

"Chief, we have arrested Stefan Balto at his home in Birtavarre. He has a massive stash of weapons and plans for each of the attacks in Norway over the past three months. We found a list of members for Stefan Balto's organization and plans for an attack on the Nobel Peace Prize Ceremony. The threat is real, Chief."

"As soon as we end this call, I'm going to send patrol cars and tactical weapons teams to the home of Jusse Balto and the Balto residence at Maridalen Lake. I'll have Jens Tofte coordinate the roundup of the men on that list. Anything else?"

"That's it, Chief. We're taking Balto back to Trondheim now."

"This was great work, Kari." Chief Nord signed off.

Kari watched the officers load Stefan Balto into the back of the transport van.

Martin walked up to Kari. "I agree with Nord. This was excellent work. Let's get that bastard back to Tromsø and make provisions for a nice jail cell." He smiled and started walking to the BMW.

"Uh, Martin," Kari said. Martin stopped and looked over at her. She held out her right hand, palm up. "The keys. I'm driving."

CHAPTER 44

Lyfjord, Norway

The mountains on the far side of the inlet faded to a soft blur. The early evening sky had draped the distant peaks in a twilight cloak. Demetrius Wolffe's first few breaths after waking were short and labored. A voice spoke to him. The words seemed distant, clouded by the haze that filled his head. "Demetrius, how do you feel?"

"Like shit," he mumbled. "Will this pain ever go away?" Even his own words sounded muffled.

"It might take a day or two, but you'll recover." Asgeir sat down in the armchair next to the sofa.

"Doesn't feel like it right now." Demetrius eked out the words. The mere act of speaking was a struggle.

"The protective veils of Vayla Isarrus enabled your enrichment to occur in one step. We are ahead of where we'd be otherwise. Once you recover, we can move quickly."

Demetrius shifted his position on the sofa and managed to sit more upright.

Asgeir stood and extended his hand toward Demetrius. "Come with me. Let's walk outside. There is something I need you to experience."

Demetrius grasped Asgeir's hand and somehow found the strength to stand. "You feel different. Not like before. It feels like I can perceive your thoughts—like we are connected in some way."

"Your second soul has been infused with the primordial energy from an ancient source, Demetrius. You'll become more aware of your interactions with the world around you at a much more visceral level." Asgeir picked up Demetrius's winter coat and helped him put it on.

The moment Demetrius stepped outside, he stopped. It felt as if the world had changed.

"Things feel different, don't they?" Asgeir asked. "You're going to have a much more heightened sense of the natural world."

Demetrius inhaled deeply. "I can smell scents that I never experienced before." He reached out and touched the branch of a small maple tree near the door. "I can feel its pulse."

"Come! Let's walk to the shore." Asgeir led him down a narrow footpath to the shoreline.

Demetrius sat on a boulder at the water's edge. "Everything around me is alive."

"Everything is connected, Demetrius. Now for the first time in your life you can actually experience that."

"I never want to be without this feeling." Demetrius embraced the cool breeze that washed over his body. Even the air that bathed his skin felt vital.

"Demetrius, what you are feeling now is what every living, sentient being on this planet will feel after you activate the Ebony Sphere. This is how the Moirae followers of Vayla Isarrus intended it to be. This is what it is like to feel the natural harmony and balance of existence."

"Everyone should be able to experience life this way. It's joyous. The rapture I feel is unlike anything I could have imagined. I'm hearing and feeling rich, sympathetic vibrations from the sounds around me, from the breeze rustling through the branches of trees, from the water lapping up on the shore. I know my days are numbered, but I feel so blessed to have experienced this. Even if you told me this was my last day on Earth, I would die a happy man. Why couldn't it have been this way for everyone from the start?"

Asgeir smiled. "The cosmos is an amazing, boundless place." He stood at the edge of the water and swept his arm across the sky. "There are so many worlds out there teeming with life, Demetrius. On many of them, the inhabitants do feel this, every day of their existence. They live enlightened lives. Vayla Isarrus and her followers saw this. We believed all life should experience this harmony and balance. It's why the Ebony Spheres were created. But the old-order Moirae believe every soul should have the free will to evolve and fulfill its destiny unhindered by outside influence. And that's the shortcoming of their belief system. Life evolves differently everywhere. And here, on your world, an insidious disease has metastasized among your society, where the hatred and distrust of anything that is different, no matter how little, eats your culture away from the inside— to the point that all of the good in the world fades to the edges and cannot overcome the disease that is slowly killing it."

"Is that why you brought me outside? To experience this?"

A tear ran down Asgeir's cheek. "This is what Vayla and her followers wanted. All life should experience this connection. But our vision violated the core hands-off tenets of the old-order Moirae. Demetrius, if you activate the Ebony Sphere, you can bring this feeling to all the people of this planet."

"This is so glorious. Words cannot adequately capture what I'm feeling." Demetrius paused for a moment to soak in the radiance of his surroundings. "Asgeir, when I was about to enter the flow of the Quintessence, I saw you run toward the second soul of Jade Hendrix. What happened?"

"She was attempting to put an end to your second soul in the Otherworlds. She and the people she is working with are trying to prevent you from blessing the people of your planet with the enlightenment you are now experiencing. Is that what you want?"

Demetrius felt the cold surface of the boulder on which he was sitting. It was resonating with energy. He felt its harmonies in the tips of his fingers. "No, it's not what I want. Everyone should experience this."

"Even if it means thousands, maybe tens of thousands of lives will be sacrificed to make that future world a reality?"

"You had said it is a small price to pay and that the benefit so much outweighs the loss. After experiencing these sensations, I'm more convinced than ever. This is the best path forward."

"It's unfortunate that the woman you knew as Jade Hendrix had to be eliminated. It's not the way I would have wanted to do things. She was part of the sacrifice that had to be made. I released her into a nexus where three veins of the Quintessence crossed. By now, her second soul will have been shredded. We don't have to worry about her anymore."

CHAPTER 45

Tromsø Police Station

"David," the voice whispered. "Wake up."

He had dozed off. Must have been more tired than he thought. "What time is it?"

"11:45," Kari Salversen whispered.

The light from the hallway flooded into the holding cell. David Skye sat up, still groggy. "What's going on?"

"We arrested Stefan Balto. I owe you a great deal of thanks for what you've done."

David squinted as his eyes adjusted to the light. "Good. I'm glad the information I provided was of help."

"It certainly was. Police from our Oslo precinct have been sent to apprehend and arrest Stefan's brother, Jusse, and the men working with him. And as you predicted, we now have a list of members for the Daggers of a New Dawn organization."

Kari handed a document to David.

"What's this?" he asked.

"It's a formal release document. If you and Jade agree to the conditions and sign it, you'll be free to go."

David looked at the document. He was tired, and after being woken up at this hour of night, he wasn't in a state to concentrate. "Can you summarize them for me?"

"You need to surrender your passports and driver's licenses, remain in the municipality of Tromsø, and check in with the Tromsø police station every Monday and Friday."

"Is that everything?"

"There's one more thing. You'll tell me, in detail, how you and Jade Hendrix had advanced knowledge of these recent events. And I expect to receive that information first thing tomorrow morning. Otherwise, I'm returning both of you to your holding cells, and we'll proceed with the request to have both of you remanded in custody."

David considered the options. "If I sign this, I can go?"

Kari nodded and handed him a pen.

David signed the document and handed it back to her. "Can we get Epiphany?" He rubbed his lower back as he stood. "I'm not going to miss that cot," he said as he followed Kari into the dimly lit hallway.

Kari unlocked the door to Epiphany's holding cell. David slipped by her and went to wake Epiphany. He touched her shoulder and gently nudged her. "Epiphany, we're getting out of here." He reached down and touched her forearm to nudge her again. "Jesus, she's ice cold."

Kari touched Epiphany's forehead. "She really is."

David knelt down beside her bed and felt her wrist. "I can feel her pulse. It's pretty weak."

Kari bent over Epiphany and listened. "I can hear her breathing."

David nudged her several more times, a little more forcefully this time. Still nothing.

"I'm calling an ambulance. We'll get her to the hospital," Kari said.

———

The waiting was unbearable. David stood at the windows in the lobby area of the emergency center at the University Hospital of North Norway. He gazed lazily at the outside world. Piles of snow had been plowed along the perimeter of the parking area. A smattering of vehicles were parked under the lampposts. He turned around quickly when the door to the examination and triage area swung open, and a doctor who appeared to be in her forties came out to talk to him. Detective Salversen walked over to join them.

"How is she?" David asked, rubbing his arms to shake off the cold and some of the nervous energy.

"She's in stable condition. Her heart rate has settled down into an acceptable range. Blood pressure's a little high. We're keeping her warm, and her body temperature is slowly getting back to a safe level."

"Is she awake?" Detective Salversen asked.

"No, she's still unconscious. From the tests we've done, her brain activity is normal, so we don't see any concern there. We're going to run some more tests in the morning. Right now, we want to keep her warm and let her rest until we figure out what's going on."

Detective Salversen pulled a business card out of her wallet and wrote a number on the back of it. "This is the phone number of the place where I'm staying. My business phone is on the front. Please have someone call me if there is any change in her condition."

David watched the doctor slip the card into her pocket and disappear behind the door to the examination area. He hated the feeling of helplessness that had overtaken him. There was nothing he could do for Epiphany right now.

"It's pretty late," Detective Salversen said. She looked at her watch: 1:35 am. "Judging by the baggage we removed from your rental car after the incident in the tunnels, I'm guessing you and Jade checked out of your hotel rooms before going to the café to meet Demetrius Wolffe."

"That's right. We were planning to head back to Stamsund to meet Johannes, had everything gone as anticipated."

"Do you have any other place to stay?"

David shook his head. "Not unless the hotel has a vacancy, and it was pretty well-booked when we made our initial reservations."

"We have a lot going on in Tromsø this time of year. Most of the hotels will be at capacity, and to be honest, I'm tired as hell and don't want to wait around on the hope that you'll find a place to stay."

"What do you suggest?"

"You're more than welcome to use the holding cell," the detective said coyly.

David looked at her suspiciously, "Really?"

"I have two spare bedrooms at the place I'm staying. You can stay there—provided you deliver on the details regarding how you and Jade had gotten the information about the attack in Overgård and the Daggers of a New Dawn."

David extended his arm and shook hands with the detective. "You have my word." He smiled and followed her to the car.

CHAPTER 46

The Otherworlds

The shifting currents of the Quintessence swept Epiphany through the meandering vein. Fighting against the raw power of the turbulent flow quickly proved to be pointless. But she wasn't going to give in either. Instead, she relaxed her body and let the flow of ancient energy infuse her second soul. She embraced the very thing that could annihilate her. An eerie sense of calm overtook her mental and physical states. The stabbing pain she initially felt when Asgeir released her into the nexus had ceased. Although she felt at peace, a troubling thought worried her: *Perhaps this is what death feels like when it grows near.*

A hazy beacon flickered in the distance as the flow of the Quintessence carried Epiphany along. She focused every ounce of energy on moving toward it. The Moirae who had been her guide through childhood, who had eased her through the experience of having a second soul, pulled her from the turbulent flow.

Epiphany rolled over onto her back. She gazed up at the deep blue sky. "Where am I?" she managed to ask.

The Moirae guide knelt by Epiphany's side. "You are in the Realm of the Forever Sun."

"How am I still alive?"

"I could not let you remain trapped in the bounds of the Quintessence. When you entered the Otherworlds, the harmonies of your second soul led me here."

Epiphany sat up. Her focus was slightly blurred. She grasped the Moirae's arm. "Thank you for saving me."

"You saved yourself. Rather than fight the flow, you welcomed the ancient energy into your second soul and became one with it. Had you not done that, your existence would have ended. There is something you should know, however: You will be different now."

"How so?" Epiphany asked.

"When you leave the Otherworlds and return to your reality, you will experience an enhanced connection to the natural world around you. Things will feel alive in ways you never knew were possible. Your body will be shielded by a veil of force that will protect it against spiritual energy that could be used against you."

"Like from the Ebony Spheres?"

"Yes, and from the likes of Asgeir. He has the power to rob the human body of its soul, but you will be protected from that. There is more you need to know. The man who has the sphere has also been infused with the same ancient energy that flows through your body. He will use the Ebony Sphere very soon. Unfortunately, it will take some time to recover from the trauma you've been through. When you return to Earth, your body will require rest and will be in a sleeping state for at least one of your days."

The Moirae spirit remained kneeling beside Epiphany. "I am breaking the Moirae vow of not interfering in the ways of humanity. In giving you the information you need to stop Demetrius Wolffe, I will be influencing your destiny, and that violates everything the Moirae stand for. For this, I fear I will be punished." She reached down and cupped her hand around the back of Epiphany's head, just above her neck.

Epiphany felt the warm flow of energy seep into her mind.

The Moirae removed her hand and smiled. "Please do not fail." She stood and vanished among the shadows of the forest.

Epiphany lowered her back onto the warm ground and looked skyward. The air was warm in this realm. Long beams of light streamed through the canopy of branches and leaves overhead. She closed her eyes. Vivid imagery of the information that had been released into her head spilled forth. It was snowing heavily. Demetrius Wolffe was standing in an open area holding the Ebony Sphere of Vayla Isarrus in his outstretched hand. Asgeir stood next to him. The exact location of where he'd be was firmly implanted in her head. At 9 pm, two days from now, Demetrius would make his attempt to change eight billion souls.

CHAPTER 47

Salversen family vacation home, Tromsø, Norway

Kari put her feet up on the ottoman and took in the view from the armchair in her living room. Street lights illuminated the entire length of the Tromsø Bridge. A cargo ship eased its way between the tall pillars of the long structure. The serenity of the early morning hours was something to be savored—a chance to clear the mind and simply enjoy a peaceful moment before the inevitable chaos of the day begins.

Her thoughts returned to last night. She had interrogated Stefan Balto briefly before Jade Hendrix was taken to the hospital, but the man had refused to say a word without an attorney present. That wasn't much of a concern. The evidence they had gathered would support an unassailable case against him. She hoped to accomplish two things this morning before her second go-around with Balto later today. One, she needed to know how David Skye and Jade Hendrix knew about the attacks and the men behind them. And two, she wanted background information on Demetrius Wolffe to better understand who she was dealing with. It was the latter of the two that she started with.

The Citizens for a Peaceful Planet website provided a good starting point for material pertaining to Demetrius. He was fifty-five years old, born and raised in Bremen, Germany, and grew up in a small house along the Weser River. He attended City University of Applied Sciences in Bremen, where he received Bachelor of Arts degrees in business and social services. After university, he had stints in London and Dublin before settling down in Oslo. It was in Oslo, at the age of thirty, that he and a partner, Christian Slagg, founded Citizens for a Peaceful Planet.

The sound of David Skye lumbering into the kitchen interrupted Kari's concentration. She glanced at the digital clock on the wall in the living room. It had just switched from 5:33 am to 5:34. "You're up early," Kari said softly. "There's a fresh pot of coffee on the counter."

David shuffled over to the coffeemaker, poured a cup, and meandered into the living room. He plopped down onto the sofa across from Kari.

"How'd you sleep?" Kari asked.

"Not that great, Detective."

"Please call me Kari. Sorry to hear that. Was it the bed?"

"No. The bed was comfortable—a hell of a lot better than the cot in the holding cell. I know you were tired last night and didn't want to haul me around town to find a hotel room, but I've got to ask, why did you offer to have me stay here at your place? I'm in a holding cell one day, and the next I'm sleeping in one of your guest bedrooms."

"David, do you mind if I call you by your first name?"

"That's fine by me."

"First of all, the background checks we did on you and Jade Hendrix were illuminating. The great things the two of you are working on are exemplary. You have provided the police with information that will lead to the arrests of the men behind a horrible string of attacks. And if you remember, you signed a release document agreeing to the condition that you'd tell me how you've come across that information. I don't feel you are a threat to me, and I felt the comfort and privacy of my home would be a good place to tell me what you know."

David took a sip of coffee. "That makes sense. Thanks for allowing me to stay here."

"Were you worrying about Jade Hendrix? Is that why you couldn't sleep last night? If it helps, I called the hospital this morning. Her vital signs have pretty much returned to normal. The doctor said she has been drifting in and out of consciousness briefly, but she has not yet been awake for more than a few seconds. They will continue to keep a close eye on her condition."

"Thanks for doing that. I really appreciate it. Oh, and you might not know this, but she prefers the nickname her sister gave her. Epiphany."

"Given what she told me about the attack in Overgård, I can see how she must have earned that name. Epiphany mentioned that Demetrius Wolffe is the man we should be focusing on. I've been digging into his background online. He doesn't seem like the type of person to be involved in any of this. How well do you know him?"

"I've met him a few times and talked to him on the phone on occasion. It doesn't take long to realize how much of a humanitarian he really is. Epiphany and I did not want to believe he'd have anything to do with this. But after he set us up to be killed by that man in the coffee shop. What did you say his name was? Anders something?"

"Gustason."

"Yeah. Demetrius called us and wanted to meet at the coffee shop, and the next thing we know, we're being shot at and then chased through the tunnels of Tromsø by Anders Gustason."

"Wolffe was behind that?"

"Yeah, but it's just not like him. I don't know what's changed," David said.

"Did he give a reason for why he wanted to meet you at the coffee shop?"

"He wanted to give us the sphere."

Kari set her cup of coffee down on the end table, took her feet off the ottoman, and sat upright. This was getting interesting. "What sphere? Do you mean the orb from the statue in Tjeldsund? What does a five-hundred-year-old orb have to do with anything?" The question she asked made her smile. Martin Kolbeck's insights never ceased to amaze her. He had suggested that maybe the crime at the Tjeldsund Church was to steal the orb and the deaths had been secondary. *It looks like his instincts might have been right,* she thought.

David stood and walked over to the picture window. He watched the cargo ship that Kari had seen moments earlier. He turned to face her. "Kari, there are things that happen in this world that no one will ever know about. It's how Epiphany and I know the things about these crimes and these men. The only way for you to fully appreciate what I will tell you is to experience who Epiphany and I really are. *What* we really are."

Kari looked at David with an eye of skepticism and intrigue. She watched him walk over to the sofa. This time, she really concentrated on the measure of the man she had invited into her house. He was about six feet tall, with an athletic build, wavy dark brown hair that fell to his shoulders, and chestnut brown eyes. When he spoke, his voice was soft and at times silky smooth. "Who you are and what you are?" she asked.

"I want to show you how we know the things we've told you. Once you see that, you'll better understand what I will tell you. The thing is, I've never done this before."

Kari furrowed her brow. "Never done what before?"

"The best way I can explain it is that I'm going to take you on a spiritual journey. Everything you see, you will see through my eyes, but the emotions and senses you feel will be your own as if you were actually there with me."

"Okaaay," Kari said, drawing the word out to emphasize her skepticism.

"I need you to come over here and sit next to me."

Kari paused a moment to consider what he was asking her to do. She got up, walked around the coffee table, and sat next to David.

"I want you to lean back, relax, and close your eyes. I'm going to lightly grasp your wrist with my hand, and then you'll see what I mean."

Kari looked at David for a moment. He must have sensed how uncertain about this she was, so he said, "Don't worry. I have zero intention of hurting you in any way."

Kari leaned back and closed her eyes. She felt the warm touch of his hand around her wrist, and then everything went black.

Kari drifted through an immense void, engulfed in a suffocating darkness. The silence was overwhelming. It felt as if she was spinning, but there were no reference points from which to gauge any sense of motion. There was no sense of time. Her pulse accelerated. Panic consumed her emotions. Someone or something reached out to steady her soul, to ease her thoughts. Its touch was warm and soothing. It whispered its name: Moirae. The Moirae guided her across the void. When Kari crashed through the abyss, into the Otherworlds, a grand symphony filled her ears. Its beauty brought tears to her eyes. Images faded in and out of view. Then silence again.

The shimmering light of a faraway sun reflected off the glassy smooth water of a pure blue lake. Kari gazed upward at the mountain peak on the far side of the water. Steep cliffs rose skyward. The peaks of the jagged rocks disappeared among the cottony white clouds. A waterfall spilled over a rocky ledge high up on the side of the mountain range. A spectrum of colors shimmered in its mist.

Kari turned and walked into the woods. Interspersed throughout the forest were trees taller than any she'd ever seen.

David's voice drifted in the wind. "I'm looking for men with a tattoo of Earth with a dagger through it and a rising sun in the background."

The landscape around Kari shifted. She followed a narrow footpath that had multiple branches, but she always stayed on the one that was illuminated by a soft glow of light. The path came to an end at the edge of the forest. When she stepped beyond the woods, the landscape shifted again. Kari stood on the road facing Stefan Balto's house and the large, red garage. She knelt down and touched the earth at her feet. The words "Birtavarre, Norway" instantly appeared in her head. She walked to the front door and opened it. The voices of several men talking from somewhere upstairs could be heard.

Kari walked up the steps and down the hall to the room where the voices were coming from. When she entered, no one flinched or noticed she was there. The big man by the table was Stefan Balto. The bigger man that looked just like him she recognized as his brother, Jusse. Another man stood alongside the two brothers, all of whom were staring at the large computer monitor. A man sitting at the desk was keying in a location. She watched him type Oslo City Hall. A map on the computer screen zoomed out a great distance and then zoomed back in, rotating in a three-dimensional view around Oslo City Hall. The man at the keyboard stopped the 3D image from rotating to view the front of the building. Jusse Balto pointed to the image on the screen. "Me and one of my men will enter the plaza from Roald Amundsens Street. Another of my men will enter over here from the left entrance to the plaza, and a third man will come in here from the right entrance. We'll have control of every way in and out of the plaza. When I start shooting, all hell lets loose." Jusse and the others started laughing.

Kari left the room and exited the house. She walked to the garage on the property and entered through a door at the back. Once inside, she went into the room where the weapons were stored. The room was fully stocked with a complete arsenal of rifles, shotguns, and pistols, just as she had seen it in person. She exited the garage and walked back to the forest.

The release of David's hand from Kari's wrist woke her instantly, as if someone had jabbed a finger into her ribs. She immediately leaned forward and jumped up to her feet. "Jesus fucking Christ. How'd you do that? It was so real!"

"It *was* real, Kari. We were actually there," David said.

Kari walked over to the window, folded her arms, and shook her head in disbelief. She looked out the window at the waterway, at the island of Tromsøya on the other side. The Tromsø Bridge was lit up, still where it had always been. She reached out and touched the cold glass of the window to reassure herself that it was in fact real. "That was beyond belief."

David stood and joined her at the window. "And now for the really incredible part."

CHAPTER 48

Salversen family vacation home, Tromsø, Norway

"You asked how I did that," David said. He walked back to Kari's kitchen to top off his coffee and then sat down at the table in the dining area. Kari had done the same and was seated across from him. "I was born with a second soul. It allows me to travel to a place called the Otherworlds—a collection of spirit realms hidden in the folds of space-time, beyond our physical reality. If you really want a detailed explanation, Johannes Stinar could explain it better than I can." He stopped to let that soak in with Kari.

"You expect me to believe you have two souls?" she asked. "How's that even possible?"

"I told you this would be incredible, maybe unbelievable is a better way to put it. A second soul wasn't something I asked for or earned through some gallant feat. It's just the way it is. I was the beneficiary of cosmic probability. Spirits known as the Moirae allocate a soul to each sentient being at the time of birth when the spark of life is first ignited. They also create a limited number of *second* souls that are bestowed upon individuals every generation or two."

"Are those the same Moirae that guided us through the dark void when you took me to the Otherworlds?" Kari asked.

"Yes. Second souls are given to people who are expected to act as apostles to help guide society toward a peaceful coexistence, to achieve the harmony and balance the Moirae want to see. Epiphany and I are those apostles. So are Demetrius Wolffe and Johannes Stinar. Aidan McCallum, the man who was chasing after the bomber in Trondheim, was also an apostle."

"How many of you are there?"

"Just the five of us. We're all doing our bit to make the world a better place. Epiphany founded an organization to help refugees and immigrants start a new life. I started a company focusing on cleaning the oceans and atmosphere. Demetrius launched Citizens for a Peaceful Planet. Johannes is doing groundbreaking research in physics that will advance society in leaps and bounds. Aidan had been doing great work in bringing clean water and food to impoverished nations."

"Five people doesn't seem like it would even come close," Kari commented.

"You're absolutely right about that, but the Moirae do not want to interfere in the direction the souls of this Earth take. Five was probably a stretch for them."

Still a bit skeptical, Kari asked, "If Demetrius is one of these apostles, how do you explain what he is doing?"

"To answer that, I need to give you a little background." David talked about the message that Aidan had received from a Moirae spirit, requesting that he find and destroy the only surviving Ebony Sphere of Vayla Isarrus. He explained how the breakaway faction of Vayla Isarrus and her followers had created the Ebony Spheres and provided a brief overview of what they were designed to do. David ended his story by explaining how all of the spheres had been destroyed except for one. "The only one to have survived is here on Earth. Care to guess where it was?"

"The orb that was taken from the church in Tjeldsund?"

"That's it."

"It went missing the day all of those people were killed," Kari said.

"And Demetrius is the person who has it."

"You touched on it briefly, but can you tell me more about the Ebony Sphere?"

"If a society drifts too far from harmonious existence, a person with a second soul could use it to alter every soul on the planet. But if the sphere is misused, it can actually rip the souls out of people's bodies."

"Is that what happened in the church?" Kari asked.

"I think so. It might have been activated accidentally by Demetrius when he took it. It tore the souls out of each living being in that church."

"And the same thing happened in Overgård?" Kari asked.

"Yes. Epiphany and I believe that Demetrius is testing the sphere. If I know him, he's trying to figure out how to use it for its intended purpose. Something must have gone wrong in Overgård."

"In what way are souls changed if it's used properly?" Kari asked.

"If a person with a second soul can master the power of the sphere, he or she could use it to basically do a global reset. I believe Demetrius is trying to reshape humanity to change every soul on the planet to his specification. He could use it to eliminate the ability of humans to kill each other, to end racism and hate, and whatever else he believes would result in a perfect world."

"Who wouldn't want that?" Kari asked, thinking aloud.

"What if Demetrius's view of a better world isn't what everyone else wants, or even what the majority of us want? If he makes that change," David paused and then added, "and we don't know that it will work, how will you and I be different? Will you be the same person you are now? How will your values change, and will you embrace those changes? Would your personality be different? There's a lot we don't know."

Kari was speechless.

David could see she was thinking deeply about what he had said. "Here's the kicker. To power the sphere, to change the eight billion souls on the planet requires the spiritual energy from a thousandth of one percent of the souls to be changed. It doesn't sound like much—until you do the math. To change eight billion souls will require sacrificing eighty thousand people. Ever look at the population of Tromsø and the surrounding towns and villages?" David asked.

"No, don't tell me. It's eighty thousand," Kari said.

"Pretty damn close. Imagine all of the people in this entire area dead in the blink of an eye. Is killing all of those people okay if it means changing the world for one man's perception of better?"

Kari shook her head in astonishment. "Wow. This is unbelievable."

"Given the consequences, if you could wield that power, would you do it?"

"All of those ideals you mentioned—no more killing, no more hate—are clearly worth pursuing. It does make achieving them with this sphere seem like it would be worth doing." Kari was silent for a moment. "You're making my head swim. To answer your question: No, I wouldn't do it. Every life is important and should have a chance to shine."

"That's how Epiphany and I feel. That's what the old-order Moirae believe. It's why we're trying to retrieve the sphere: to prevent it from being used."

"Do you know for sure Demetrius is going to use the sphere in Tromsø?" Kari asked.

"No, not for sure. He's somewhere in the area, but he might head to a bigger city for the final usage of it."

Kari shook her head. "Maybe we should evacuate Tromsø."

"What do we tell city officials? Some lunatic with an ancient artifact is going to kill eighty thousand people so he can create a better world for everyone else on the planet? Besides, from what we have learned about this thing, it's going to take the souls of the *closest* eighty thousand people. It doesn't matter where they are. It doesn't matter if they are five feet away or five hundred miles. There's no safe place they can go."

"We have to find some way to stop this." Kari paused and thought for a moment. "Is it possible to stop this?"

"We think we have a plan. Johannes Stinar has a working prototype of something he calls a quantum-well device, which can tap into the primeval energy that flows through the whole of the universe. If we can throw the sphere into the quantum well, it will destroy it. Or at least, that's what we hope."

"There were a series of individual killings that occurred in the region. The faces of the victims had the same horrified look as the victims of the church attack and the one in Overgård. Was that Demetrius using the sphere?"

"No, one of the spirits who was in league with Vayla Isarrus came through a void caused by a trial run of Johannes's quantum-well device. He's here to help Demetrius. In order to survive, he needs the energy from human souls. He literally tears them from the bodies of his victims. That's who caused those deaths."

"He nearly killed me in Tromsø, but Epiphany chased him off," Kari said. "When is Demetrius planning to use the sphere to change every soul on Earth?"

"We think it could happen any day now."

"And you're telling me we need Johannes and that device of his, right?" Kari asked. "Is he still in Stamsund?"

"As far as I know. Why?"

"Have you seen the weather forecasts lately?"

"No," David admitted.

"A huge snow storm is rolling in tomorrow. It's supposed to start sometime after midnight and could go on for two to three days. If we don't get Johannes here today, using his quantum-well device won't be an option."

CHAPTER 49

The Arctic Cathedral, Tromsø, Norway

Demetrius sat quietly, lost in his own thoughts. The white van reached the halfway point on the Tromsø Bridge. He looked out the passenger's side window to his right and gazed at the waterway separating Tromsøya from the mainland. The view from this elevation was amazing. Small boats were scattered across the water. Snow-covered mountains rested under the blanket of a twilight sky as the city began its day. Early morning traffic was light. He glanced at his watch, barely 6 am. "Where are you taking me?"

"Up ahead," Asgeir said. "The church."

Demetrius turned to look at the roadway ahead. The Arctic Cathedral was lit up inside, gleaming like a jewel. The aluminum-coated concrete and glass structure looked like an accordion of layered triangular building blocks of varying sizes laid end to end. The entire front face of the church was constructed of rectangular glass panels. A giant cross was part of the external structure. It rose up from the ground and culminated inside the apex of the front façade.

Asgeir crossed the bridge and followed the road to the back of the church. He pulled into a parking spot and turned off the engine.

"Why here?" Demetrius asked.

"I'm thinking this is where we use the Ebony Sphere. It's been housed in a church for close to five centuries. I think it's only fitting that its first use be at the site of a church, don't you?"

Demetrius sat calmly and nodded.

"You are about to initiate the most ambitious event in the history of humankind, one that will change it for millennia to come. I think this is where we should do this," Asgeir suggested. "Come! Let's walk around the church, get a feel for the lay of the land, and pick the spot where you will change the future."

Demetrius got out of the vehicle and stood at the edge of the roadway. The church was an impressive piece of architecture. He thought it looked like a jagged piece of ice jutting up out of the ground. The aesthetic of its shape seemed fitting for the snowy arctic city in which it had been built.

Asgeir opened the rear door of the van. He grabbed the backpack containing the Ebony Sphere and handed it to Demetrius. "Carry this with you while we walk around the church. I want you to experience things as they will be tomorrow night."

Demetrius took the backpack and flung it over his right shoulder. He had longed for the touch of the sphere, to hold it in his hand. Having the sphere this close to his body was rejuvenating. Its energy warmed his soul. Demetrius followed Asgeir along the side of the building and then up an inclined, paved walkway to the front of the church.

"What do you think, Demetrius?" Asgeir asked. "We activate the sphere right here where you are standing."

Demetrius took a step back and leaned against the railing at the top of the hill. It was a breathtaking view of the front face of the church with the giant cross in front of the glass panels. He turned around to view the waterway and the mountainous terrain. "This feels right. When do we do it?"

Asgeir replied, "9 pm tomorrow."

CHAPTER 50

Salversen family vacation home, Tromsø, Norway

"Come on, Johannes, pick up," David Skye said as he waited impatiently for an answer. Getting Johannes Stinar to Tromsø tonight before the snowstorm began dumping what would be an impressive amount of snow was imperative. The helicopter that flew Kari into Tromsø was not an option for transporting Johannes; it was needed in Oslo for the mission to apprehend Jusse Balto and his men. David wasn't looking forward to convincing the sometimes-grumpy physicist to make the long drive on his own.

Johannes picked up on the third ring. "I'm kind of busy." The bothered tone in his voice was pretty evident.

"Sorry to call you at this hour, but we have an emergency on this end."

"I've been awake for two hours working in my lab. What's the emergency?"

"We think Demetrius is really close to using the sphere for the big event. He did a trial run in a small village southeast of here. Epiphany thinks his final run will be soon," David said.

"How soon?"

"Tomorrow or the next day."

Johannes didn't answer right away. "I've got work to do. I'm not finished with everything. If I leave today, some of the critical problems will not get fixed," Johannes said, the tone of his voice noticeably more heated.

"Will your device still work if these issues aren't corrected?" David asked.

"Yes, it will work, but it will be dangerous to anyone anywhere near it."

"There's a major snowstorm heading for Tromsø. It's supposed to start after midnight tonight and could last for two to three days. We're talking upward of two feet of snow. When can you leave?"

"It's an eight-hour drive."

David expected that response. "Johannes, we need you here. Today!"

"Yeah, I get that. I will be there. You have my word. I've got one, maybe two hours of work to finish up. Then I need an hour or two to pack everything. I can be on the road by ten o'clock. That'll put me there around six this evening. Maybe a little later with stops."

David gave Johannes the address for Kari's house. *I hope like hell Johannes gets here before the snow starts falling*, he thought.

CHAPTER 51

Salversen family vacation home, Tromsø, Norway

Kari read through her notes for the interrogation with Stefan Balto, which was scheduled for 1:30 that afternoon. Balto's attorney, a local public defender, would be sitting in. After her scheduled phone calls with Jens Tofte and Martin Kolbeck, she'd head into the office.

Her cellphone chimed. The home screen indicated an incoming call from Jens. "Hi, Jens. Good to talk with you."

"Likewise," he said. "I've got a lot to report on. The information you passed on really came through in a big way. Jusse Balto and three of the men working with him were apprehended around 3:30 this morning."

"How'd it play out?"

"They were picked up at the family property on Maridalen Lake. Not a shot fired."

"Good! So no one hurt then?" Kari asked.

"No one hurt. They were totally taken by surprise. I think they were shocked that we knew anything about it. One of the rooms at the back of the house was packed with guns and explosives. They even had grenades if you can believe it."

"This is a big deal. We both had a sense that these guys were just getting started. How about the list of operatives that we got from Stefan Balto?" Kari asked.

"Over the early morning hours, we've picked up seven of the twenty-plus members. My guess . . . within the next three to five days, we'll have all of them in custody."

"How's Chief Nord? Happy with the results?" Kari asked.

"I don't know that I've ever seen the man happier. This morning, he stopped by my desk to offer his congratulations to me and you with an ear-to-ear smile. I'll keep you posted with any new developments on this end."

"Great. Thanks," Kari said, then ended the call. Kari called Martin Kolbeck.

"Hi, Kari. Ready for the Balto interrogation this afternoon?" Martin asked.

"Very," she said. "He's got no room to maneuver on this."

"Yeah, should go pretty smoothly."

"I'm going to head over to the station in about fifteen minutes. Did you hear about Jusse Balto?" Kari asked.

"No, I haven't gotten any updates on that."

"Just talked to Jens. Jusse and three of his men were taken into custody early this morning. They've already picked up seven of the members on Stefan Balto's list."

"That is great news. I'll buy the first round tonight. See you soon," Martin said and then ended the call.

Kari was scheduled to interrogate Stefan Balto that afternoon, but her mind would be elsewhere. Finding a way to stop Demetrius Wolffe from changing every soul on the planet would be consuming her thoughts. She walked outside onto the front deck overlooking the water. Second souls, spirits that inhabit other realms, an ancient artifact that could change every soul on the planet, and a man from a place called the Otherworlds that resembles a sixteenth-century statue. She placed her hands on the rail around the deck and attempted to steady her nerves. The information that David Skye unloaded on her this morning was so utterly unbelievable. But after seeing the Otherworlds for herself, at the moment anyway, it was the only way she could make sense of everything that had transpired over the past week.

CHAPTER 52

The residence of Filip Elstad, Tromsø, Norway

Filip Elstad was the type of man who had a singular focus for the task at hand. Once he set his mind on a project, he saw it through to the end. The project that consumed his focus tonight was preparing for the snowstorm. Weather forecasters were giddy about breaking snowfall records. "One of the biggest snowstorms to hit Tromsø since we entered the twenty-first century," they were saying.

Bring it on, he thought. He'd seen a lot of harsh winters in his forty-nine years. *How bad could this one be?* No matter how much of the white stuff they got, he'd be ready for it. Filip rolled up the garage door and brought the trash can inside next to his stealth gray Tesla sedan. He placed two snow shovels inside next to the garage door, wheeled the snow blower into the space behind the car, and checked on his supply of ice melt.

Filip stepped outside. The dark night sky was filled with large puffy clouds, and the air had a damp cold feel to it. It felt like snow was coming. Filip's house was at the end of a road that bordered Vardentoppen, a large, wooded area at the top of the island. Interlaced with trails, the forested area was used year-round for hiking, mountain biking, and cross-country skiing. Filip looked at his watch: 7:37 pm. There just might be time for a quick walk to the high point of the island to enjoy a nice view of the city at night and then walk back for a late dinner.

Everything was where it needed to be: snow shovels, snow blower, and several bags of ice melt. Filip pushed the button on the wall and watched the garage door slowly lower to the ground. Something felt odd; a static charge filled the air behind him, tingling the back of his neck. He turned around to see a vaporous haze take human form. "What the hell!" he exclaimed. The words had barely left his mouth when a large right hand gripped his face and tore the soul from his body.

Asgeir fished the keys out of Filip's pants pocket and laid his dead body across the backseat of the car. He left the house and walked to the trailhead at the end of Filip's road. From there, he'd make the short hike to the van, pick up Demetrius Wolffe, and bring him back here for the night. He entertained a pleasing thought as he walked: *Tomorrow night, not much later than this, the world would be a different place, and the grand plans that Vayla Isarrus and her loyal group of followers had devised will finally be realized.*

CHAPTER 53

Salversen family vacation home,
Tromsø, Norway

The rapping on Kari Salverson's front door brought David Skye out of his catnap. He had dozed off momentarily after another failed attempt to find information about Demetrius Wolffe in the Otherworlds. The continued failures were becoming more than just frustrating; they were demoralizing. David got up off of the sofa and went to the window to see who was at the door. He saw the familiar face of Johannes Stinar and quickly let him in.

"Johannes," he said. "I'm so glad you're here."

"That's a long damn drive by yourself," Johannes said grumpily. "Got something to eat? I haven't had anything since lunch."

"Let's get your stuff out of the car, and we'll see what we can find in the fridge."

David opened the rear hatch to Johannes's Range Rover and reached for a stuffed, oversized duffle bag. It looked like Johannes had packed every piece of clothing he owned. David carried the bloated bag and a backpack into the house. Johannes was right behind him with a hard-shell case containing the quantum-well device and an assortment of instruments. They piled everything in Kari's living room.

David was about to shut the door when he saw Kari pull into the driveway. When she got out of her car, he noticed she was staring at the large, black Range Rover. He called out to her, "Kari, Johannes is here. That's his car." She nodded and came inside, carrying a plastic bag.

"Sorry I'm late. The interrogation ran longer than expected, and Martin and I decided to get as much of the paperwork done as we could." She set the bag on the dining room table. "Have you eaten anything? I got some Thai takeout."

"No, I haven't." David pointed to the refrigerator. The door was wide open, and Johannes was rummaging through it. "And, neither has he. Johannes, get the hell out of her fridge and come over here." Introductions were made, and the three of them sat down around the table and ate.

"David, I stopped by the hospital before I went for takeout. Good news. Epiphany is doing much better today. All of her vital signs look okay. She's been drifting in and out of consciousness much more frequently, although she's never awake long enough to say anything yet. But the doctors are very encouraged."

"What?" Johannes interjected, his mouth stuffed with Thai street noodles and shrimp. "Epiphany's in the hospital? What happened?"

"Sorry, Johannes. I should have mentioned it earlier," David said. We found her unresponsive in her holding cell. She was taken to the hospital by ambulance. We don't know what happened to her." David looked over to Kari. "Was she awake when you saw her?"

"No, she was asleep again. The doctor I talked to said she was awake briefly, just long enough to acknowledge their presence, about an hour before I got there."

"She's going to be okay?" Johannes asked.

Kari reached for another helping of fried rice. "The doctor I talked to said they can't find anything wrong with her. All of the tests they ran came back negative. He thought she'd be back on her feet tomorrow or the next day. Just needs to get some rest and nourishment."

"That's great to hear," David said.

"I dropped off her bag and cellphone at the hospital, so when she feels up to it, she can get dressed in her own clothes and call us when she's released."

After they finished eating, Kari showed Johannes a second guest bedroom where he could sleep, and then they adjourned to the living room.

"Johannes, Kari knows about us—about having second souls and the Otherworlds."

"You told her?" Johannes asked, somewhat bewildered. "Why would you do that? No one is supposed to know about it."

"I didn't have much choice. Epiphany and I were looking at being held in custody for four weeks." David explained the background about providing information that led to the arrest of the Balto brothers and the men in their Daggers of a New Dawn organization. "Besides, I think she can help us stop Demetrius."

"David tells me you have some sort of device that can help," Kari said.

Johannes retrieved his backpack and took out his laptop. He fired it up and navigated to a folder containing videos of the latest test runs.

"This is the video from my most recent test." Johannes talked them through it. "That small canister you see is the quantum-well device. It will open a well at the quantum level, allowing me to tap into an infinite source of ancient energy known as the Quintessence."

David and Kari leaned in close to the laptop. David watched the golf ball–sized sphere of light appear from out of nowhere. It quickly expanded to a sphere measuring ten meters in diameter. Multi-colored light swirled around the surface of the shell.

"When I approached the well, it appeared to be stable," Johannes said. "Well, it was stable until I tossed the ball into it to simulate what would happen with the Ebony Sphere."

David watched the video play out. He saw Johannes turn and run. "The outer shell is expanding."

"It almost killed me. I'm lucky to be sitting here."

"What would have happened if it would have reached you?" Kari asked.

"My body would have been shredded into its constituent parts—torn apart into atoms, and the atoms torn apart into quarks and electrons. I would have been consumed by the energy within the well and scattered throughout the universe."

"Well, that's not too melodramatic," David said.

Johannes smirked but didn't reply.

"How do we use this device of yours to stop Demetrius?" Kari asked.

"A lot of things need to happen. First, we need to find Demetrius and get the sphere from him." Johannes looked over at David. "Any luck with that?"

Dejectedly, David looked down at the floor and said, "I've been trying but can't find anything."

Johannes continued. "Assuming we can find Demetrius and get the sphere from him, then we can throw it into the quantum well. And if we can find the spirit helping him, we can push him into the well along with the sphere. So we need to know where they will be and when they will be there. I need to activate the device in close proximity to them. One thing I did manage to change is the activation time. When I hit the ignition button, the well will form within ten to twenty seconds, instead of the forty it had been taking. The well will only stay open for a limited amount of time, so once it's open, we have to move quickly."

"Johannes, when we talked this morning, you mentioned problems you were working on that would not be fixed in time. What are they?" David asked.

"The first problem is that once the quantum well opens, we have no more than five minutes to get the sphere and the spirit into the well before it collapses. I didn't have the time I needed to figure out how to keep the well open longer than that. The other problem that I partially fixed is the rapid expansion of the shell caused by an influx of energy."

"Help me out here," Kari said. "What influx and what are the implications?"

"When something is thrown into the well, it causes a localized swell of energy that will make the quantum well expand. The greater the amount of energy, the faster the expansion. I've managed to slow the rate of increase for modest-sized amounts of mass. But the Ebony Sphere however has a significant amount of energy. Whoever throws the sphere into the well won't have enough time to get away if they are sufficiently close to it. A few seconds at best."

"So essentially this is a death sentence for whoever does that," Kari stated matter-of-factly.

Johannes responded with a simple nod and said, "Yes."

CHAPTER 54

Salversen family vacation home, Tromsø, Norway, Next day, early evening

David Skye pulled the hood of his winter coat over his head, zipped his coat, and ventured out onto the deck. Somehow the cold breeze still managed to find a way to chill his bones. It looked like the weather forecasters had gotten it right: Snow was falling at a slow, steady rate, and the wind had begun gusting again. The view of the waterway and Tromsøya Island had taken on a mystical appearance while it was being drenched in large white flakes. Plows had been through earlier in the day in an attempt to stay ahead of the snowfall, focusing on the major arteries. The residential roads remained unplowed, covered in six inches of snow.

The events of the past week had occurred at a dizzying pace. He couldn't let go of the devastation in Trondheim. Images of the little girl with the blonde ponytail and the red hat, sitting on the pavement next to her mother, continued to haunt his thoughts. David hoped like hell that she and her little brother would come out of this okay. The information he had provided to Kari led to the arrests of the men responsible for the heinous acts that put young children like them in such grave danger, and for that he was extremely grateful.

Right now, however, he needed a change of perspective. His attempts to uncover where and when Demetrius Wolffe would use the Ebony Sphere of Vayla Isarrus had been fruitless. And Epiphany, the only person able to come close to determining what Demetrius was planning, was laid up in the hospital, unconscious. David stood motionless, staring into the distance, not focusing on any one thing. Several minutes had passed, and as much as he tried, he couldn't settle his racing mind. Not having found the inspiration he had hoped for, David turned around and went back inside to the warmth of Kari's living room.

Kari was seated at the dining room table, working on her laptop, hoping to find anything that would help them locate Demetrius. When David walked in, she looked up and asked, "Any luck?"

"Nothing," David mumbled in a disgusted tone.

"How does this thing with your second soul work? I mean, I experienced how you found out about Stefan Balto, but we never really talked about the mechanics of it."

David removed his coat and took a seat in an armchair across from Kari. "As you saw when I took you through the Otherworlds, I began by concentrating on a specific topic. I focused on the tattoos that each of those men had, and the Otherworlds reacted to me, revealing different threads. It constantly evolves as I change my focus and delve more deeply into specific areas."

"So your primary focus in that instance was on the tattoos, at least initially, not the men who had them?"

"Yeah, that's right. Following that approach ultimately led me to Stefan Balto."

"How have you been approaching what you're doing now?" Kari asked.

"I've been focusing on Demetrius and trying to follow his probable timelines. But they're all so vague and haven't led anywhere. At a minimum, I should have been able to find out where he is staying, but even that is unknowable at this point."

"Instead of concentrating on Demetrius, what about focusing on threads associated with the Ebony Sphere as the primary target? Ultimately, you want to know where the sphere will end up, right?"

"That's a great observation." David smiled in appreciation of the insight. "I've been so fixated on Demetrius and what he might do next that I totally overlooked that approach."

"So next time, start with the sphere in the Tjeldsund Church, follow its timeline to Overgård, and then see where it leads to from there."

"Thanks, Kari. That's a great idea." David walked back to the den on the ground floor to make another attempt.

───────────

David closed the door to the den and sat down in an armchair. A single window provided the only light in the room. He closed his eyes and crossed the Black Void into the Otherworlds. The object of his focus was the Ebony Sphere, where it had been used and where it might be used in the future. His journey took him to the scene of the Tjeldsund Church. That timeline led him to the open fields of Overgård. From there, he followed a possible future path to a familiar place.

David's second soul stood in the triangular patch of land bordering the road behind the Arctic Cathedral. It was in the early morning hours when the city of Tromsø was awakening. Two men got out of a van that had just pulled into the parking area behind the church. The first man was instantly recognizable. Demetrius Wolffe stood by the vehicle observing the grounds around the cathedral. The driver came around to the back of the van. David had seen him before in Tromsø. He and Epiphany had chased him through the streets of the shopping district after the man had murdered a young woman. David moved closer. He focused on finding the second man's name. Within seconds the name Asgeir drifted through his head.

Asgeir retrieved a backpack from the rear of the van and spoke as he handed it to Demetrius. "Carry this with you while we walk around the church. I want you to experience things as they will be tomorrow night."

Tomorrow night, David repeated to himself. When did this trip to the cathedral occur? The Mesh quickly revealed the answer. Demetrius and Asgeir had come to the cathedral yesterday. *Demetrius is going to unleash the power of the sphere tonight.*

David followed them up an inclined walkway. He heard Asgeir speak again. "What do you think, Demetrius? We activate the sphere right here where you are standing."

Demetrius's response was quickly forthcoming, "This feels right. When do we do it?"

Asgeir replied, "9 pm tomorrow."

David watched the men get back into the van and drive away. Finally, he had the information he desperately needed.

———

David came out of his trance and immediately glanced at his watch. It was nearly 7:30 pm. He raced from the den into the living room where Johannes was packing the quantum-well device into his backpack. "Where's Kari?" David blurted out.

"She's in her study."

"We're going now. Pack everything up. It's happening soon," David said hurriedly. He bounded back down the steps and nearly knocked Kari over as she was coming out of her study. "It's going down at nine o'clock at the Arctic Cathedral."

It took ten minutes for everyone to gather their winter outerwear and get dressed in clothing appropriate for the stormy conditions they were about to endure. They congregated in the narrow, single-car garage. David and Johannes stood next to Kari in the cramped space around her sedan, as she opened the roll-up door. A frigid gust of air greeted them with the subtlety of a cold slap in the face. David glanced at Johannes. He could sense the worry and nervousness the man was feeling. David reached out and gently squeezed Johannes's left shoulder. Once they stepped across the garage threshold, they'd be carrying the weight of eighty thousand people on their shoulders.

"They still haven't plowed the back roads yet," Kari said.

David stepped to the edge of the garage to peer out. "There's at least half a foot of snow out there already."

Kari grabbed a measuring stick and walked into the driveway. "Nineteen centimeters."

David did the conversion in his head, *Between seven and eight inches.*

Kari walked back into the garage. "Johannes, we're taking your Range Rover. It'll do better in the snow than my sedan." Johannes nodded his acceptance. Kari handed him a snow brush and took one herself.

"I'm going to call Epiphany. She needs to know," David said.

Kari and Johannes brushed the snow off the Range Rover. "Everyone in," Kari ordered. "Johannes, I'm driving."

Johannes gladly handed the keys to Kari, then jumped into the backseat with his backpack.

David got into the front passenger's seat and pulled the door shut with a loud thump. "I tried several times. No answer."

Kari backed out of the driveway and put the large vehicle into drive. David felt the four-wheel drive kick in as Kari accelerated slowly and headed in the direction of the Arctic Cathedral.

"Try the hospital desk. Tell them you're calling on behalf of Detective Salversen. Say it's an emergency."

David did as Kari instructed and waited while the woman who answered the phone checked on Jade Hendrix. When the woman came back with an update, David replied, "Yes, I'm still here." He paused while she updated him. "What? She's not there? Where the hell is she?"

University Hospital of North Norway

Epiphany had been disoriented when the Moirae pulled her out of her deep sleep. It had taken a few seconds for her to realize she was in a hospital, without any recollection of how she got there. The Moirae had also given her two vital pieces of information: the time and location where Demetrius Wolffe would deploy the Ebony Sphere.

She had little time to act. After disconnecting the leads to the monitoring equipment, she grabbed her duffel bag and ran down the hall to another room where she got dressed as quickly as she could. The commotion in the hallway had grown in intensity once the nursing staff realized what she had done. When the opportunity arose, she darted away unseen and made her way to the ground floor.

It was snowing heavily outside. She'd need some heavier outerwear than what she had brought with her. Epiphany waited near a set of entrance and exit doors to a staff parking area. Two of the grounds crew came in from clearing the sidewalks. They came down the main hallway and turned into a room on their right. When they came back out, they were not wearing their coats or their boots. She overheard one of the men talking about getting a hot cup of coffee. When they were suitably far enough away, she hurried to the room where they had left their outerwear.

The room was cluttered with winter clothing. Parkas hung on wall hooks, and boots were piled in the corner of the room. She found a coat that fit and checked the pockets to find a pair of gloves inside. Epiphany grabbed several pairs of boots and took them over to a bench. She had just finished putting on a pair that actually fit pretty well when two of the maintenance crew walked in.

"Who are you?" the younger of the two asked. "What are you doing in here?"

"That's Karl's coat," the older man said.

Epiphany stood and approached the two men cautiously. "Hey look, there's something I need to tend to. It's a bit of an emergency. Please, I promise I'll return this stuff as soon as I'm done."

The two men looked at each other. The younger one said. "We have a job to do too. We need to keep the walkways clear in case there's an emergency. You're not going anywhere with that coat."

The older man called security on his radio.

"Hey, look guys, I don't want any trouble, but I'm going, and I'm taking the coat and boots with me."

Both men looked at each other again and moved closer together to block the doorway. The older of the two said, "You're staying with us until security gets here."

"Move out of my way, or you're both going to get hurt."

The younger man started moving toward Epiphany.

She backed up, "If you're dumb enough to fight me, I'm smart enough to kick your ass."

He lunged forward and attempted to grab her by the coat. She sidestepped his attempt and blocked his arm. As he moved past her, she hooked his lead ankle with her right foot and took his feet out from under him. The full weight of his body brought him down hard on the tile floor with a loud thud. The clunk of his skull smacking against the floor was unsettling.

The second man immediately charged toward Epiphany. She had no problem outmaneuvering him and dropped him onto his buddy. Then she sped out the door and headed toward the exit. A security guard running down the hallway yelled, "Stop!" She raced through the exit doors into the storm.

Arctic Cathedral

Kari turned left into a parking area for a building across the street from the Arctic Cathedral. The momentum of the Range Rover carried it to a sliding stop on the icy pavement. It had taken fifteen minutes to reach the church. During the course of the trek, they had seen only a few brave souls who dared to take to the roads.

"They said they'd activate the device at the front of the church," David said.

"We have a clear view of it from here." Kari kept the engine running to allow the ventilation system to keep the windows from icing over. They waited fifteen minutes, but there was no sign of Demetrius or Asgeir.

"I'm going to take a closer look," David said. He pulled his hood up and swung the passenger's door open. Cold air quickly invaded the inside of the vehicle. He jumped out and shut the door. David kept his eyes glued to the front of the church. The only sounds were those of the cold snow pelting the ground. David walked to the edge of the roadway, then looked up and down the length of the road. The city was eerily quiet. At that hour, it appeared that everyone was content to stay inside in the comfort and safety of their own homes.

David jogged back to the Range Rover and got inside.

"Do you think they might have gotten held up in the snow?" Johannes suggested.

"It's possible," Kari said. "But you'd think they would have known about the storm rolling in. How certain are you about the vision you had in the Otherworlds, David?"

"Very. This has to be the place."

David's cellphone rang. He fumbled with his coat and fished it out from one of the inside pockets. "It's Epiphany," he said excitedly. "Epiphany, you're on speaker with Johannes and Kari."

"Where are you?" Epiphany shouted.

"We're at the Arctic Cathedral. Demetrius is going to use the sphere at this location, tonight. Soon!" David said.

"No. Not there. At Vardentoppen, the wooded area at the top of the island, near some structure that looks like a radio antenna."

"Epiphany, I had a vision of Demetrius and Asgeir at the cathedral. This has to be the place."

"It was a false lead, David. It's what Asgeir wanted you to see. I don't have time to explain. Do you have a way to get here?"

Kari chimed in. "We're in Johannes's Range Rover. We can get there in twenty minutes. Maybe a little longer."

"Hurry!" Epiphany shouted.

Vardentoppen, Norway

Epiphany navigated the trails through the Vardentoppen woods. She moved as quickly as she could over the rough terrain that would lead to the high point of the island. The Moirae who had pulled her from the flow of the Quintessence mentioned that her connection to the natural world would change. Until now, Epiphany hadn't appreciated by how much that would actually be the case. Everything around her was resonating with energy, almost to the point of being overwhelming. As amazing as these feelings were, she needed to push them aside and focus on finding Demetrius and the sphere. Epiphany stopped and retrieved her cellphone. She turned her back to the wind to keep as much snow off the screen as she could. Her hands trembled from the cold as she zoomed in on the map application. She was a little more than halfway into her 1.6-mile trek from the hospital to the pinnacle of Vardentoppen.

Trudging through more than half a foot of snow would slow her down. Epiphany figured no less than thirty minutes in these conditions. She looked at her watch. It was 8:30. If she could make the trek in thirty minutes, she'd have a fighting chance to stop Demetrius. Anything more than that, and the world would be changed in ways she couldn't begin to fathom. Epiphany gazed out over the landscape on the east side of the island and shuddered to think about all of the lives that would be lost if she failed.

———

Demetrius stepped outside into the full brunt of the storm. Gusting winds blasted his body with frozen pellets of snow. His moment to step up and be counted, to do something that perhaps few others would be brave enough to do, was waiting at the end of a kilometer-long hike into the woods at the top of Tromsøya. Asgeir shut the door, and they veered to the right to an access trail leading into the Vardentoppen woods. Demetrius figured it would take twenty to thirty minutes to reach their destination.

Asgeir had explained that their trip to the Arctic Cathedral was a ruse to keep David and the others out of the way. Demetrius imagined them waiting at the church, wondering what they would be feeling once they realized they had been deceived.

"Focus on your view of the world as you wish it to be," Asgeir said as they ascended the incline in the trail that skirted the outer perimeter of Vardentoppen.

The melodious hum of the Ebony Sphere, which was nestled in the backpack over his right shoulder, provided a calming effect. Demetrius longed to hold it in his hand, to feel its power coursing through his soul. It felt as if its hold on him would be a permanent one, something he'd never be able to let go. Demetrius paused along the trail and looked out over the west side of the island. Lights from neighborhoods and the airport flickered through the large flakes of snow. The island on the other side of the waterway bordering the west side of the airport was barely visible now.

"What's bothering you, Demetrius?" Asgeir asked.

"All of these people will be gone thirty minutes from now."

"But many more than that will be saved for generations to come. Don't lose sight of that!"

Demetrius turned and looked into Asgeir's eyes. He saw no sign of compassion looking back at him. "That's what I keep telling myself." Demetrius moved past Asgeir and continued his hike along the trail.

———

Kari sped around the long curve in North Island Road, bordering the eastern side of the woods at the top of the island. She fishtailed coming out of the bend.

"Up ahead on the right. Stop at that parking area," Johannes instructed from the backseat. He had been following the directions from the map application on his cellphone.

Kari pulled off of the road and came to a stop.

"It should be about a six-hundred-meter hike up that hill," Johannes said as he reached between the two front seats and pointed in the direction they needed to head.

"Time! What time is it?" Kari yelled.

"8:40," David said. "That's a lot of ground to cover in twenty minutes in these conditions."

"Fuck! Let's hope these guys aren't punctual," Kari blurted out as she exited the Range Rover. She came around to the front of the vehicle and yelled to David, "Call Epiphany and let her know we're twenty minutes out."

David made the call, but there was no answer. He dictated a text message, then followed Kari and Johannes up the slope over the rough terrain.

Demetrius came to a stop at one of the highest points of the island. Asgeir helped him remove the backpack and extracted the Ebony Sphere of Vayla Isarrus. Its outer surface was encased in a velvety orange glow as it absorbed spiritual energy from Asgeir's touch. Demetrius watched Asgeir hold the sphere out in front of him, raising it up as if making a toast to the night sky. He couldn't help but notice the uncanny resemblance of Asgeir to the statue in the church at Tjeldsund. Had Tiorvi Eiken foreseen this event nearly five hundred years ago? Was this moment in time a fait accompli? Maybe it really was meant to happen this way.

"I envy what you are about to do," Asgeir said as he handed the Ebony Sphere to Demetrius.

The feelings Demetrius was experiencing ran the full gamut of human emotion. His pride swelled, knowing that he was about to wield the full might of the ancient artifact. He was sad about the sacrifice that would be made by tens of thousands of innocent lives, and yet he was enraptured by the thought of the peaceful new world that sacrifice would bring. The moment Demetrius grasped the sphere in his right hand, a burst of brilliant orange light erupted from its surface.

———————

The burst of light stopped Kari in her tracks. David and Johannes halted behind her. They were less than fifty meters from Demetrius. The orange light of the Ebony Sphere flickered like a firefly. It was barely visible through the heavy snowfall battering the dark, unlit section of the trail.

David moved past Kari onto the trail. "He's started."

Kari grabbed David by the arm. "Are we too late?"

"We still have time," David replied, "but not much. He needs to channel the energy of the Quintessence into the sphere. That could take a few minutes."

"Johannes, fire that thing up!" Kari demanded as she pointed to the backpack containing the quantum-well device.

"I need to set it in place, get the correct angle," Johannes shot back.

"No time for that. Fire it the fuck up. Now! You're going to have to hold it yourself," Kari yelled.

"But I've never done that before," Johannes said worriedly.

Kari stepped toward him and grabbed him by the coat with both hands. "Take that thing out! Fire it the fuck up. Now, Johannes!"

Johannes removed the quantum well and flipped the switch. He felt the soft hum of energy swell through his shaking hands.

Kari took charge of the situation. "Johannes, David, where's a good place to set up the device?"

Johannes pointed to a clearing twenty meters ahead on the right.

"Okay, let's go," Kari ordered.

She and David situated Johannes at the chosen spot along the trail. David knelt down next to him, trying to calm Johannes's nerves. Unexpectedly, David jumped up and shouted, "Behind us. He's behind us." David stepped into the trail and looked over his shoulder. Asgeir rammed into him.

As Kari watched David stumble and roll through the snow, she shouted, "Johannes, open the well!"

David slid to a stop at the base of the hill, ten meters from where he had been hit.

Johannes pushed the ignition button. Kari wheeled around; it was difficult to see. The snow was falling rapidly, and the winds were gusting. Asgeir was on top of her before she had time to react. His first strike was a right jab to the ribs. The impact knocked her backward. Asgeir followed that with a left hook. She managed to deflect it, wincing at the pain in her ribs. Kari landed a lightning-quick right jab of her own to the left side of Asgeir's head.

A brief flash of light lit up the trail, illuminating the look of pain that filled Asgeir's face. The quantum well had opened.

Three hundred seconds. The clock had started. Johannes was seated on the ground in the snow. His hands trembled from the bitter cold and gusting winds. The tiny bits of icy snow felt like bees stinging his face. The quantum-well device was clenched between his knees. His ribs ached as he shivered. In Johannes's best estimation, the quantum well had opened twenty, maybe thirty meters from Demetrius.

Brilliant shades of violet, green, and yellow radiated across the outer shell of the quantum well. The sound of the struggle between Kari and Asgeir behind him was unnerving. In his hurry to activate the device, he had misjudged. It was too dark, and the snow made it difficult to see. The bottom of the quantum well was too low. It had taken a bowl-shaped gouge out of the ground, about two feet deep. The swell of energy consumed from the earth that was swallowed up would cause the well to expand sooner than desired. They'd have less than the five minutes he had hoped for.

———

Kari and Asgeir continued to exchange punches as their struggle consumed the better part of a minute. She never saw the right cross that hammered her left shoulder. Kari stumbled and landed on her back. Her head was nearly swallowed up by the cold, icy snow. Asgeir was on top of her holding her down with both hands. She struggled with all her might to get out from under him but didn't have the leverage needed to push him off. He let go of her left arm and reached for her head. With her free hand, she clasped him around the wrist and managed to keep him from gripping her face. The muscles in her arm strained to hold him back. She knew her arm would eventually give out, and her soul would be his.

———

David woke with a gasp. In addition to knocking the wind out of him, the crushing blow from Asgeir had driven him backward into the trunk of a tree before he tumbled down the hill. His head had smacked the base of the tree hard enough to cause a momentary blackout. David had drifted in and out of consciousness several times. He had no idea how long he had been out. David got to his feet and scrambled back up the hill. He was shocked by the size of the quantum well as it rotated in the air above the trail. He sped toward Demetrius.

Kari's arm gave out. Asgeir wrapped his large hand around her face. Her vision blurred. Waves of intense pain flowed over her body as it fought to prevent the release of her soul.

Asgeir looked up in surprise when his right hand was pulled away from Kari's face before he could rip her soul from her body.

"Not today!" Epiphany yelled.

Asgeir jumped to his feet. His face lit up in dismay as he gazed upon the woman he had thought perished in the torrents of the Quintessence. Anger swelled as he swung at her. Epiphany easily dodged his attempted punch. She outmaneuvered him, swung her right foot to the back of his ankle, and took the large man off his feet.

Asgeir got up quickly. "I will make you suffer before I rip both of your souls from your body."

Epiphany slowly backed up toward the quantum well, luring her prey closer to its doom.

Asgeir kept moving toward her. "Say your last good-byes to your sister. Once I take your souls, you'll have no chance of seeing her in the afterlife." He charged toward her, reaching out with his right hand and latching onto the underside of her jaw as he had done in the Otherworlds.

Epiphany let him grab her. Her back was three feet from the outer shell of the quantum well. She knew Asgeir wouldn't push her into it. He wanted to taste the energy of her souls. She stared into his deep black eyes, reached up, and clasped her fingers around his neck. His face lit up in shock. The ancient energy that had infused her second soul flooded over Asgeir in a torrent of pain. She squeezed harder around his neck and turned, pushing his back to within inches of the outer shell of the quantum well. His hands fell to his sides, and he dropped to his knees.

Demetrius continued to funnel the ancient energy of the Quintessence into the Ebony Sphere. It felt as if he would succumb to the crushing strain.

Vayla Isarrus spoke to him as he struggled to maintain consciousness. "The sphere will be ready soon. You must not give up."

Demetrius had underestimated the effort this would take. Asgeir did not mention that the energy needed to change every soul on the planet would be orders of magnitude greater than what had been needed for the trial run in Overgård. Once the Ebony Sphere was at capacity, it would consume the eighty thousand souls needed to ignite it.

The voice of Vayla Isarrus made its way through the haze that clouded Demetrius's mind. "Twenty more seconds, Demetrius. Hold on for twenty more seconds."

David reached the top of the hill. "Demetrius, please stop. You don't have to do this!" he yelled. Less than twenty feet separated the two men. The brilliant glow of the Ebony Sphere illuminated Demetrius's face. He was clearly in pain. The resemblance of his facial expression to the statue in the Tjeldsund Church was undeniable.

The intensity of the Ebony Sphere increased dramatically. David was running out of time. He knew how the sphere would work. It would drain the life energy of the nearest people one at a time—until it claimed eighty thousand souls.

As David charged toward Demetrius, a thought ran through his head. *No, I wouldn't sacrifice tens of thousands of lives to make the world a better place. But I would sacrifice one life—mine—to give eight billion lives a fighting chance.* David rammed into Demetrius, knocking him to the ground. The Ebony Sphere flew through the air, landed in the snow, and rolled to within a few feet from the outer shell of the quantum well. David got back to his feet quickly and sprinted toward the sphere. Demetrius got up and sprinted after him.

———

Asgeir was on his knees, staring up at Epiphany. "You don't know what you're doing," he shouted. "You're on the wrong side of this."

"Good-bye, Asshole!" She unleashed a roundhouse kick that sent him backward into the quantum well. Its surface flared in brilliant violet light. The slow expansion of the outer shell began to accelerate.

Epiphany turned and sprinted toward David.

———

David got to the sphere first, but was tackled from behind by Demetrius. Demetrius clawed at him, attempting to pull him back, away from the

Ebony Sphere. David rolled onto his back, pushed Demetrius away with his right foot, and grabbed the sphere. He tossed it through the outer shell of the quantum well.

Demetrius got to his feet and shouted, "You have no idea what you've just done. You've robbed this world of its only chance for a peaceful future."

To David's shock, Demetrius charged into the quantum well.

———

"Shit!" Johannes shouted as he observed Demetrius end his life. He dropped the now purposeless quantum-well device in the snow. The well had become self-sustaining for the past four minutes. Grim thoughts ran through his head: *David's too close. He'll never make it.* Johannes turned and ran toward Kari, who was still struggling to get back to her feet and steady herself. He grabbed her by the arm and pulled her down the hillside to a position safely away from the expanding shell of the quantum well. They both stumbled and rolled through the snow.

———

David stepped back, away from the expanding outer shell of the quantum well as he watched it roil through every color of the spectrum. Johannes had told him the sudden influx of energy from the Ebony Sphere would accelerate the expansion, and once that happens, it wouldn't matter how much time the quantum well had remaining to stay open. A new clock would start ticking. He'd have a few seconds to get away.

"David, run!" The words reached his ears through the blanket of heavily falling snow.

He looked to his left. A weak smile crossed his face. Seeing Epiphany running toward him reminded him of what she had told him about that day when her sister was killed. Epiphany wrapped her arms around him and drove him backward into the deep snow.

The last thing David saw before the outer shell of the quantum well rolled over them were the tears running down Epiphany's face as she held him in her embrace. The snow was falling effortlessly to Earth from the dark sky above. A moment of bliss washed over him—a fitting way to die, in the arms of someone else who believed that somehow, the people of this world might someday make a difference and turn things around.

The quantum well expanded outward another five meters and then collapsed back in on itself. The tiny violet sphere at its core exploded, lighting up the night sky.

CHAPTER 55

Vardentoppen, The Epitaph, Two months later

Epiphany stood in front of a memorial plaque at the peak of Vardentoppen and read the epitaph.

"He made great strides in bringing the world to a better place," Kari said. "A person should be remembered for what he or she accomplished—not necessarily for what they could have done."

"I didn't really get to know him as well as maybe I would have liked, but in the end I do think you're right." Epiphany looked at the memorial one more time.

Demetrius Wolffe
Humanitarian
"I'd like to think I touched this world in a way
that had meaning."

"You and David are lucky to be alive," Kari said.

Epiphany nodded as she recalled the events of that night. "The energy of the Quintessence that infused my second soul acted as a protective veil that kept David and me safe when I wrapped my arms around him."

"It was like being in a cocoon," David added. "When the well washed over us, I thought for sure we'd be killed."

"Kari, I know after all of this happened, we spent the remainder of that night framing out what the official story would be. Was that how it ultimately got written up?" Epiphany asked.

"Pretty much. I said that we believed Demetrius had been kidnapped in Overgård by the person behind those killings and the ones in Tjeldsund. There were tire tracks next to the tour bus and a passenger list showing that Demetrius had been one of the people on the northern lights excursion. It wasn't a stretch to suggest he was taken from the site of the attack. The evidence supported that notion. After managing to escape from his captor, here in Vardentoppen, Demetrius called David, who then alerted me. When I got here, I reported that I saw a struggle between Demetrius and his kidnapper— the man we had seen with long hair and a beard and wearing a red-and-black plaid coat. Their confrontation ended in a massive explosion, which also explains why the sky lit up in flashes of light late that night."

"What was said about how those people were killed in the church and in Overgård?" David asked.

"Information about the method used to kill those people died along with the killer. It's one of those unfortunate things. We'll never know," Kari said.

"Did anyone question the final report?" David asked.

"No. Everything hung together pretty well. Case closed," Kari said. "And given we won't see any more incidents like the ones in Tjeldsund and Overgård, no one will revisit it."

Epiphany reached out and touched the smooth surface of the plaque. "Given everything that's happened, I was initially dead set against this. But you're right: Demetrius should be remembered for the good things he accomplished in his lifetime. One bad week out of twenty-five years of good work shouldn't color history's view of him. He had grand ideas for this world, but down the final stretch of his life, he tried to implement them the wrong way."

"In the end, it wasn't his problem to face alone. It's a problem eight billion of us need to work together to solve." David's expression turned to one of inner reflection after he finished talking. He thought about what Demetrius had said before plunging into the quantum well: "*You've robbed this world of its only chance for a peaceful future.*" He hoped like hell the man was wrong.

Acknowledgments

Many thanks to Mary Edwards, Zach Edwards, Laurel Delaney, and Barbe Fogarty for reviewing earlier drafts of the manuscript for this story. Your feedback helped shape the final version of my first novel. Laurel, you made me a better writer, and Barbe, you made me a better storyteller.

I owe a great deal of gratitude to Amelia Beamer. Her detailed and keenly perceptive developmental editing greatly influenced the final draft of this story.

I know I made the absolute best choice in working with Vickie Boff of Boff Consulting Ltd. Thank you for an outstanding, comprehensive marketing plan.

A great deal of appreciation goes to the team at Bright Communications. Special thanks to Jennifer Bright for her unbounded energy and enthusiasm in guiding me through the end-to-end process of publishing this book. You helped me bring my first novel to life. It was an absolute pleasure working with you!

About the Author

The notion of writing a novel first took root when Harrison Edwards was a sophomore in high school. Finally, a half-century later, he actually accomplished it: *A Reckoning of Souls* has become his first published work as an author. He is developing ideas for multiple novels, all of which are in the science fantasy vein. Themes for his writing are drawn from a broad array of interests, ranging from physics, quantum mechanics, and technology to mythology and spirituality.

Music has been a lifelong passion. Harrison is a multi-instrumentalist who plays the piano and drums and dabbles with entirely too many other instruments, which have included Native American flute, acoustic guitar, harp guitar, highland bagpipes, and uilleann pipes. He plays electronic percussion for a local Celtic band, has released five CDs of original contemporary instrumental music, and is working on new music for his next release.

He enjoys traveling with his wife and son. You might see them walking among the giant redwoods of northern California or exploring the fjords of Norway.

To learn more about Harrison's work as a musician and author, visit harrison-music.com.